Frozen
in Motion

Lori Roberts Herbst

Editor: Lisa Mathews, Kill Your Darlings Editing Services

Cover Designer: Molly Burton, Cozy Cover Designs

ISBN-13: 978-1-7362593-5-1
First printing: January 2022

Electronic edition:
ISBN-13: 978-1-7362593-4

*For my daughters, who have grown up to be my friends.
You make my world a brighter place.*

The Callie Cassidy Mystery series:

Suitable for Framing, Book 1
Double Exposure, Book 2
Frozen in Motion, Book 3
Photo Finished, Book 4

Subscribe at **www.lorirobertsherbst.com** for fun stuff
(including FREE Callie Cassidy prequel stories).

Acknowledgements

With every book I write, I am further reminded that nothing is truly created by a single person. I'd be lost without my team and my support system. Many thanks to the following people:

My editor, Lisa Q. Mathews, at Kill Your Darlings Editing Services: patient, kind, and so very skilled. I'm so thankful for her constructive and instructive criticism.

Cover designer Molly Burton of Cozy Cover Designs. What beautiful art she produces.

Jonna Rathbun, faithful reader and proofreader extraordinaire!

The best group of beta readers I could ask for: Grace Budrys, Becky Sue Epstein, Syrl Kazlo, Jane Meyers, Harini Nagendra, Sharon Roth, and my darling daughter Katie Shapiro. I'm grateful for your thorough reading and your oh-so-helpful input.

My ever-patient and always supportive husband, Paul. There would have been no first book without him, much less numbers two and three. He's my encourager, my cheerleader, my psychiatrist, and most of all, the love of my life.

Finally, I hope you know how grateful I am to each of you, Dear Readers. Writing can be a lonely pursuit, but your emails, Facebook comments, and reviews make me feel like I'm writing for an extended group of friends. Thank you, thank you, thank you!

1

Tiny snowflakes fluttered onto the top rail of the wooden bridge that spanned Rock Creek. The water beneath gurgled and churned across the rocks, splashing past patches of ice that glistened near the banks. Combined with the gray clouds hanging low in the sky, the scene felt both serene and ominous. I cradled my camera in the crook of my arm as I considered how best to capture the mood.

Taking a step back, I framed the shot and snapped the shutter. Then I adjusted the lens an inch to the left and snapped again. When I studied the results on the camera's LCD screen, I smiled with satisfaction.

A glance at my watch melted the smile away fast, though. I'd agreed to meet a friend at the Rocky Mountain High coffee shop at nine o'clock, and I had only one minute to make the five-minute walk through town. I tucked my camera in its bag, zipped it, and slung it over my shoulder.

"I hate being late," I muttered. Still, I knew this morning's impromptu photo shoot had been worth it. The overcast morning had generated such dramatic diffused lighting—how could any decent photographer resist?

I powerwalked across the Event Center staff parking lot, my

boots crunching on the powdered gravel. Turning right, I strode down Evergreen Way. I peeked through the window of the Snow Plow Chow cafe but didn't spot the handsome owner, my boyfriend Sam.

Boyfriend? The word screeched in my head like fingernails on a chalkboard. It might have been appropriate for the teenage versions of ourselves who'd walked hand-in-hand through the halls of Rock Creek Village High School a quarter of a century ago. But now boyfriend and girlfriend sounded too…well, *juvenile* to describe the rebooted romance we'd been carefully navigating this past year. But since I couldn't figure out how else to refer to our relationship, it would have to do.

As I passed the next shop, Yoga Delight, I noticed my friend Summer Simmons seated guru-style on a mat, leading a morning class. I waved, and she wagged a finger, silently scolding me for my recent absence from meditation class. I wrinkled my nose and touched my watch, indicating that I simply didn't have time. She pursed her lips, and I scooted off, making an internal vow to recommit. After all, the classes always improved my attitude. Why did I perpetually find ways to avoid them? *Tomorrow*, I said to myself. *Or maybe Monday…*

A few steps later, I paused in front of my photo gallery. *My photo gallery*, I repeated to myself. I'd opened the place last year after resigning from my career as an investigative photojournalist, and I still reveled in the undiluted thrill of what I'd created. I traced the words etched on the door: *Sundance Studio, Callahan Cassidy, Photographer.*

I examined the window display, trying to assess it as a tourist would. In keeping with the village's current Valentine's Day motif, I'd selected a large canvas photo of two mule deer—a buck and a doe—nuzzling in a snowy meadow. A dozen red foil hearts framed the canvas, glittering as they swayed from silver strings affixed to the overhang. Cheesy, in my opinion, but everyone else in the world seemed enchanted by Valentine's Day, so I'd felt an obligation to go along with the pack.

Next door, the bookstore with the clever moniker A Likely

Story also embraced the V-Day concept, with its exhibit of romance novels and relationship self-help tomes. But instead of a warm, fuzzy response to the display, I wrestled with a spurt of unease. I attributed my negative reaction to the store's owner, David Parisi, who'd recently become engaged to Tonya Stephens, my lifelong best friend. Everyone in town adored the charming Italian man, but I couldn't let go of my vague, unexplainable misgivings.

There was just something about him… I didn't have time to fixate on David, though. Another peek at my watch showed me I was now officially late, so I scurried past the Fudge Factory without so much as a glance at the marshmallow-topped s'mores brownies.

Well, maybe just a quick glance…

At six minutes past nine, I skidded to a halt in front of Rocky Mountain High and peered through the plate-glass window. My friend wasn't among the smattering of customers—all tourists, I surmised from their designer sweaters and ski boots. I breathed a sigh of relief that I hadn't kept her waiting.

My cellphone vibrated in my pocket, and I pulled it out to read a text from Sam: *Morning, beautiful. Thinking of you. How is your day?*

Smiling to myself, I moved to enter the coffee shop, but before I could grab the knob, the door slammed outward. A squatty, wide, Mack truck of a man in an expensive-looking navy blue parka barreled out, striking my shoulder with enough force to jar the phone out of my hand.

Though the collision was clearly the stranger's fault, I politely said, "Excuse me." The man barely broke stride. "You're lucky you didn't make me spill this overpriced coffee," he growled. "What is it with the people in this stupid town?"

My mouth gaped open. By the time a burning retort dropped onto my tongue, the man was already out of earshot, and I was left feeling angry and, what was worse, weak.

I scooped up my phone and stomped into the shop, where the aromas of rich brewed coffee and sweet, yeasty pastries soothed my nerves. From behind the tile serving counter, Mrs. Finney, the shop's proprietor, looked at me with concern.

"That boorish man practically trampled you, dear. Are you all right?"

"I'm fine," I said, shrugging out of my coat. "Who is that guy, anyway?"

"The bloody wanker wasn't kind enough to offer his name," she said in her British accent. Everyone in the village knew the dialect was fake, but at this point, it was so deeply entrenched in her persona we'd be confused if she dropped it. "I've never seen him before, and I'll be just as pleased to never see him again." She leaned across the counter and lowered her voice. "If I were still with The Company, I'd consider ordering a covert op to teach that young man a lesson."

I grinned. Mrs. Finney—a real live former CIA agent—had the stature of a curly-haired gray army tank trussed in a lavender pantsuit. I estimated her age to be late-sixties, but despite my well-honed skills as an interviewer, I'd been unable to get the eccentric woman to divulge specifics. Still, in the year we'd known each other, she'd served as protector, dispenser of wisdom, and above all, loyal friend.

I set my camera bag on the counter and settled onto a stool. "Well, no harm, no foul, I suppose. Maybe he'll make it up to both of us by dropping wads of cash in our shops."

She lifted an eyebrow. "One can hope—though he didn't bother with a tip." She inspected me and changed the subject. "Your cheeks are extra rosy, dear. Let's get you warmed up."

While she bustled around the silver coffee urns preparing my beverage, I stripped off my gloves. After a moment, she handed me a steaming paper cup of dark roast with a squirt of vanilla and a pinch of cinnamon, just the way I liked it. "Wrap your hands around this."

I laced my fingers over the paper cup and lifted it to my nose, inhaling the steamy fragrance. My hands and cheeks tingled. "Ah, that's nice."

"You haven't read the new adage." In addition to her accent, Mrs. Finney was known for her sage axioms. She'd even made

4

them a theme of her coffee shop, revealing a fresh one on her cups every few weeks. I read the printed inscription. *"Bears are treated with respect because they demand it."*

"Love it," I said. "Perhaps the giant who just ran me over could use an interview with one of our Rocky Mountain bears."

Mrs. Finney's attention shifted to a customer, who gestured from one of the bistro tables. As she bustled across the room to tend to the woman, I pulled off my knit ski cap and glanced in the mirror hanging on the wall. I grimaced at the sight. My cheeks were indeed rosy and my green eyes bright, but everything else about me appeared rumpled. I tugged at my wrinkled sweater and ran fingers through my dark, shoulder length hair, trying to fluff some life back into it. Useless. In a mountainside town like Rock Creek Village, hat hair loomed high on the list of winter hazards—right up there with chapped lips and flaky skin. The challenge had been real when I was a teenager, but now, at forty-four, it was fast becoming a losing battle.

Mrs. Finney returned and lifted the cover off a glass pastry dome. With a set of tongs, she selected a cream cheese bear claw, placed it on a stoneware plate, and slid it in front of me. I tore off a bite with my teeth and wallowed in the rich sweetness. "Delicious, as always," I said, licking my fingers. "Thank you. You are a genuine artist."

She beamed. "I appreciate that, dear. And may I say the same about you? Three customers have complimented my new photo display already this morning."

I followed her gaze to the arrangement of canvas photos on the wall: winter landscapes of snowy mountains, a herd of elk drinking from the partially frozen creek, pine trees dappled with rays of sunshine. Beneath the photos, a discreet sign touted: *On loan from Sundance Studio, Callahan Cassidy, Photographer.*

In a rare burst of sentimentality, I reached across the counter and grasped the woman's hand. "Mrs. Finney, I may not tell you often enough how much I appreciate you. Your support, your friendship…I'm just so glad you're here. You mean so much to me."

Her face flushed a bit, and she wiped her hands on a towel. "I feel the same, dear. Now, enough mush. I noticed you scanning the room earlier. Are you waiting for someone?"

I nodded as I popped the last bite of bearclaw in my mouth. "Renata Sanchez asked me to meet her here at nine. Said she had an important topic to discuss. Very cryptic."

"I didn't realize the two of you were friends."

"We're not besties or anything. I don't know her all that well. She's good friends with Jessica, though, so she's joined our group get-togethers occasionally. And…" I leaned in conspiratorially. "No one's informed me of this officially, but I suspect she and Ethan are seeing each other."

Ethan MacGregor was Rock Creek Village High School's business teacher, and also Sundance Studio's part-time marketing guru. I hoped soon he'd be my full-time partner.

"She could certainly do worse." Mrs. Finney took my plate and dropped the crumpled napkin onto it. "Her brother was here a short time ago. I must tell you, he seemed agitated."

I rolled my eyes. "Shocker. When isn't Raul agitated? That man expresses cheerfulness about as often as my pets decide to behave—once in a blue moon."

Mrs. Finney chuckled. "Be that as it may, he's turned out to be an excellent detective. I admit, at first I wasn't certain about his aptitude, but I've been pleasantly—"

Just then, the coffee shop door banged open with such force it made me jump. A gust of wind swirled inside, along with a few floating snowflakes. In their wake, Renata burst across the threshold.

Her eyes traveled around the room, dark as storm clouds. When she spotted me, she marched over and plopped down on the stool next to mine. "I swear, if that man moves here for good, I'm going to kill him."

2

R enata, keep your voice down," I said, swiveling on my stool to make sure no one was dialing 9-1-1. Fortunately, none of Mrs. Finney's customers seemed to have overheard my friend's threat. Even more fortunately, the town's resident gossip columnist, Sophie Demler, had embarked on yet another cruise with her elderly mother and wasn't around to add this little tidbit to her blog, *Sophie's Scoop*.

I turned back to Renata. "Since you've been gone a while, you may have forgotten, but people in this town have big ears and loose lips. They won't care if you were just kidding."

"Sorry," she muttered, not looking sorry at all. "Jeffrey just makes me so mad. I can't believe I ever married him."

Her brown eyes flashed, making her look so much like Raul I would have sworn they were twins. They weren't—in fact, Raul was eight years older—but their olive complexions, high cheekbones, and the tiny cleft in their chins made it obvious they were related. That and the way they both clenched their jaws when temper got the better of them. Like now.

Another customer entered the shop and approached the counter, honing in on the pastries. I nudged Renata. "Let's go get a table," I said.

Gathering our things, we settled in at a small round bistro table in a remote corner. I rested my elbows on the table. "I didn't realize your ex was in town. Remind me of his last name…"

"Forte. Jeffrey Forte. And don't you dare call him Jeff. He's way too fancy for a nickname." She sighed. "He showed up in town a few days ago. I'm surprised you didn't feel the ground shudder. He's like an earthquake."

"That might be slightly melodramatic," I ventured.

"Just wait and see." She paused. "He seemed so charming when we met. I fell head over heels. But now…" Her face tightened into a scowl. "Now, I despise him."

Mrs. Finney appeared and placed a cup of coffee in front of Renata. She leaned toward me. "Don't worry," she whispered. "It's decaf."

When our proprietor left, Renata sipped her coffee and composed herself. I used the time out to revisit what I knew about her. Like me, Renata had grown up in Rock Creek Village before moving away for college. There, she'd met and married Jeffrey, a union that lasted only five years. Following their acrimonious divorce, Renata had returned to the village last summer and taken a job as a science teacher—as well as the first-ever female assistant coach for the high school boys' hockey team. She'd been a premiere player herself through college, earning a spot as an Olympic alternate. Her knowledge and skills had helped guide the team to a 4-0 start on the season. She seemed to be acclimating well to her new/old home, and I considered it a shame that her ex-husband was still intent on disrupting her life.

After a few moments, Renata gave me a weak smile. "Sorry for the tantrum. I was already stressed over running late, and I saw Jeffrey strolling down the sidewalk in his stupid blue coat, as if he owned the place. We didn't speak, didn't even acknowledge each other, but I guess he still manages to get under my skin."

I raised my eyebrows. "Wait a minute…blue coat? I just ran into a man in a blue coat. Literally. What does Jeffrey look like?"

"Oh, he's maybe an inch taller than me. Thinning brown hair. Pale skin. About forty pounds overweight." She sipped her coffee. "He actually used to be pretty cute, back when I first met him. But now he looks…hmm. He looks like a once fancy house that's been abandoned and left to the elements."

I snapped my fingers. "That's the guy. He knocked the phone right out of my hand, then made a snarky comment." I shot her a sympathetic look. "Has he told you why he's in town?"

She snorted. "He showed up at my door day before yesterday. Said he was here on business and wanted to see Terror."

Her eyes softened at the mention of her shih tzu, an aptly named, ten-pound brindle-and-white fluffball whose innocent appearance contrasted with her yappy, domineering personality. Woody, my low-key golden retriever who topped out over forty pounds, submitted to Terror's every whim when they played together at the dog park. He loved her—and she him—but playtime definitely proceeded on Terror's terms. Woody seemed okay with it, though. He was used to it, after all, since he and my orange tabby cat, Carl, operated under the same unwritten rules.

Renata ran a hand through her hair and continued. "So I asked him, 'What business?' He said it was for him to know and me to find out. When I suggested he could do business in a thousand other towns, he said, 'It's a free country. I have every right to pursue my business wherever I see fit.' Such a jerk."

Her knuckles were white as she clenched her cardboard cup, and I envisioned its imminent collapse, coffee streaming across the table. I patted her hand. "That must be upsetting, Renata. But sadly, he's right. If he chooses to be here, there's not much you can do about it."

"That may be true," she said. "But he's not allowed to break the law."

"What do you mean?"

She whipped her ponytail over her shoulder. "Well, I can't prove it was him. Not yet. But there have been a few suspicious events in my life lately, and I'm sure he's behind them."

"Such as?"

"Yesterday morning, I was ready to drive to work. I went outside and headed to the spot where I almost always park. But yesterday, my car wasn't there."

My eyes widened. "Jeffrey stole it?"

"Not exactly. I found it a few spots away. But he moved it. I know he did."

"But why would he—?"

"To mess with my head. He's mad I got that car in the divorce. I bet he kept a copy of the key." Her voice had risen, and I motioned for her to quiet down. "Anyway," she said more softly, "I blew it off, went to school, and tried not to think about it. But when I got home yesterday after practice, my apartment door was unlocked. I'd been rushing around that morning, running late, so I couldn't be a hundred percent sure I'd remembered to lock it. And when I walked inside, nothing seemed out of place. Until I went into the kitchen."

Visions of wreckage and chaos littered my imagination—an open refrigerator door, food strewn across the floor, drawers askew and contents scattered. "Vandalism?" I asked, my mind flashing back to last summer, when vandals had waged an attack on my gallery.

Of course, now the vandals responsible—twins Banner and Braden Ratliff—were rehabilitated. In fact, they worked for me.

"No, nothing like that," Renata said. "But Terror's crate was in a different corner of the kitchen. And her food bowl was full."

My pulse raced. "Full of what? Poison? Blood?"

She squinted at me. "Dog food." Then, reading my confusion, she hurried to explain. "The thing is, I feed Terror twice a day, morning and night. I watched her finish her morning meal, even lick the bowl clean. Then I crated her and left for work. Someone refilled her bowl while I was away. It had to be Jeffrey."

"Your ex-husband broke into your apartment to feed your dog?" I asked skeptically.

Renata threw up her hands. "Who else would have done it?"

"How did he get in?"

She drummed her fingers on the table. "I haven't unraveled that part yet, but he's very resourceful."

"What would be his motive?"

"Control. Revenge. Take your pick." She sighed. "During our divorce negotiations, I agreed to almost all his stipulations, but when he demanded Terror, I refused to budge. He never liked the dog. Called my baby a hoity-toity mutt. He only wanted her because he knew how much I love her. When the judge awarded Terror to me, Jeffrey blew a gasket." She stared at me, her eyes moist. "Don't you see? He's not-so-subtly telling me that if he wants her, he'll take her."

Then she placed a crumpled piece of paper on the table. "I think this will convince you. I found it on top of Terror's crate."

I reached for the paper. It was a low-quality photo, grainy and underexposed, likely printed on a desktop device. In it, a man and woman sat on a couch facing a television, their backs to the photographer. The man's arm draped around the woman, whose head rested against his shoulder. Her black mane cascaded down the back of the couch. Renata. And even if I hadn't figured out they were dating, the man's trademark ginger hair easily revealed his identity. "You and Ethan," I said. "Your apartment?"

"Yes." She bit her trembling lip. "I had no idea Jeffrey was outside. Spying on us."

I considered everything I'd heard. Taken one by one, the events could be rationalized away. Renata parked her car in a different place and simply forgot. In a rush to get to work, she neglected to lock her door. She refilled Terror's bowl herself that morning out of habit. Perpetually distracted as we were, we often completed our daily tasks on autopilot. I, for one, couldn't count the number of times I'd arrived at the studio with no conscious memory of actually driving there.

But that photo was the difference maker. The tangible evidence that tilted the scale.

I clasped my hands on the table. "Okay, first things first. Are you afraid Jeffrey might harm you physically?"

She quickly shook her head. "No. I'm much stronger than him, and he knows it. Anyway, physical threat is not Jeffrey's style. He's more of a…a gaslighter, I think they call it."

I nodded. "I know what you mean. I once covered a crime in

which the offender was diagnosed as a narcissist. My background research taught me people like that aren't wired to accept blame or even acknowledge their own shortcomings. They thrive on control and harbor a deep-seated need to win every dispute. They often see competition where it doesn't exist. The psychologist I interviewed said there's no way to reason with a full-blown egomaniac."

"Exactly," she said. "But I've also learned you can't give in. You have to stand up for yourself. Like this says." She lifted her cup and pointed at the message there.

"So you want to demand respect," I said. "How do you plan on doing that?"

She tilted her head and smiled. "I was hoping you'd do a little snooping. I've heard you're good at that."

"Me?" I shook my head. "Renata, your brother is the detective. You need to be talking to him about this."

She groaned. "Callie, do you know Raul even a little? If I so much as mention Jeffrey's name, my brother explodes."

I could see that. Over the past year, Raul and I had forged a friendship based on mutual respect. In fact, I sometimes even thought of him as the little brother I'd always longed for. But even if he *were* my brother, I wouldn't want him involved in my domestic affairs. No, Renata needed someone on her side who wasn't quite so…volatile.

"Do you need a place to stay for a while? I have a spare room, and you and Terror are more than welcome—"

"That's nice, Callie, but we're fine where we are. I'm not worried about Jeffrey breaking in again. He's made his point. Besides, I bought an alarm for the door."

"Well, then, I can recommend my therapist. She's in Pine Haven, and I've found—"

"I appreciate it, Callie, I do. But I was hoping for something more…immediate. Jeffrey is hiding something. I know he is. I've felt it since before we divorced. An unethical business dealing, maybe, or even something illegal. If I can discover what it is, maybe I can leverage the information to, well, to *suggest* that he leave town. That's all I want. Everyone says you're a first-class investigator, even Raul."

I sighed. Based on a couple of events over the past year, I'd gained a reputation as a local crime solver. These days, villagers approached me for help with issues ranging from misdelivered mail to squirrels stealing from bird feeders. Perhaps instead of a photo gallery, I should hang a private investigator's shingle.

"Renata, I no longer have access to the research tools I used as a journalist. I can't uncover any information you can't dig up yourself on Google." I snapped my fingers. "Wait, what about Tonya? Her newspaper subscribes to a few research databases."

"I thought of her. But Tonya's busy with wedding planning. Besides, I don't want my life story recapped in the local paper. I want it all…off the books."

I grinned. "Now you sound like a mobster."

The corner of Renata's mouth turned up. "Yeah, right. Listen, Callie, I know you still have contacts from your time at *The Washington Sentinel*."

She was referring to Preston Garrison, my former boss. Someone must have filled her in on the saga of his visit to the village last summer—and the reason he owed me more than a few big favors.

I studied Renata as I considered what to do. Her expression was pleading. And I did feel sorry for her. The woman had been through an ordeal and emerged on the other side. Here in Rock Creek Village, she'd found a job she loved. Friends and family. The seedling of a new relationship. She deserved peace, not the tumult of her ex-husband's presence.

I made up my mind. "I'll give Preston a call."

She whooped, and I held up a cautionary hand. "I can't make any promises. He might not agree to help, but if he does, he'll want to start by conducting a background check on your ex-husband. For that, he'll need some basic information. Why don't you come to the gallery with me so I can jot down some details?"

She glanced tentatively at her watch. "I have to be at the rink in an hour for warm-ups."

The high school was hosting a league tournament this weekend. I knew that because they'd hired me to shoot team photos. "I need to be there too. We'll make it quick."

Energized, she leapt to her feet and put on her coat. "Thank you, Callie. I can't tell you what this means to me."

"One thing, Renata," I said. "Your brother tends to get a little irritated when I butt in. If—or rather when—he gets wind of this, he won't be happy with either of us."

She gave me a lopsided grin. "My brother, irritated and unhappy? Story of his life. And by extension, mine."

I chuckled. "All right. If you can take it, I can too."

3

Outside, I inhaled the crisp, thin air, the kind found only in mountain climates. In the distance, Mt. O'Connell lifted its peak skyward, as if inviting observers to gather round. A brisk breeze gusted, and I pulled my scarf tight around my neck and looked at the sky. I hadn't heard any predictions of snow over the next few days, but those of us who lived in the shadow of the Rockies knew forecasts could change in an instant. For now, temperatures in the twenties meant layers of snow would stay put on the mountains, which glistened like divas drenched in diamonds.

Renata and I hurried down the sidewalk toward the studio. When we were two shops away, we heard a voice call out and turned to find Ethan jogging toward us.

"Morning, boss," he said, giving me a mock salute. "Reporting for duty."

By the time I'd readied my response, his attention had already pivoted to Renata. "Good morning," he said, his voice husky now. "You look amazing."

The temperature seemed to shoot up twenty degrees. I gave an amused snort. Renata looked away, and Ethan flushed. After a second, he cleared his throat and said, "So, Callie, what's on your agenda today?"

"Hockey team photos at eleven. Should take a couple of hours." I paused. "Renata will be there, too, in case you wanted to know."

Ethan's cheeks tinged pink again. I was enjoying this far too much.

"Will Tweedledee and Tweedledum be in today?" he asked, changing the subject.

His sarcasm was lighthearted, and I figured the twins had earned the teasing. Banner and Braden had incurred Ethan's wrath during last summer's series of misdeeds, and though the boys had reformed, Ethan still hadn't quite forgiven them. He was getting close, though.

"Yes, full day. Can you play nice?"

He chuckled. "I'm surprised I'm saying this, but they're doing a great job. But, Callie, they won't be enough in a month or two. You still need to hire more staff."

Ethan had been pushing me for weeks now to start interviewing, but I'd resisted. I'd come to trust the twins, so hiring them hadn't caused me much angst. But the last person I'd brought on board before them…well, suffice it to say it hadn't worked out, and I was still raw from the betrayal.

Ethan was right, though. With him teaching weekdays and the twins enrolled in morning college classes, I was frequently on my own at the gallery. This time of year wasn't too busy, but when spring arrived, bringing an influx of tourists, I'd never be able to keep up. I vowed to hang a help wanted sign first thing Monday.

We'd reached the studio by then. I was digging the key from my pocket when a voice bellowed from above. "Well, well. If it isn't the harlot and her latest conquest."

Renata stiffened, and Ethan looked around quizzically. My brow furrowed. *Harlot? Who even used that word anymore?*

I followed the words to a man standing against the railing outside Willie Wright's second-floor realty office. When I spotted the blue coat, I groaned. It was Renata's ex-husband, Jeffrey Forte.

This wouldn't be pretty.

I shot a worried glance at Renata. She wore an expression of barely contained rage. Ethan's face paled. "Ignore him," I said to them. "Let's get inside."

Jeffrey's expensive boots squeaked as he trudged down the stairs. "Hanging out with your latest boy toy?" He spoke loudly, almost yelling, and I figured it was his intention to create a scene. And it was working. Several window-shopping tourists paused to gawk. Pamela emerged from The Fudge Factory to see what the ruckus was about, and David appeared in the door of A Likely Story. The potential confrontation was fast becoming a spectator event.

Jeffrey made it to the sidewalk and planted himself in Renata's path. "You two seem tired. Guess you've worn the poor guy out." He sneered at Ethan. "I understand how that goes, buddy. Enjoy it while you can. She'll leave you high and dry in a few months' time."

I moved to Renata's side. "All right, that's enough. Time to move along, Mr. Forte."

To my surprise, Jeffrey elbowed me aside. "Mind your own business, lady. This is between me and my wife. And Loverboy here, of course."

Ethan's nostrils flared. "You need to get out of here."

"Or what?" Jeffrey stared at Ethan, daring him to make the first move.

Just when I thought he'd get his wish, we heard a shout and saw Raul thundering down the sidewalk. He ground to a halt in the space between Ethan and Jeffrey. His face was hard. "I'm warning you, Forte. You need to leave. Do it now."

Jeffrey hesitated. A flicker of fear crossed his face. For a hopeful moment, I thought he'd comply. But his eyes flitted to the crowd, which had grown to at least a dozen. Aware of his audience, he dug in.

"So big brother swoops in, is that how this goes?" he said. "The big bad cop, wielding his power against the evil ex-husband." He reached out and poked Raul's chest, baiting him.

As if in slow motion, Raul clenched his fist and cocked his arm.

I held my breath, waiting for the inevitable swing.

But Renata beat him to the punch. Literally.

She pushed her brother aside and socked her ex-husband in the nose.

***

There wasn't much to the punch. In fact, it was more of a slap, open-handed and lightly delivered. A warning that something more intense awaited.

Still, it was enough to make Jeffrey clutch his nose and stagger backward, his eyes wide. For a moment, everyone froze. The air crackled with tension. Then the crowd emitted a mutual gasp, and Jeffrey looked at them, embarrassed. A man like him didn't take kindly to being shown up by a woman.

He drew himself to full height, threw his shoulders back, and bellowed like a bull. As he rounded his shoulders and prepared to charge, a clump of wet snow plopped onto his balding head.

Jeffrey stopped in his tracks. I looked up to see Willie on the balcony, gloved hands grasping the rail. Surely, he hadn't...

But when I noticed his smug smile, I realized he had. *Willie Wright*, I mused. *Who knew you had it in you?*

Jeffrey swiped off the snow. He stared at the crowd, some of whom had out their cell phones to document the brawl. A flash of shrewdness crossed his face, and he jabbed a finger Renata's direction. "This woman attacked me without provocation." He turned to Raul. "You're an officer of the law. Do your job. Arrest her for assault."

Raul's face turned purple. I decided to intervene—before Raul completely lost his cool.

I crossed my arms and glared at Jeffrey. "No provocation? You started this whole thing. First, you verbally attacked your ex-wife. Next, you physically assaulted her brother. We all witnessed it." I gestured toward the crowd. A few of them nodded.

"I saw it," David said. "This man pushed Detective Sanchez."

"Me too," Pamela chimed in. "He might have been going for his gun."

Others began adding murmurs of agreement. I crossed my arms. "If anything, Detective Sanchez should arrest you."

Jeffrey's head swiveled and a wild look came into his eyes. Then his body deflated. The swagger had left him, but he made one last-ditch effort to save face. "I did no such thing," he grumbled. He stared at Renata. "This isn't over. I'd advise you to contact your lawyer."

He glared at Raul. "As for you, your boss will hear from my attorney. You failed to intercede in the attack of a citizen. I'll have your badge."

This was sounding like a bad cop movie, and I was over it. "Mr. Forte, stop with the threats. There's nothing further to be said. It's time for you to walk away."

He turned his cold eyes on me, and a shiver skittered up my spine. When he leaned toward me, his words emerged in a frosty haze. "I don't know what your stake is in all this, but I suggest you watch your back. I'm not a man to be trifled with."

Without waiting for a response, he stalked off. The spectators parted to let him through. Raul watched him go, then took Renata by the arm and pulled her aside. I felt a wave of sympathy. I'd been on the receiving end of enough of his lectures that I could paraphrase the content. But Renata wasn't having it. She stood toe to toe with her brother and wagged a finger at him.

I noticed a few people raise their phone cameras again, and I hurried over to the siblings. "Knock it off, you two," I whispered. "You're about to go viral."

Renata dropped her finger, and Raul took a step back. "Later," he hissed at his sister. He turned to me. "As for you…" Pausing, he squeezed his eyes shut. His lips moved, but no sound came out. I knew from experience he was counting to ten. When he opened his eyes, he said simply, "I'll be in touch." One last frown at Renata, and he was off down Evergreen Way.

Ethan moved beside Renata while I turned to the crowd and smiled. "Show's over, folks," I said. "Come back in half an hour when Sundance Studio opens. I can promise you some amazing photo deals. Until then, enjoy this gorgeous winter day."

4

I unlocked the door and flipped the switch, bathing the gallery in subtle light. A second switch unleashed a series of spotlights accentuating the canvases displayed on the walls. An immediate sense of calm settled over me. Despite a murder on the premises a few months ago, this was still my happy place.

A glance at Renata's trembling hands told me she wasn't experiencing the same sense of serenity. I gave her a sympathetic smile. "That was intense," I said. "You must be wrung out. We don't have to do this right now. I can get Jeffrey's information from you tomorrow."

She shook her head. "I'm not wrung out. I'm pissed off. Give me paper and a pen. I'll write everything I know and even make up more if it helps get that man out of town."

I couldn't help but grin. Renata was a firecracker.

"Sounds good," I said. "I need to prepare the gallery for opening, but Ethan can get you set up in the office. Make a list of whatever identifying information you might remember—driver's license, social security, previous places of employment. Anything Preston's researchers can use for their background check."

She nodded. "I can do that."

After the two of them walked through the arch, I let my eyes roam across the gallery's large, open space. The cleaning crew had visited last night, leaving the polished concrete floor gleaming and every surface sparkling. I studied the photo displays. The landscapes, wildlife, and candids hanging on the walls reflected the optimism and peace of my current life.

I reflected that I hadn't always felt so hopeful. Just over a year ago, I'd been a big-city photojournalist at a major newspaper, tasked with documenting the world's sound and fury. My career had taken a hard toll on me, enveloping me in a cloak of stress I hadn't fully realized I'd been wearing until I removed it. Now, as I stood beside a photo of a moose peering through a thicket of fir trees, I knew I was where I was meant to be.

Heading behind the sales counter, I booted up the computer we used to ring up purchases and chart sales. That done, I returned to the entrance and repositioned the postcard racks filled with Callahan Cassidy originals. Next, I flipped through trays of matted photos on the display table. The stock would be sufficient for the weekend, but I'd need to replenish it by mid-week.

Once I'd completed my tasks, I put my hands on my hips and surveyed my kingdom, satisfied that all was well in Sundance Studio.

Next stop was the office, where I found Renata at my desk, tapping a pencil against her chin. Ethan perched on a chair he'd pulled next to hers. I watched them for a moment and decided the combination of her feistiness and his laid-back demeanor created a good balance. I hoped Jeffrey didn't drive a wedge between them that their newborn relationship couldn't survive.

Renata pointed at the legal pad in front of her. "I've written everything I can think of. There's probably more, but I need to get to the rink. I preach punctuality to the team. If I turn up late, I'll never hear the end of it."

"I'm sure it's fine," I said. "I'll be at the rink myself in a while. If you remember anything else, you can let me know then."

She hopped up from the chair and came around the desk to

hug me. Her powerful arms nearly squeezed the breath out of me. "Thank you so much for helping me with all this and for standing up for me. I hope it doesn't end up biting you in the butt with Raul. I told him not to get on your case, but he can be stubborn as a toothache."

I smiled, figuring he'd say the same of her. "No worries. I was a journalist, remember? Raul's a pussycat compared to a lot of the people I've met. Remind me to tell you about this rabid school nurse I interviewed…"

She laughed and headed toward the office door. Ethan trotted after her. "Hey, boss, I'm going to drive Renata to the rink. After what just happened—well, her ex could be lurking anywhere. I'd rather she didn't go alone."

Renata spun on her heel to face him. "Ethan McGregor, don't you dare patronize me. I'm not some sweet little girl that needs a big man to defend her."

As she stalked through the door, my mouth dropped open. It was like watching a video replay of more than a few interactions I'd had with Sam. Witnessing the scene as an objective observer made me see Sam's protectiveness in a new light. Though misguided, perhaps, Ethan's intentions were good—and I realized Sam's were as well.

Ethan turned to me and raised his hands, palms up. "I was only trying to help."

"I get that," I said. "But try to see it from Renata's perspective. She's just had a fight with her nasty ex-husband. Then her overbearing big brother berates her. She doesn't need another man in her life implying she's weak."

"That's not what I was doing." He pouted, and I cocked my head. He puffed his cheeks. "I guess you're right. So what can I do to fix it?"

I considered. In his shoes, how would I handle…me? "It's pretty simple," I said. "Give her some time. Then go to her and apologize. Tell her you know she can handle things on her own, and you're there for whatever she needs. And mean it."

Ethan sighed, then went to the gallery's small kitchen to make himself a cup of tea. I heard the back door open as the twins reported for work, chattering cheerfully. It was a pleasant sound, especially considering their belligerence a mere six months ago.

They stopped at the office door to say good morning. Though the Ratliffs were identical twins, down to their shaggy brown hair and thick eyebrows over wide, hazel eyes, I could tell them apart now, even when they dressed the same. The trick, I'd learned, lay in the small, pale scar on Braden's upper lip, the result of a bicycle accident when he was six.

The scar creased as Braden popped the last bite of a muffin into his mouth. Banner took a sip from his Rocky Mountain High cup and handed another cup to me. "Brought you an espresso, Callie. Figured you could use more caffeine."

"Yeah," Braden said. "Especially after the big brawl this morning."

"You heard?"

A few crumbs fell to the floor as he wiped his mouth, and he crouched to clean them up. "Who didn't? This is Rock Creek Village, remember?"

I nodded. News traveled at lightning speed in our town. "What's the buzz?"

He looked over his shoulder as Ethan returned to the office. "Everyone's saying Ms. Sanchez's ex-husband started it. What a jerk. That guy could use a good *ubuntu*."

Braden's words sent a wave of warmth through me. He was referring to an evening's intervention my friends and I had dispensed when we'd caught him and his brother sneaking in and vandalizing the studio. Summer had suggested that the boys' hostile actions originated from the pain of their mother's death. Instead of pressing charges, she recommended *ubuntu*, a cultural philosophy espousing the belief that all people are essentially good and benefit from affirmation more than punishment. A group of us—Summer, her wife Jessica, Tonya, and me—had organized the *ubuntu*, and that day, the boys' lives changed course.

Now they were kind, productive young men. Both took classes at the community college, with Banner majoring in accounting and Braden determined to pursue—of all things—photography. They'd even gotten the word *ubuntu* tattooed on their inner wrists as an affirmation.

But as successful as the experience had been for them, I realized not everyone could be that easily transformed. What was the joke my therapist told? *How many counselors does it take to change a lightbulb? Just one, but the bulb has to want to change.*

"It's a nice idea," I told Braden, "but *ubuntu* only works when the person on the receiving end is open to it. From my observations, Jeffrey Forte is not open. Not even close."

"Yeah?" Banner said. "Then maybe a little tough love is in order." He smacked a fist into his palm. Uh-oh. Perhaps the twins hadn't achieved Summer's level of pacifism yet. But then, few of us had.

I saw Ethan's mouth twitch. Time to change the subject. "Enough talk of conflicts and controversies. We open in ten minutes. Let's hit the ground running."

I rose from my chair, and Ethan took my spot at the desk so he could go through invoices. The twins and I walked into the gallery, and Banner headed to the computer behind the sales counter.

He clicked on the keyboard. "Yesterday was big," he said. "Fourteen online orders."

I shook my head in wonder. It was still hard for me to comprehend that so many people wanted Callahan Cassidy originals. This gallery had been the best decision I'd ever made, and it had come on the heels of one of the worst. Vinegar to wine, as my mother would say.

Braden opened the blinds on the door. "Hey, Callie, if it isn't too busy, can I work in the darkroom? I want to develop some photos for a class assignment."

I beamed. "More than okay, especially if you'll do me a favor after you've completed your homework. The print bin could use restocking. Would you mind? It'd save me some time later."

He nodded with enthusiasm, looking like a little boy who'd earned an extra recess. "That'd be great."

I joined Banner behind the counter and wrote up a list of prints I wanted. Then I went to the storage closet in the darkroom and gathered the requisite negative strips. When I handed them over, I said, "Don't forget, you'll need to—"

He rested a hand on my shoulder. "I got this, Callie. You taught me well."

I smothered a smile at his serious expression, but I knew he was right. I'd walked him through the process and watched him enlarge and develop a dozen photos on his own. It was time to let the little bird fly from the nest.

The alarm on my phone beeped, indicating opening time. I turned the sign in the window and unlocked the door, an unceremonious event since exactly zero customers streamed inside. Owning a small business could be a roller coaster ride, I thought. I headed to the office to organize the equipment for the hockey shoot, tucking my Nikon DSLR into a padded camera bag, along with a wide-angle lens for team photos and a zoom lens for everything else. Next, I added a couple of extra memory cards, a stash of batteries, and a microfiber cloth to clean the lenses. In another, larger bag, I packed a free-standing flash, a folded directional umbrella, and a sturdy tripod.

Banner appeared at my office door. "Want a hand?" He took the equipment bag and the tripod case. I slung my camera bag over my shoulder and led the way out the back door to my red Honda Civic in the alley. We arranged the bags in the back seat, and I locked the car. Back inside, I took one last look around as I pulled on my coat.

"Okay, troops. Hold down the fort, batten down the hatches, take care of business—"

"We get the picture," Ethan said. "No pun intended. Go do your thing."

5

Five minutes later, I pulled into the visitors' parking lot at The Ice Zone, Rock Creek Village's ice skating rink, which did double duty as the local hockey arena. I took a moment to study the arena's impressive exterior. The architecture was tasteful, with a gray brick and glass window facade. Surrounded by clusters of pine trees, the building blended into its surroundings without diminishing the glorious view of the Rockies in the distance.

Built a few years ago, the rink provided yet another lure for the Rock Creek Village tourism business. It wasn't a massive structure, but it was large enough to serve as home to the Rock Creek Village High School Rockets, as well as small-scale tournaments, such as today's regional eighteen-and-under championship. I made a mental note to use the arena as a focal point in an upcoming Chamber of Commerce photo shoot.

As I turned off the ignition, I caught a flash of motion in my peripheral vision. When I looked through the windshield, I noticed two men near the arena, their bodies rigid with what I assumed to be confrontation. One wore a black leather jacket completely impractical for our snowy climate. The other I recognized right away. Even if he hadn't been wearing that "stupid blue coat," as Renata put it, I couldn't mistake the superior tilt of his chin and the aggressive posture. After all, I'd seen it a couple of hours ago.

Jeffrey Forte.

Had he come to further antagonize poor Renata? If so, he'd have to get past me to do it.

A rap at the car window made me jump. If I'd been one of those big-haired Texas women I'd gone to college with, I'd have flattened my hairdo on the roof of the car.

I turned to see Jessica, her green eyes sparkling with merriment. "Didn't mean to scare you," she mouthed.

I got out of the car. At five-five, I was considered average height for a woman, but I towered over my petite, pixie-like friend. But the energy she generated made her seem like a giant. Being around Jessica was like shuffling across a shag rug in your socks. She filled the atmosphere with static electricity.

"What are you doing here?" I asked.

"I came to watch Renata coach. Plus, I have students playing and thought I'd offer my support." She threw back her hood, revealing a shock of spiky red hair. "What's got you on edge?"

I looked toward the spot where the two men had been arguing, but they'd disappeared. "It's been a tense morning in general."

"Yeah, I heard about the fight between Renata and her horrible ex." Jessica's lips curled up in a small smile. "Sounds like she threw a mean right hook. Good for her."

I tsked-tsked at her. "Summer wouldn't be pleased to have you talking that way. Besides, it was more of a smack."

She folded her hands into a meditative pose, mimicking her wife. "Your heart will celebrate if you hold love and forgiveness there," she said. Then she dropped her hands. "Let's be honest. *My* heart would be more likely to celebrate if the man fell off the face of the earth, maybe following a slight shove. Just sayin'."

I grinned. When it came to her friends, Jessica possessed the protective instincts of a German shepherd. Her bond with Renata made perfect sense. The two women were peas in a pod, each with a layer of plucky, rugged strength covering an inner core of compassion and loyalty.

Jessica helped me lug my equipment into the arena. Lars Eggars, the rink manager, met us at the boards. "I vill carry," he said in his Swedish accent. He took the bags, hoisting them as if they were balloons, and walked across a non-slip liner to a large, square rubber mat positioned center ice.

With a wave, Jessica headed into the stands to join the fans. I trotted after Lars. Teenaged boys whizzed around us like missiles on skates, so close my hair ruffled in their breeze. Lars deposited my bags on the mat and, after asking if I needed anything else, took off for other duties. I unpacked the equipment and positioned the pieces in the proper spots. Once I'd screwed the camera onto the tripod, I took a couple of test shots. Everything was ready.

"Attention, players!" I called. "It's time for team photos. We'll start with the Rock Creek Rockets…"

Whoosh. The players continued to fly past me, whooping and chattering, oblivious to my command. I furrowed my brow, trying to achieve an air of authority. "Rock Creek Rockets! Line up!" I yelled, louder.

Still no response.

I searched the rink for Renata, another coach, or any adult who might help me corral the young heathens, but it seemed I was the lone representative of the twenty-and-older club. Just as I started to imagine myself as prey in a frigid *Lord of the Flies* sequel, a shrill whistle cut through the chatter. Turning toward the blast, I saw Jessica leaning across the boards, her face stern.

"Cameron Lane, get your teammates lined up. Right now. Don't make me come out there!"

The boys came to sudden, snow-spraying stops and turned toward Jessica with respect. Or was it fear? "Yes, ma'am," Cameron said, his voice squeaky with puberty. He glided into place in front of the camera and called for his teammates.

"Is this where you want us, ma'am?" Cameron asked me.

"Move forward a bit," I directed. "Okay, that's good. Now, you boys line up, tallest in the back. Those in the front row, kneel on your left knee."

As the boys scrambled to follow directions, I glanced at Jessica, who winked at me. The woman was dynamite wrapped in a small package, and I knew the boys would behave under her watchful eye.

Once I was satisfied with the arrangement, I set the camera's aperture to f/8, focused the lens, and took hold of the remote.

"Smile on three. One, two, three."

Frowns covered each face as the boys worked to appear fierce.

"Okay, let's try again. Smile for the camera! One, two, three…"

This time, they scowled.

Boys. Always with the machismo.

To be fair, girls displayed their own conceits. I'd recently photographed the girls' volleyball team, and from them I got hands on hips, cocked knees, and fish lips. Sigh.

Once I determined the group scowl was the best result I'd achieve, I released the Rockets and summoned the next team. When they assembled, I snapped the shutter, only to hear it jam.

Ugh. This glitch happened on occasion with a DSLR. I held up a finger, indicating the boys should stay put. I unscrewed the camera from the tripod, opened the back, and gave the shutter a gentle jiggle. Good as new.

As I prepared to reattach the camera, a loud clank grabbed my attention. It seemed to come from the catwalk, and I shifted my focus upward just in time to see a long, slender object fly over the guardrail. By the time it clattered to the ice, I'd identified it as a hockey stick. Then I heard a wrenching noise, and the boys began yelling and pointing. Out of habit, I lifted my camera to my eye. In the process, I stepped off the rubber mat and felt my feet scramble for traction on the slick ice. They didn't find it. With a painful jolt, I landed on my backside. My camera flew from my hand, skidding several inches across the slick surface.

For a moment, everything was silent. Then people began yelling from the stands. A few screams pierced the air. Jessica's voice called my name, telling me to get out of the way. I looked up to see a shadowy shape hurtling downward from the catwalk, coming straight at me. My first impulse was maternal—save my baby. I stretched my arm as far as I could. My fingers grazed the camera strap, but I couldn't quite get hold.

The object descended, closer, closer, picking up speed even as time seemed to stand still. I made out a man's form, headed straight for me. No time to escape.

Then I noticed the blue coat and realized…

The hulk about to crush me was Renata's ex-husband, Jeffrey Forte.

6

J effrey's bulky girth landed on me, knocking the wind out of me. The impact caused my head to jerk up, and it thudded back onto the ice. Tiny stars flashed in front of my eyes. I heard a pop, followed by a sharp, stabbing pain in my left wrist. *Uh-oh*, I thought. I'd never experienced a broken bone before, but I assumed it felt—and sounded—like this. My vision went black for a second. When it cleared, I saw a pair of sneaker-clad feet rushing toward me with a grace I'd never muster on solid ground, much less ice. Dropping to her denim-covered knees, Jessica slid the last few inches, and her face appeared above me.

"Callie!" She swatted my cheek lightly.

I jerked back to avoid another slap. "Stop it," I snapped. But the contact carried the desired effect, and clarity returned. With a vengeance.

Because it was then that I truly comprehended my state: I was immobilized beneath a lumpy mass of human being. "Get off me!" I writhed in a futile attempt to free myself. My squirming triggered additional pain in my wrist, a dull throbbing in my head, and an angry ache in my abdomen. *Uh-oh*, I thought again.

Jessica put her hands on my shoulders, gently restraining me. "Callie, Jeffrey…can't move. You're only going to hurt yourself worse if you keep jerking around."

I took a deep breath and held it, willing myself not to hyperventilate. I stopped focusing on my pain long enough to look at the man pinning me down.

He'd landed on his stomach on top of me, and his body lay perpendicular to mine. His legs splayed out to my right, his head and shoulders to my left. His neck twisted at an unnatural angle, and his face was turned away from me. I saw a bloody gash on the top of his head.

I knew in my gut the man was dead.

I squeezed my eyes shut, reopening them at the sound of skates approaching. Two legs the size of tree trunks skated across the ice, stopping a few feet from me. An angular face, pale and creased with concern, dropped into my line of vision. With surprising gentleness, Lars rested a hand the size of a goalie's glove on my cheek. "Hang on, Ms. Cassidy. Help is on ze way."

He looked at Jessica and tilted his head toward Jeffrey, a question in his eyes. She had already scrambled to Jeffrey's side and placed two fingertips against his wrist. After a moment, she looked at Lars and gave a small shake of her head.

It was official, or at least confirmed. Jeffrey Forte was dead. Did Renata know? My eyes darted around, searching for her. Where was she? I couldn't think…

I saw the players huddled together a few feet back. Lars rose and turned to them. "Boys, go wait in ze stands. Police and paramedics are on ze way. You vill help best by moving aside."

Once the boys had complied, Jessica clutched Lars's arm. "Let's get him off her," Jessica said. "Can you help me lift him?"

He stood tall and waved her off. "Stay back, Ms. Fannon. I vill do."

Even in my wounded state, I found myself charmed yet again by Lars's Swedish accent and his ice-blue eyes, not to mention his scent. Whatever cologne he wore always reminded me of the forest on a winter night. Still, there was no mistaking his power. At six foot five and an estimated two hundred fifty pounds of solid Alpine muscle, Lars' brawny arms strained the fabric of his black flex jacket. The red tubing down the sleeves looked like wriggling veins as his biceps flexed. Despite Jeffrey's tubbiness, I didn't doubt Lars could grab the man by the scruff of the neck and lift him off me with one hand.

Instead, he dropped to his knees, and with a tenderness approaching reverence, slid his arms beneath Jeffrey's lifeless body. He lifted the dead man off my torso and rested him on the nearby rubber mat.

Immediately, I tried to roll onto my knees, intending to stand up, but my body rebelled. My wrist shrieked in agony, and the pain in my side escalated. Worst of all, I was woozy and disoriented. For a moment, I even feared I was going to throw up.

Jessica plopped cross-legged on the ice and positioned my head in her lap. "Don't move, Callie. You might have a concussion. We'll wait here for the paramedics," she said, brushing strands of hair from my forehead. I nodded, feeling tears leave warm trails down my cheeks. I wondered idly if they'd freeze when they dropped to the ice.

Then I began to shiver, whether from the chill or shock, I wasn't sure. Jessica looked up at Lars. "Can you get her a blanket?" Without a word, he skated off toward the locker room.

Renata came flying across the ice and executed a quick hockey stop. Her eyes locked on Jeffrey, and she dropped to her knees. "Oh, god. Is he…is he…?"

Jessica took her hand and squeezed. "He's gone. I'm sorry, Renata."

Renata's other hand flew to her mouth. A series of emotions flashed across her face: confusion, fear, disbelief. Next came a rush of grief. Despite their estrangement, it made sense to me. He'd been her husband once, after all. They'd shared a life, however brief. For a while, anyway, she'd loved him.

After a moment, she drew a breath. "Well, then," she said simply.

She turned her watery eyes to me, as if noticing my presence for the first time. "Oh, Callie, you're hurt." She looked at Jessica. "She must be freezing. Shouldn't we get her off the ice?"

"I don't think we should move her," Jessica said. "Let's wait for the paramedics."

Lars returned with a blanket, and Jessica pulled it tight across me. Renata shot another quick glance at Jeffrey. Her eyes scanned the ice behind him, and she cocked her head. She got up, skated to a spot a few yards away, and bent over, hands resting on her knees. I squinted, finally figuring out she was examining the hockey stick I'd seen plummet from the catwalk. Suddenly, she stood bolt upright.

The sound of sirens filled the arena, and I saw Lars hurry toward the rink's entrance to meet the first responders.

***

Two paramedics headed straight toward Jeffrey, followed by police officers Kevin Laherty and Vicki Tollison. The four of them huddled over the man's inert form, checking for a pulse I knew they wouldn't find.

A pair of familiar faces—EMTs Maddie and Roland, both of whom I knew—made their way to me, moving Jessica aside so they could perform an examination. After determining I didn't have neck or spinal injuries, they lifted me onto a stretcher. Though they tried to be gentle, I had to ball my fists and suck in my lips to keep from moaning in pain. Once I was secure, they half rolled, half slid the gurney across the ice and onto solid ground. Maddie rustled in her duffel bag and removed a bag of liquid, which she hung from a pole attached to the gurney. "We're going to give you fluids and pain meds."

"I don't need any of that," I protested. "I'm okay. I think I sprained my wrist, and I'm sure I'll have a few bruises, but nothing I can't handle."

Roland smirked. Maddie rolled her eyes. "Since when did Rock Creek Village's famous photographer earn her medical license? Let's see…"

She kneaded the lump on my head as Roland moved my wrist back and forth. I bit my lip hard as tears welled in my eyes. Then Maddie slid her hands under my shirt and across my rib cage. The groan I'd been suppressing escaped. To their credit, neither paramedic said I-told-you-so.

"This wrist is broken," Roland said to Maddie.

She nodded. "I'm guessing at least a couple of her ribs are fractured, too. Plus, I'm thinking concussion." She turned her gaze on me. "Now, how about those pain meds?"

I nodded meekly. While Maddie inserted a needle into the vein on the back of my right hand, I distracted myself by watching the buzz of activity on the rink. The EMTs in charge of Jeffrey had done their part, and now they stood back and let the officers take over. Soon, I knew, the coroner would arrive to pronounce the death officially. They would encase Jeffrey in a black plastic body bag and transport him to the morgue to await an autopsy. A pit formed in my stomach. An hour ago, Jeffrey had harbored plots and schemes and emotions and desires. Now he was a shell. No matter what kind of man he'd been, I still felt a kernel of sympathy for him.

Officer Laherty snapped pictures of the body and the area surrounding it. His actions made me remember my camera, and I craned my neck looking for it but didn't spot it. I had other cameras, of course, but that Nikon held an esteemed place as my favorite—and the most expensive.

I called to Jessica and Renata, who stood a few feet away, watching the paramedics work on me. "I'm worried about my camera. I dropped it when I fell, but now I don't see it."

Jessica glanced toward the spot where Jeffrey had squashed me. "Maybe the cops have it," she said. "It'll turn up."

My blanket had fallen to the side, and Jessica rearranged it across me. The painkillers kicked in, and a light, soothing fog softened all the sharp edges. I felt like I was floating, or rocking in a cradle. I let my eyelids droop shut. My mind drifted, trying to make sense of all that was happening. A series of images rotated in my head: Renata smacking her ex-husband's nose. Jeffrey arguing with a black-coated stranger. A hockey stick on the ice. Jeffrey falling from the catwalk.

What was he doing up there, anyway?

"Was this an accident?" I murmured. "Or was it...?" Then I dozed off.

***

When I opened my eyes again, a lanky figure in a cowboy hat was leaning over me. I smiled drowsily at Frank Laramie, Rock Creek Village's current chief of police and my father's partner many moons ago. "Fancy meeting you here," I said.

Frank removed his wide brimmed Stetson. "Callahan Cassidy. What have you gotten yourself into this time?"

"Why do people always say that? I did nothing but get smooshed."

He chuckled. "Seems you have a habit of being in the wrong place at the wrong time."

"I'd like to protest, but I'm afraid I'll slur my words." My eyes still felt so heavy, but I fought the urge to drift off again. I wanted to be alert for this.

"I talked to your dad on the phone. He said, 'Tell Sundance to stay out of it.' So I'm passing it along."

Hearing my father's pet name for me perked me up. Charlie Cassidy, who'd acquired the nickname Butch when the same-named Paul Newman movie was released, had referred to me as his sidekick since before I could walk.

Frank turned to Renata. "Any idea where your brother is? Been trying to call him."

Her voice sounded concerned. "No, I...I assumed he was around here somewhere."

"Haven't seen or heard from him all day," Frank said.

"I'll try to call him," Renata said. "My phone's in the locker room. I'll be back in a minute."

As she skated off, Frank and I heard a scuffle break out across the arena. Frank immediately took off in that direction, and my eyes followed him. Near the entrance, I saw Officer Laherty grab hold of someone—a man in a black leather coat.

Not too many black leather coats populated Rock Creek Village. This had to be the same man I'd seen earlier in that angry encounter with Jeffrey—minutes before his nosedive from the catwalk.

7

The agitated man in the black coat pushed past Officer Laherty and scrambled onto the rink, headed for the gurney on which Jeffrey Forte lay encased in a body bag. "Hey there," Frank called, his voice calm. He stepped in the man's path. "Take it easy, fella. What is it you want?"

"Open that bag! Let me see him," the man cried. Behind him, Laherty approached, reaching out to grab him with a meaty hand. The man dodged his grasp, but the move backfired. His feet began spinning on the ice. He struggled to regain his balance, but it was no use. He toppled backward, bashing his head on the ice.

Now three of us had cracked our skulls against that ice today. They could declare this place an official disaster zone.

Maddie and Roland darted across the ice to the man's side. The adrenaline that rushed into my blood overpowered the lightheadedness caused by the painkillers. I resisted the urge to yank the IV needle out of my hand and chase them. Given my experience with ice today, it was just as well I was a prisoner of a gurney—and of Jessica, my iron-handed caretaker. "Calm down, Callie," she said in her teacher voice. "You're not going anywhere."

I sighed and leaned against the thin pillow. My body vibrated. Or at least, my rear end did.

It took me a second to figure out what was happening. Then I remembered I'd shoved my phone into my back pocket prior to the photo shoot. I was surprised it still worked, after the force of hundreds of pounds crushing me—and it. I'd be sure to write Apple a nice review.

Ignoring my injuries, I reached for the phone. Though the painkillers had dulled the ache in my ribcage to a tolerable level, my left wrist told a different story. Screamed it, in fact. And since I found my right hand incapacitated by an IV, I feared I was facing a lost cause.

Jessica came to my rescue, dislodging the phone from my pocket and placing it in my right hand with a grin. "Pathetic," she teased. "Want me to answer it for you too?"

"I can do it," I said stubbornly. After checking the caller ID, I swiped the screen and pressed a button.

"Hi, Dad. You're on speaker."

"You are too. Mom's here. They tell us you've found another body."

"Fake news," I protested. "The body…well, it found me."

He paused. "From what Frank said, that may be true."

My mother's voice came through the line. "Butch, you haven't even asked my baby how she's feeling."

"Hi, Mom. I'm okay. No big deal."

"Are you kidding? That enormous man dropped on you like the house in Oz!"

"Wait, am I the wicked witch in this scenario?"

"Stop joking. Frank told us they're transporting you to the hospital."

"Well, I think that's the plan, but we've been delayed. I'm sure we'll be leaving soon."

There was a long pause. "Delayed?" Dad asked.

"Yes. I don't want to get into it right now. I'll fill you in later. Or I'm sure Frank will."

"No matter about that," Mom said. "Darling, how badly are you hurt?"

"Really, Mom, it's nothing. Sprained wrist, I think. Bruises on my abdomen. Maddie says they'll be checking me for a concussion."

Mom gasped. "Nothing, you say? You've been bruised and battered. I've left a message for Jamal. As soon as he can get here to take over the front desk, we'll head to the hospital."

"No!" I said, with more force than I intended. "I mean, that's unnecessary, Mom. You know how long these things take. Anyway, I'm pretty woozy from the pain medication. I'll probably doze the whole time."

There was a long pause, and I listened as my parents conferred. "All right," my mother finally responded. "But promise you'll call if you get any…unexpected news. We can be there in half an hour."

I made the promise.

"In the meantime, I'm off to prepare the guest room. You'll stay here tonight."

I could have objected, I suppose, but I didn't have the energy. Plus, it would be nice to be fussed over and pampered, at least for one night.

"If you're thinking of arguing, don't bother," Dad said. "Your mother is already up the stairs."

"I won't argue. It sounds like a good idea."

"Good. Also, I'd urge you to get in touch with Sam. He's called here twice, said he left you a bunch of voicemails. It's not…well, it's not kind of you to leave him hanging."

I shot an embarrassed glance toward Jessica. "I've been kind of busy, Dad."

"Callahan Maureen Cassidy. We're never too busy for the people who care about us, right?"

"Okay, Dad. Point taken. I'll call him."

As I pressed disconnect, the phone buzzed again in my hand. Sam's name appeared on the screen, along with a picture of his handsome face, tousled blond hair tousled, and sexy grin. Jessica smirked at me. "Better answer that. You don't want your daddy grounding you."

I hovered my thumb above the connect button. Jessica sensed

my hesitation and stepped away, giving me a bit of privacy. As much as possible in this beehive of activity.

I steeled myself and pressed the connect button. "Hi, Sam. I was about to call you—"

"What's going on, Callie? Where are you? They said you got hurt, and when I couldn't get through to you…" His breath hitched, and I was hit with a wave of guilt.

"I'm fine, Sam. Don't worry. A couple of minor injuries. Nothing too bad."

There was a moment's silence. "You should have called me."

His demeanor had shifted from worried to hurt. In response, I turned defensive. "I'm sorry. I really haven't had time. Everything happened so fast, and the paramedics have been poking and prodding me. And the painkillers…I've been pretty groggy."

More silence. I gave it a beat, but when he didn't speak, I did. "Sam, I get the idea you're angry with me, but I'm not sure what I did wrong."

"I'm not angry," he said. His voice was soft, barely more than a whisper. "It's just…Callie, you and I are supposed to be in a relationship, but I had to get this news about you from someone else. It's…well, it's par for the course." He sighed. "Sorry. Now's not the time for that conversation. I can be at the rink in ten minutes. Is that okay?"

I knew he wanted me to say yes. To lean on him. Depend on him. But the old, independent Callie balked at that. Instead, I tried to compromise. "Listen, they'll be taking me to the hospital in a few minutes. Why don't I call you from there? If you wouldn't mind, I'll need a ride when they release me."

"That'll be fine," he said, his voice monotone. "Just call me when you're ready for me."

"Thank you." I hesitated. "And Sam, everything you do for me…it doesn't go unnoticed."

"Yeah. Take care of yourself, Callie. I'll see you soon."

***

While I'd been on the phone, Maddie and Roland had gone to the ambulance and returned with another stretcher. Now, as they lifted the man in the black coat onto it, he appeared conscious and alert. I got a better look at him as the paramedics rolled him across the ice toward us. Stringy blond hair, thin eyebrows, pale complexion. Young, maybe mid-twenties. Nothing familiar about him.

"Have you seen that guy before?" I asked Jessica.

She shook her head. Renata returned then, wearing sneakers in place of her skates. "Can't locate Raul," she said, her brow creased. She caught sight of the third gurney. "What's going on?"

Jessica started filling her in, but by then the color had drained from Renata's face. "What is it?" I asked.

She shook her head as if she couldn't comprehend what she was seeing. "That's Theo," she said. "Theo…Clement, I think it is. Jeffrey's half-brother."

He caught sight of her at the same time and pointed at her from the stretcher. "Don't let that woman near me," he shouted. "She'll kill me too!"

8

One pair of EMTs was required to stay with Jeffrey's body until the coroner arrived, so Theo and I shared an ambulance ride to Pine Haven Hospital. The space was so tight between my stretcher and his that our slender paramedic barely fit between us.

Maddie leaned over Theo's gurney, checking his IV line. The odor of antiseptic circulated through the air, mingling with what smelled like body lotion (probably Maddie's) and sour sweat (no doubt Theo's).

Once Maddie finished checking Theo, she turned to me and began fiddling with my IV line. "Doing okay, Callie?"

The speeding ambulance hit a pothole, sending the three of us bouncing. Theo and I both groaned. "Roland, take it easy!" Maddie shouted. "In case you've forgotten, we're transporting head injuries." She shrugged. "Male drivers. What're you gonna do?"

Satisfied that we were stable, she pulled down a Murphy-style seat near our feet, sat, and began tapping in our vitals on a tablet. Rock Creek Village wasn't large enough to warrant its own full-service hospital, so we made do with a couple of primary care physicians and a walk-in clinic. Serious injuries and illnesses required a thirty-mile trek to Pine Haven, a booming metropolis compared to our little town. Even more serious situations meant a trip to Boulder, an hour's drive south of the village. But from the looks of things, neither Theo nor I had sustained those kinds of injuries.

With Maddie's attention diverted, I stole a glance at Theo. Questions percolated in my brain, and here I had a captive audience who might be able to answer a lot of them.

Before the paramedics had kicked Frank out of the ambulance, he'd conducted a brief interview with Theo. I'd eavesdropped, of course. I mean, I was only inches away—what else could I do? The mini interrogation had yielded no information of value, not in my estimation. Theo said he'd been walking in the park across the street when he'd seen emergency responders race into the arena. So he hadn't even been present at the time of the...what? Accident? Murder? I glanced at him and wondered if he could be trusted at his word.

I decided to assume—for the moment, anyway—that his story was true and he hadn't witnessed the occurrence. Even so, I believed Theo harbored some useful information—knowledge Frank hadn't had time to dig out of him. Maybe I could.

As I drummed my fingers on the blanket, I consulted the angels and devils on my shoulders. Little devil Tonya would encourage me to dive right in, knowing she and her newspaper would be first in line for a scoop. I figured Jessica, a journalism teacher, would land on the devil side as well. From the other shoulder, Raul would tell me not to stick my nose into police business. Frank would concur. Sam would jump on that bandwagon, too, as would my parents. They'd all say this was none of my business.

We hit another pothole, and the resulting spasm of pain reminded me the dead man had fallen on *me*. Didn't that give me a right to prod? I mean, Fate clearly wanted me involved.

Mentally, I patted the devil shoulder. No time like the present.

I glanced at Maddie, who remained deep in concentration over her tablet. "Theo?" I whispered. I remembered Renata mentioning Jeffrey's refusal to be called Jeff and amended myself.

"Do you go by Theo? Or is it Theodore?"

His head lolled toward me. "Just Theo. Plain old ordinary Theo."

I gave him my best sympathetic smile. "My name is Callahan Cassidy, but I'm just plain old Callie. Looks like you and I are in the same boat. Or rather, ambulance."

"Hummm," he said. A bit of saliva drooled from his open mouth, and he stared at me vacantly.

I studied the rubber tube attached to his arm, wondering just how much morphine Maddie had given him. Far from serving as a deterrent, though, his drugged-up status might make him more compliant.

"How are you feeling?" I asked. Kind of a lame question, considering the man lay strapped to a gurney in the back of a speeding ambulance, but experience had taught me that asking the obvious often started the conversational ball rolling.

He lifted a hand and touched the back of his head. "They said I banged my head on the ice. Don't remember it. Hurts, though."

"I'm so sorry to hear that."

"My brother is dead."

"Yes."

His eyes locked with mine, and I glimpsed an alertness I hadn't seen there a moment ago. "Did you know my brother?" he asked.

"Not really." *I met him when he screamed at his ex-wife in front of my shop. And, of course, we were pretty close when he landed on me.* "Just in passing."

The dazed, half-lidded stare returned, and another question occurred to me: *Was Theo faking?* A little voice inside told me the man might not be as confused as he wanted me to believe.

"Six minutes out," I heard Roland call.

"Roger," Maddie said, looking back at her patients. "You two hanging in there?"

"I'm good," I said. Theo nodded. Maddie turned back to her tablet. Time was short. My subject needed a firm nudge.

"I saw you and Jeffrey arguing earlier, outside the arena. What was that about?"

Theo looked at the ceiling. Precious seconds passed before he responded. "Jeffrey decided to set up his new business venture in Rock Creek Village. It was a stupid choice, and I told him so." He paused, a sad smile playing on his face. "My big brother never took kindly to being contradicted."

I could only imagine. Jeffrey hadn't struck me as the type to appreciate anyone else's input. "Why did you think coming here was a bad idea for him?" I asked.

His lips tightened. "That ex of his. Renata Sanchez. I told him to forget about her, that she'd only cause him trouble. Turns out I was right."

Well, this piqued my interest. "What do you mean? They'd finalized their divorce a while ago, right?"

"Yeah, but Jeffrey wanted to get back together. It was the main reason he came to Rock Creek Village."

I was stunned. Outside my studio this morning, Jeffrey hadn't seemed at all interested in reconciliation. Then again, jealousy sometimes caused people to act irrationally.

"I had no idea he wanted Renata back," I said.

Theo snorted. "Sure. Nothing to do with love, though. He just couldn't stand that she's the one who left him. He never enjoyed losing."

"You opposed the idea?"

"Of course I did. Renata's nothing but a gold digger. I figured she'd jump at the chance to get back with Jeffrey, especially now that our mom died and left him everything."

Huh. Renata hadn't mentioned Jeffrey's inheritance. Interesting…

Still, the gold digger label didn't jibe with the Renata I knew. I thought about the affection that softened her features when she looked at Ethan. And then the smack she'd delivered to her ex-husband's nose. Neither suggested a desire to put her marriage back together. I couldn't believe she'd been considering reconciliation, even for financial gain.

"I have to say, my conversations with Renata don't lead me to believe she had any designs on Jeffrey or his money. In fact, she asked me to help get him—"

I stopped as Theo began thrashing against the straps of the gurney. His heart rate monitor beeped wildly. "Shut up!" he cried. "You don't know what you're talking about. She hated my brother. All she wanted was revenge!"

Maddie leapt up from her seat and rushed to Theo's side. His cheeks puffed in and out as he gasped for air, and she slid an oxygen mask over his face. After a few seconds, the beeps from the monitor came more slowly. Maddie took a breath and turned to glare at me. "I think that's enough of the interrogation."

"I wasn't interrogating," I objected. "We were just talking…"

"Well, the conversation is over." She positioned herself between us and didn't budge for the rest of the ride.

***

Two hours later, I'd been poked, kneaded, X-rayed, and groped, all the while being directed to "relax" and "take it easy." So many people handled me that I felt like a lump of Play-Doh at a kid's birthday party. Now, I was resting on a hospital bed in the ER, waiting for the elusive doctor as I listened to the whir of emergency room machinery and inhaled bitter medicinal odors. My attire consisted of an attractive gown tied loosely in the back, thick yellow gripper slippers, and a thin blanket that smelled of bleach. Aside from the flimsy garb, I was relatively comfortable, thanks in large part to the painkillers flowing through my veins.

Crammed alongside the bed in the tiny curtained cubicle, two plastic chairs held Jessica and Renata, who had shown up in the emergency room soon after my arrival. Jessica had assumed the role of patient advocate, ordering medical personnel about as if she were chief of staff. Renata was quieter, and I figured she was still trying to process the reality of her ex-husband's death.

Now that the procedures were complete and we were in sit-and-wait mode, all of us were calm. In fact, Jessica was so calm that she was snoozing. When I lifted my phone to snap a picture of my slumbering friend, Renata looked up from her own screen and grinned wryly.

As I snapped the almost-silent shutter, Jessica straightened in the chair. "Two can play that game," she said. She pulled her own phone from her pocket and turned the screen to me. In the picture, shot from the back as I was getting settled on the bed, a semi-profile of my face was visible. The embarrassing part, though, involved an expanse of pale skin visible through my hospital gown's opening—along with the slightest hint of butt crack.

"Give me that!" I reached across the bed with my good arm but was stopped short by the IV attached to the back of my hand.

Jessica laughed and wagged a finger at me, holding the phone just out of reach. "One little swipe, a couple of clicks, and this baby is all over social media."

I moaned and squeezed my eyes shut. My head fell back on my pillow, and my face contorted in agony. Jessica leapt to her feet. "Callie? What is it? Should I call the nurse?"

When she leaned over me, I opened my eyes, darted out my good hand, and snatched her phone.

She scowled and pried the phone from my fingers. Renata began laughing then. It was such a welcome sound from her that Jessica and I joined in. I wondered if the medical personnel found it odd to hear laughter floating through their emergency room. With everything they saw in their jobs, maybe they'd consider it a welcome respite. I knew I did.

9

J essica yawned. "I'm going to scout some coffee and look for your doctor. Want anything, Ren?" Renata shook her head, and Jessica parted the curtain and squirmed through it.

Renata settled back in her chair. Her amused expression morphed back into a thoughtful, distant gaze.

"How are you holding up, Renata?" I asked.

My voice brought her back from wherever she'd been, and she gave me a sad smile. A single tear dripped down her cheek, and she swiped it away. "I don't understand why I'm reacting like this. It's not as if I loved the man. Not anymore."

"But you did once. It's only natural to feel shaken over his death."

"I suppose you're right." She sighed. "It was so weird that Theo turned up in town, too. I didn't even realize he was here."

"How well do you know him?" I asked.

"Not well. I hadn't seen him in over a year. Before that, I'd only met him a few times over the course of the marriage. He had some...issues. Drugs, I'm told, though Jeffrey didn't talk about him much."

"They didn't get along?"

She scoffed. "Not hardly. They're half-brothers. Same mom, different dads. Theo is about ten years younger. From what Jeffrey told me, rehab served as Theo's second home from the time he graduated high school. I wouldn't say Jeffrey hated him, but he had no respect for him, and he certainly didn't love him. Then again, Jeffrey never cared about anyone but himself."

I twisted in the bed, trying to get comfortable. "In the ambulance, Theo mentioned that Jeffrey recently inherited their mom's estate. I'm wondering why she excluded Theo from the will. Because of the drug problems, you think?"

Renata shrugged. "Could be. But their mom's money came to her courtesy of Jeffrey's father. When he died, he left a substantial fortune, all to her. Theo's dad came into the picture afterward. He was kind of a loser, never kept a job. Could be she felt the money rightfully belonged to Jeffrey. Who knows? That family was the epitome of dysfunction."

I hesitated but decided Renata deserved to hear what else Theo had said. "Renata, Theo told me something in the ambulance…"

"Uh oh," she said. "Whatever it is, just say it. It can't be worse than Theo screaming at everyone that I'd killed his brother."

She had a point. I filled her in on Theo's speculation that Jeffrey wanted Renata back and that she'd been considering the proposition—so she could get her hands on his money.

Her face scrunched up and turned red, and once again I noticed her resemblance to her brother. "A gold digger? Ugh." She clenched her fists in her lap. "Guess his brother didn't bother to tell him I gave up any claim to Jeffrey's money when we divorced. The only things I demanded were the dog and the car, even though my lawyer said I could have gotten much more."

She paused, tossing her long, dark hair over her shoulder. "Do you think anyone will believe him? I won't be a suspect in Jeffrey's death, will I?"

I hoped not, but I knew spouses—and ex-spouses—were always among the first people police investigated. "It could still turn out to be an accident," I said. "Maybe he tripped on the catwalk and fell over the guardrail somehow. But for the sake of argument, where were you when Jeffrey fell?"

She looked away, replaying events in her memory. Then she blinked. "I was in the locker room," she said. "Preparing for coaching duty."

I stayed silent. Renata's demeanor made me doubtful I was getting me the full truth from her. Her hands twisted in her lap. "Callie, there's something you should know."

I braced myself. Was Renata about to confess? Please no.

"There was a hockey stick lying on the ice…"

I remembered seeing Renata skate over to the stick. The way she'd stiffened at the sight of it. "I saw it. It flew down from the catwalk, just before Jeffrey…"

She shot me a dark look. "It belonged to me. And the blade was covered in blood."

***

Our conversation left me with more questions than answers, but Jessica returned, putting the conversation on hold.

"Couldn't find your doctor, but I brought you a visitor," she said, pulling back the curtain with a flourish to reveal Frank, who squeezed into the cramped space beside my bed. His eyes moved from the IV in my right hand to the sling on my left arm, finally resting on my face. "None the worse for wear, huh?"

His smile didn't align with the somberness in his eyes. He wasn't here to check on my well-being—not entirely. Frank was here in his capacity as Chief of Police. Still, it wouldn't do any good to press him. He'd reveal his intentions in his own time.

I replied in the same cheerful tone he'd used. "I'm fine, Frank. Nothing to worry about. Just waiting for the doctor to release me, but I'm not high on her list of priorities."

"Mmm hmm. Well, your mother said to tell you she's been to your house, packed you a bag, and rescued Woody and Carl from their lonely plight. All you have to do is show up when you're done here."

I smiled, knowing Woody and Carl were living the high life as we spoke. My parents owned and operated the Knotty Pine Resort, Rock Creek Village's top-tier vacation spot, and they lived in a lovely condo above the lodge. My mother kept tins of treats all around the place, as well as comfy beds for her grandpets' frequent visits.

A sudden thought occurred to me, and I winced. "Oh. Sam's my ride. I said I'd call him. He's going to be worried. And mad."

"We can give you a lift home," Renata said. "Plenty of room in my Explorer, in case they send you home with a wheelchair or something."

I swatted her arm. "My drunk uncle," I said, using one of Mrs. Finney's favorite expressions. "There's nothing wrong with me that a glass of wine and a good night's sleep won't cure."

"We'll see about that," Frank said. "But I do think you should call Sam for that ride." He turned to Renata. "I'll need you at the station to answer some questions."

Renata slid me an "I-told-you-so" glance.

Jessica's jaw tensed. "What kind of questions?"

Frank's eyes never left Renata. "The hockey stick that fell from the catwalk? The one covered in blood? It belongs to you."

Renata's gaze dropped to the floor. She nodded. "I don't know how it got there, I swear."

Jessica gripped Renata's forearm. "Don't say anything else," she cautioned.

"Yes, best to keep quiet," I told her, giving Frank a scowl. "Does Renata need a lawyer?"

Frank shoved his hands into the pockets of his jeans. "I can't offer any advice on that. But I can say, Renata, your cooperation is voluntary. At this point."

Renata gave herself a shake. "I'll answer whatever questions you have. No lawyer necessary. I have nothing to hide."

Frank nodded. "All right, then. Before we go, have any of you heard from Raul?"

"Raul?" I said, surprised. "You still haven't talked to him?"

"I've tried several times to reach him. My calls go straight to voicemail. He hasn't contacted any of you?"

I shook my head, and Jessica lifted her hands, palms up. Renata wouldn't meet anyone's eyes. "I've called him over and over and sent texts. He hasn't responded."

My eyebrow shot up. It was unlike Raul to be off the grid, especially where his sister was concerned. But even more worrisome was Frank's expression. Something was up. "It's not like he'd be working the case anyway, since the victim was his ex-brother-in-law," I ventured. Then I thought of the argument outside the gallery, and alarm bells clanged in my head.

"Is he…are you thinking Raul might've…"

Frank held up a hand. "Don't go borrowing worries, Callie. I just need to talk to him, that's all. If he gets in touch, have him call me. Right away."

Yeah, right. Mom used to say worry was my middle name. What did Frank know that I didn't?

Renata picked up her bag. "Chief, is it okay if I drop Jessica at her house before I come to the station?"

"Oh, heck no," Jessica said. "I'm coming to the station with you." Frank sighed, and Jessica turned to me. "That is, if you don't need me to stay, Callie."

I waved. "No, what I need is for you to be with Renata. I'll call Sam. He'll be here in no time. Keep me posted, okay? I want every detail."

"Can you tell Ethan what's going on?" Renata asked. "I don't want him to worry when he can't reach me."

"Of course," I responded.

Then the three of them disappeared through the curtain. I laid my head against the pillow, my head spinning. Renata in the crosshairs? And Raul? I needed to figure out how to help.

10

Anurse popped in, checked my monitors and IV line, and assured me the doctor would be along shortly. Ha. I'd heard that before. Once she left, it was time to tackle my next stressor: Contacting Sam. I didn't expect my delay had settled well with him, and I wasn't looking forward to the call. But it had to be done, so I tapped his number on my phone.

He picked up on the first ring, and I told him they'd completed all the tests, and the doctor still hadn't been by to give me any results. "I'm sure there's nothing to be worried about," I said. "I'll be fit for duty by tomorrow."

"Uh huh," he responded, his voice terse. "I'll leave now and see you in a half hour."

The conversation felt businesslike and distant, leaving me with the sense that the current bump in our romantic road wouldn't be easily patched. Unfortunately, I wasn't even sure I had the tools to make the repair.

Putting relationship worries aside, I called Sundance Studio. Not only did I need to inform Ethan of Renata's plight, but I also wanted to check on my business.

"Sundance Studio. How may I help you?"

Though I took pride in knowing which twin was which in person, their voices still sounded identical to me, so I took a shot in the dark. "Hi, it's Callie. Braden?"

"Hey, Callie. Yeah, it's Braden. Heard you almost got crushed by a body! That sucks."

"I'll be fine. Back to the gallery by tomorrow, I bet."

"Yeah, well. We'll see." No one seemed to put much stock in my medical self-diagnosis.

"How'd it go in the darkroom today?" I asked.

"Didn't get in there. Kind of busy, and Banner needed my help with customers while Ethan was gone."

"Ethan left?"

"Yeah. Had a couple of things to take care of, he said. He's been back for a while, though."

"Can you put him on the phone?"

"Sure thing." Braden clicked a button, treating me to soft jazz on-hold music. My head pounded, and I shifted in the bed, trying to get comfortable. *Why had Ethan left?* I wondered. It wasn't like him to abandon the gallery when he was in charge. Still, when he picked up the phone, I didn't mention his absence. We had more important things to discuss.

***

After I gave Ethan the details, I told him to put Banner and Braden in charge of the evening lock up and head over to the station. Though they'd never done it on their own, the twins knew the closing routine. I felt certain they could handle it.

Now, lying on the hard bed, I found myself at loose ends. The beeping of the machinery and the murmured conversations at the desk outside my cubicle provided my only companionship. If the doctor didn't show up soon, I feared I'd require a psychiatric consultation as well.

I used the down time to reassess my physical status. My headache had intensified slightly, probably due to my spate of activity, as well as the adrenaline wearing off. Some soreness around my ribcage, but that was milder now. The problem area was my wrist. I still experienced sharp pain every time I moved it. Besides that, the joint had swollen to twice its normal size. Despite what I'd told Sam, I thought the medics were right about it being broken. How on earth would I be able to shoot pictures if I couldn't even hold a camera?

The thought triggered a memory—the last time I'd held my precious Nikon. Just before Jeffrey's body landed on top of mine. I closed my eyes and replayed the scene. I'd watched the hockey stick fall to the ice. Then I'd heard another noise from the catwalk. Instinctively, I'd lifted the camera to my eye and aimed it upward…Hadn't I? The memory was hazy, but one thing was clear. I needed to get my hands on that camera.

I reached for my phone again, determined to get in touch with someone who could help me. Frank, maybe, or Lars at the rink. At that moment, though, the doctor entered my cubicle. At least, I assumed she was a doctor. Her white coat and stethoscope indicated as much. Otherwise, I might have thought her a candy-striper, so youthful was her appearance. She'd pulled her red hair into a ponytail, and her makeup-free face bore no sign of wrinkles.

I suspected the person entrusted with my physical well-being wasn't any older than seventeen.

"Hello, Ms. Callahan," she said, without so much as a glance in my direction. "I'm Dr. Foster."

"Just in time," I said. "I was about to suggest they go ahead and move me to a senior citizen center." I kept my tone light, but the sarcasm dripped from my words.

She finally looked at me over the rims of retro cat eyeglasses, her expression impassive. "Sorry about the wait. These things take time. We appreciate your patience."

"*Our patient's patience*. Might make a good new hospital motto."

"What's that?"

"Never mind," I said. My attempts at wit were clearly lost on this woman. "So, doc, what's the damage?"

"I've reviewed your scans and determined a grade zero concussion."

"Last time I got a zero, it meant I'd flunked chemistry."

"It's the lowest severity on the scale," she said. "You just need to take it easy for a day or two. No heavy lifting or strenuous activity."

"You're saying I should cancel my Ultimate Fighting competition?"

Another blank look before she returned her attention to the clipboard. "Your X-rays show a couple of minor rib fractures. I'm afraid there's little we can do to treat that. Ice packs might ease the discomfort, but the only true remedy is time."

I didn't even attempt to inject levity. Just nodded and waited.

"Most concerning is the distal radius fracture of your left wrist. It'll require a cast. A nurse will be by to take care of it."

Ugh. My fear was coming to pass. "Is a cast necessary? I'm a photographer, and I need the use of both hands. How about, like, a brace or something?"

She dropped her clipboard to her side and fixed me with a somber stare. "I suppose we could do that. I just assumed you'd prefer not to spend the next forty years with limited mobility and possibly significant pain. Perhaps I was mistaken."

Apparently, I wasn't the only one who could wield sarcasm like a sharpened scalpel. I felt like a scolded child, but she'd made her point. If the doctor said I needed a cast, I'd suck it up and get one. I nodded in compliance. "If you think it's best, I'll trust your expertise."

She nodded and returned to her clipboard, scribbling on a piece of paper. Tearing it from the pad, she placed it on the bedside table. "I'm sending you home with a prescription for a mild painkiller you can take for the next couple of days. When that runs out, acetaminophen, such as Tylenol, should do the trick. No ibuprofen. Also, I'd suggest having someone stay with you for the next few days, just as a precaution. Let us know if you have any dizziness or fainting." She paused, as if considering whether to trust me with what came next. "Questions?"

"No. I understand. Thank you, doctor."

"You'll need to make an appointment with an orthopedist for follow-up care. Your discharge orders will include a list of recommended doctors. After the nurse casts your wrist, she'll give you that paperwork. Then you're free to go."

11

After Dr. Congeniality departed, I didn't have to wait long for the nurse to enter with her tray of cast-making materials. She was a plump woman with silver hair who called me "dearie" and "ducky" as she removed my IV line and detached the monitors. It was a pleasant change in the wake of the doctor's all-business attitude.

In addition to the nurse's bedside manner, she exhibited skill and efficiency, chatting affably while she worked. Just as she wrapped the last piece of fiberglass around my wrist, Sam came through the curtain, his cheeks red from the cold. My heart swelled at the sight of him. He took in the scene with a single glance and moved to the head of the bed. "Broken?" he asked simply.

I nodded. "A couple of minor rib fractures, too, and a mild concussion. Nothing major. I should be okay in a couple of days."

He folded his arms. "Guess it could have been worse."

Did I detect irritation in his clipped response? Frustration? "Sam, I did nothing to cause this. It was a simple photography gig. I just ended up in the wrong place at the wrong time. I didn't ask the man to fall from the catwalk and land on me."

He sighed, then leaned over to kiss my cheek. "I know. And I'm glad you're all right."

The nurse stood, peeling off her latex gloves. "All done," she said. "You'll need to keep the cast dry. You can buy waterproof covers for showering at any drug store. As I'm sure Dr. Foster told you, you'll need to see an orthopedist next week, then again two weeks later."

I grimaced. "So I'm stuck with this thing for two weeks?"

The nurse chuckled. "Oh, no, ducky. More like six weeks. The cast just needs to be checked every so often to make sure it's not getting too loose. They'll do X-rays, too, so they can make sure the bone is healing properly."

"But I'm a photographer," I objected again. "I need the use of both hands."

"What can't be helped can't be helped." She lifted her tray, rested it on a hip, and smiled. "It's been a pleasure, Ms. Cassidy. Now, get dressed and let this handsome man take you home to coddle you."

After she left, Sam helped me sit on the edge of the bed. He handed me my clothes, and in a burst of modesty, I asked him to turn away as I struggled into them. The jeans I managed fairly well, and I problem-solved the bra issue by fastening it in front and wriggling it around, sliding my arms into the straps. It was the sweatshirt that stopped me short. I got it over my head, no problem. And I got my right arm in just fine. But after a few feeble attempts to thrust the cast through the left sleeve, I was stuck.

Sam stood aside patiently. I knew he heard me struggling, but experience had taught him not to intervene. My discouragement threatened to turn into tears. For as long as I could remember, the desire for self-sufficiency was both my biggest strength and a huge curse. I reminded myself of my therapist's words: *Asking for help is a gift you give others.*

"Sorry, I can't do this on my own," I admitted. "Can you help me?"

Sam turned and assessed the situation. "Let me try," he said. He took the left sleeve and stretched the cuff, guiding my cast through the opening. With an endearing gentleness, he pulled the shirt over my stomach. Then he kissed me softly on the lips, and I wrapped my good arm around him and held him tight.

No doubt about it, the man was a keeper.

***

Unfortunately, our kumbaya moment was short-lived. We'd gathered my things, signed my paperwork, listened to stern instructions on the proper care and maintenance of a mildly concussed, broken-wristed, fractured-ribbed patient, and settled into Sam's car. I couldn't even fasten my seatbelt—a sign of how annoying these next few weeks were going to be—so he reached across the console and buckled me in. After he'd turned on the seat warmers, he kissed me again and pulled out of the parking lot.

I was drowsy again, so I lazily watched the landscape float by as we made the journey home from Pine Haven. It was early evening, and the sun hung low on the horizon, casting geometric shadows across the snowy meadows. The stalwart Rocky Mountains rose in the distance, exuding permanence and strength. I felt secure in their presence, reminded that time goes on and goodwill prevails.

We rounded a corner, and a scenic view of the river flowing at the foot of a mountain took my breath away. Instinctively, my hand moved to my chest, searching for the camera that usually hung there. And that reminded me: I didn't know where my Nikon was right now.

I looked at Sam, whose hands were at ten and two, his eyes focused on the road ahead. "Sam, can we make a quick stop at the hockey rink? Last time I saw my camera, it was lying on the ice. Then it seemed to disappear. I really need to find it."

He glanced at the clock on the dashboard. "I'd better not. It's getting close to event time, and I've left Rodger to handle all the prep. I need to get back."

"Event time?"

He shot me a sidelong glance and frowned. "My catering event tonight. Kimberly and Parker's party?"

I searched my foggy brain. "Oh, yeah. The early-Valentine-slash-anniversary couples-only shindig, right? That's tonight?"

Sam stayed silent for a moment, then heaved a sigh. "Yes. And I've only been talking about it every day for the past week."

My face grew hot. I'd let him down again. "I'm sorry, Sam. I just forgot. It's probably the concussion…"

"I only wish that were true," he said quietly.

I closed my eyes and took a deep breath—as deep as my protesting ribs would allow. Did we have to do this right now? "So tell me about it. What are you serving? How many people did they invite?"

Kimberly Wainwright Petrie Lyon had been a high school classmate, and a few years after I'd bolted out of Rock Creek Village for college in Austin, Texas, Sam had married her. It had been what the old-timers called a shotgun marriage, and it had lasted little more than a year after their daughter Elyse's birth. Now, the two of them maintained a cordial relationship—a good thing, since they both lived in our small town. Kimberly and I got along well, too, especially since I'd saved her life a year ago. Still, I hadn't been invited to the party—which I secretly believed might turn into some sort of swingers' thing anyway—because Kimberly didn't think it appropriate to include the caterer and his girlfriend on the guest list.

No great loss, as far as I was concerned.

Sam didn't respond, and I felt my own wave of irritation. A dead man had fallen on me. I'd been injured. And now my boyfriend was giving me the silent treatment.

I stared out the window, brooding. A herd of bighorn sheep grazed on the rocky hillside, and I fought the urge to direct Sam's attention to the creatures.

After a few more moments of silence, he blew out a breath and began filling me in on the job's details in an almost normal tone. By the time he'd finished telling me about pâté and pomegranate and pickled herring, he'd pulled into the parking lot of the rink.

"Sam, you said you didn't have time…"

He unbuckled his seatbelt. "If I don't take time to make the ones I love happy, what's my life about? Stay here. I'll check on your camera."

When he closed the door and headed toward the rink's entrance, I considered his words. He was right. What we had in this world was each other. And to me, that meant I owed it to my friends to make sure justice was served.

12

The stop at the ice rink had been a bust. After finding the place locked, Sam had knocked on the door, only to be met by Officer Tollison. She told him she knew nothing about a camera, but that I should check with Marilyn, the administrative assistant at the station, on Monday morning. Her nonchalant response annoyed me—I mean, that camera represented my living—but Sam wouldn't let me out of the car to plead my case.

Instead, he drove to the Knotty Pine Resort, and we walked through the lobby and up the stairs to my parents' home above the lodge. After a grateful handshake from my father and a tight squeeze from my mother, he handed Mom a container. "My newest dessert creation," he said. "Beary Special Cobbler. Made with locally grown gooseberries, cherries, and pears."

My father licked his lips and reached for the container. "I may skip dinner and get right to dessert."

Mom swatted his hand away and headed to the kitchen, placing the cardboard carton in the refrigerator. "Thank you, Sam," she said over her shoulder. "You're always so thoughtful. And I appreciate you for always taking such good care of our troublesome daughter."

"Hey! How am I troublesome? I'm a pleasure and a delight. The light of your life, I imagine."

Just then, a swash of gold fur streaked into the room, headed on a collision course with me. Dad reached out in time to grab Woody's collar before the pup could execute his signature leap, one that ended with his paws atop my shoulders. "Not today, Woodster," he said. "Our girl's injured. You need to take it easy on her."

The dog whined, and his liquid brown eyes displayed instant understanding. When Dad released him, Woody wriggled and wagged, but he kept all four paws on the ground. I bent and scratched behind his ears. From the corner of my eye, I saw Carl peer around the corner, then stroll coolly into the living room. He wrapped himself once around my ankles and meowed. As I stooped to pick him up, a wave of dizziness came over me, and I braced myself on the back of the couch.

Sam hurried over and took my elbow. My father scooped up the cat, plopping him into my good arm. "Lest you forget, Sundance, it's okay to ask for help."

I nodded and ran a finger down Carl's spine, earning a deep purr.

"All right," Mom said, rubbing her hands together, "time to get our girl settled in for a nap before dinner. Sam, you're welcome to stay, of course, but if memory serves, tonight's the big gala at the Lyon home. I imagine your services are required elsewhere."

Sam gave her a grateful look, and I winced. My mother had a better handle on Sam's schedule than I did. "I do need to get going," he said.

I walked him to the door. We stood facing each other, awkwardness wedged between us. He looked into my eyes, as if searching for something. I wished I knew what it was. Finally, he said, "Take it easy, Callie. Give your body a chance to recover."

"I will. Thank you, Sam, for…well, for everything."

He leaned across Carl and pecked me on the cheek, then trotted down the stairs and through the door.

"He's a good man," Dad said when I returned.

"Such a lovely boy," Mom said. "I believe I've sensed some stress between the two of you in recent days, though."

I gave her a warning look, and she waved me off. "A conversation for another time." She led me up a flight of stairs to the guest room. The thick curtains were closed. The lamp on the nightstand gave off a soft yellow glow. Mom had turned down the plump comforter, and the bed sent me a siren song, luring me into its embrace. I sat on the side of the mattress and watched my mother remove my shoes, like she had when I was a little girl. With a groan, I stretched out on my back. My mother stroked my forehead and gazed at me. "My poor baby," she said. "How do you keep getting yourself into all these messes?"

I opened my mouth to object, and she patted my shoulder. "Never mind, darling. Just rest. Jamal is going to drive your father over to retrieve your car. Then they'll stop at the drug store to pick up your prescription and get some of those shower thingies you need. I'll come check on you every half hour. If you're not exhibiting any danger signs by the time we finish dinner, the doctor's instruction sheet says it's safe to let you sleep through the night."

She sat on the edge of the bed, and I relaxed beneath her gentle touch. I marveled again at what a beautiful woman my mother was: Tall, regal-looking, silver hair framing smooth, porcelain skin. For Mom, sixty-eight was the new forty.

I drifted off, thinking how lucky I was to have her in my life.

***

It seemed only moments had passed when the mattress shifted, and a tongue licked my cheek. I reached over and buried my fingers in Woody's silky coat. "Thanks for the wake-up call, furball," I muttered.

The dog stretched out beside me, and Carl perched across Woody's shoulders, looking uncharacteristically softhearted. Turning my head, I saw Dad standing next to the bed, hands in his pockets. The room was dark except for the ambient light filtering in from the hallway. "I figured a furry reveille would be kinder than turning on the light and jacking up the volume on the radio the way I did when you were a teenager."

"No doubt about that," I said. "I remember those days, and none too fondly." I yawned, but when I lifted my left hand to cover my mouth, it felt heavy, as if tethered to the bed. I remembered the cast, and the rest of the day's events came flooding back.

"You're probably starving," Dad said. "I bet you haven't had anything since breakfast."

As if to punctuate the thought, my stomach rumbled. "I could eat."

"Always," he said.

"Careful now. I get the idea you're calling me a glutton."

"Never. As you know, I respect a hearty eater. Now, let's get you up and fed."

He shooed Woody off the bed and placed a firm hand behind my back, supporting me as I swung my legs over the side of the bed. "Easy does it, Sundance. You may feel a little dizzy at first."

He hit that nail on the head. In fact, it felt like he'd hit it on *my* head. My skull seemed to be two sizes too small. And my ribs…ugh. Had someone taken a chainsaw to them while I slept? Even my wrist, bound as it was, pulsed in angry dissent. I closed my eyes and bowed my head. "Did you pick up those painkillers?"

"I did, but you shouldn't take them on an empty stomach. Dinner first, meds after."

He grasped my arm and helped me to my feet. Through the soft edges of a dizzy spell, he looked even more like Paul Newman than usual. His thick gray hair, which he kept short around his ears, had just begun to recede a bit in the front. The lines on his forehead and around his clear blue eyes lent him an air of depth. I experienced a wave of love for the man who'd raised me. And that wasn't just the concussion talking.

Once the initial lightheadedness had passed, Dad took me downstairs and settled me into a chair. Mom bustled about, placing platters and cups on the dining table. Simple fare tonight—her secret recipe meatloaf, mashed potatoes, fresh steamed green beans drizzled with balsamic vinegar, and yeasty homemade rolls. Comfort food at its finest. I dug in fast, glad I had full use of my right hand.

After a few minutes of power eating, I glanced up from my plate to see my parents watching me—amused or horrified, I couldn't be sure. "What?" I asked, wiping a trail of gravy from my chin. "Haven't you ever seen anyone eat before?"

"Not with quite that level of...gusto," Mom said. "But I'm glad you appreciate my cooking."

"Also glad we don't have guests," Dad muttered, spearing a few green beans. "Doubt there'd be enough to go around."

"Listen, I haven't eaten all day. Besides, I'm just trying to meet the requirements for the pain pill you promised me."

Mom smiled. "You're looking better already. A little color in your cheeks. I'll be certain to pass that news along to all your well-wishers."

"Well-wishers?"

"Yes, darling. In case you didn't realize it, you've collected quite a loyal group of friends in the village. We've fielded frenzied calls from Jessica and Summer, Kimberly Lyon, Fran, Mrs. Finney...and Tonya heard the news and called from Vail."

Dad stuck a bite of meatloaf in his mouth and pointed his fork at her. "Don't forget Raul."

"Raul? He finally turned up?"

Dad nodded. "Showed up at the police station mad as a wet cat." On cue, Carl yowled from the corner of the room. "He got Renata out of there in a hurry."

"Did he say where he'd been all day?"

"Not that I heard. I don't think anyone had the hutzpah to ask him."

I picked up a roll and slathered it with butter. "What else is happening with the investigation?"

Mom made a point of looking at her watch. "Well done, Callie. Over five minutes have elapsed since you sat down at the table. Your father predicted you'd bring up the murder within thirty seconds, but I said you'd hold out at least three minutes. Guess hunger trumps nosiness."

Ignoring the barb, I tore off a bit of roll and popped it into my mouth. "Well?"

"Not much news coming down the pipeline," Dad said. "Frank's been too busy to talk. I haven't heard anything you don't already know."

I arched an eyebrow. That seemed unlikely. My father, Rock Creek Village's former chief of police, and Frank Laramie, his lead detective who'd been promoted to the position when Dad retired, talked business daily—which really meant they gossiped like a couple of old ladies. My father surely knew something I didn't.

At any other time, I'd harangue him until I wore him down. But the day's events were taking their toll. At this point, all I wanted was dessert, a pain pill, and a long night's sleep.

"If you say so," I said. "I won't pester you tonight—too tired. Come tomorrow morning, though, you're on the hook."

13

I woke twice in the night, the first time because I needed to use the bathroom. Since I'd needed my mother to help me into my pajamas like I was a four-year-old, I worried I'd have to wake her for assistance. But like a big girl, I managed on my own, cast and all.

The second awakening occurred in the aftermath of a nightmare—or rather, a memory that took on a horrifying twist in my subconscious dream state. In it, I was sitting in the stands at the hockey arena, watching another version of myself standing center ice, camera in hand. A few feet from on-ice me, Woody and Carl lay curled together in a golden ball. Suddenly, a huge, hulking figure, at least four times Jeffrey's actual size, hurtled down from the catwalk. My avatar scrambled out of the way, but I couldn't reach the creatures, and they were buried beneath the giant's bulk.

I woke up writhing and sweating, disoriented. Once I realized I was in the guest room at my parents' house, I wrangled out from under the covers and stumbled to the door. My mother had banished Woody and Carl from the room, concerned they'd end up on top of me in bed, as usual. But the two of them hadn't gone far. When I opened the door, I saw them snuggled together in the hallway like sleepy sentinels.

Woody raised his head and thumped his tail. Carl eyed me moodily. "Get in here, you two," I whispered.

They scrambled into the room, and I climbed back beneath the covers. Once I was situated, I patted the bed, and the two furballs jumped up beside me. Woody pressed his warm body next to mine while Carl burrowed into the pillow above my head.

Now I could truly rest.

***

When I woke the third time, the muted light of dawn seeped around the edges of the curtains. A glance at the clock told me it was six in the morning, and my brain told me there was no chance I'd be going back to sleep. Ten hours must have been all my battered body required.

I stretched my various body parts—arms, legs, neck, torso—expecting to be stiff and sore now that the painkillers had worn off. Apart from a spark of disagreement in my ribs, I felt surprisingly good. My headache had subsided, and even my wrist didn't complain much when I moved it inside the cast. I figured I'd be able to forgo the pain pills today and settle for Tylenol.

Pulling myself to a sitting position, I rested against the headboard. My mind turned to Jeffrey's murder. Woody continued snoring, but Carl must have sensed my thoughts. He sashayed to my side and regarded me through narrowed eyes.

I stroked his spine. "So much information to sift through." He meowed. "All these questions that need answering. Where was Raul all day? Was Renata really in the locker room when the body fell, as she told me? Why did Theo come to Rock Creek Village? For that matter, what was Jeffrey's true purpose in town? Renata said she had the idea Jeffrey was hiding something. Did one of those secrets led to his death?"

Carl yowled and nudged my hand. I grinned at him. "You're right. These mysteries aren't going to solve themselves, are they?"

He seemed to consider my words, and his head bobbed. I probably gave the cat more credit for his intelligent nature than most people would, but heck, he'd been an integral part of solving a couple of recent crimes. I figured he'd earned that respect.

By the time I'd pulled myself out of bed again, brushed my teeth, and stepped into a pair of slippers, the tantalizing aroma of frying bacon sifted beneath the bedroom door. I padded down the stairs and into the kitchen, Woody and Carl at my heels. There, I found Dad tending the stove while Mom whisked eggs in a bowl. "Morning," I said.

"You're up early," my father said.

Mom wiped her hands on her apron and guided me to a chair. "Sit down, darling. You shouldn't be on your feet too much. Let me pour you a cup of coffee. Your pain pills are on the table next to a glass of water."

"I don't think I need them," I said, yawning. "I'm feeling good, all things considered, and I don't like the wooziness they cause. A couple of Tylenol should do the trick."

"Now Sundance," Dad said. "There's no need to be hurting. Stoicism doesn't make you heroic. At least, not in this instance, when you have tools at your disposal to cope with the pain."

Mom's forehead creased. "On the other hand, darling, you could always try going without. The pills will be there later if you find you need them. I've read stories about people getting addicted to these prescription painkillers."

"She's not going to get addicted, Maggie," Dad said. "She's legitimately injured."

"Now, Butch, I'm not saying you're wrong. She should take the medication if it's warranted. I'm just saying there's no sense jumping on that bandwagon if—"

"Enough," I interrupted. "All this bickering is giving me a headache. Remember, I'm forty-four years old. I think I can decide this life-changing issue on my own."

"Of course, darling," Mom said. She brought me a cup of coffee and a bottle of Tylenol. I swallowed two, along with a healthy dose of caffeine.

"Just trying to be helpful," Dad grumbled as he flipped bacon strips in the skillet. "Anyway, it's probably for the best if you keep your wits about you. Frank called this morning—"

"News on the case?"

"Not much, to tell the truth. He told me Raul won't be working the case—"

"I figured that," I said. "Witnesses saw him in a tense argument with the victim just hours before the murder. And his sister was married to the guy. Raul wouldn't make the most objective investigator."

"Murder? You're jumping to the conclusion that someone killed Jeffrey? What makes you think it wasn't an accidental fall?"

"Dad, it's obvious. The guardrail is probably high enough to prevent someone randomly tumbling over the side. Plus, there's the bloody hockey stick."

I saw Dad smile and realized he'd been testing me. "Yes, Dad, my mental faculties are in tip-top condition. So tell me, is Frank taking the lead in the investigation, then?"

"Just let me finish up here."

He pulled the skillet off the stovetop and placed it on a trivet on the counter. With a set of tongs, he transferred the crispy bacon onto a towel-lined plate. Mom placed another pan on the stove and poured the egg mixture into it. While she scrambled the eggs, Dad grabbed a mug of coffee and settled into a chair across from mine. "Okay, Sundance, here's what I can tell you."

I leaned forward eagerly.

"Frank doesn't think it would be appropriate for him to conduct the investigation himself, since Raul is under his command. Conflict of interest, he said. So he called Pine Haven and asked them to loan us one of their detectives."

An outsider? I experienced a stirring of unease and realized how quickly I'd acclimated into the village, prepared to close ranks. "Seems like it would take the new guy a while to get caught up on our village dynamics."

"New woman."

"What?"

Mom pointed her spatula at me. "Why would you assume the detective is male? From someone who touts feminist views, your response surprises me."

Dad grinned. "She got you there, Sundance. The detective's

name is Lynn Clarke."

I felt my cheeks flush, and Dad continued. "I haven't met her, but I know her by reputation. She's competent, efficient, and intelligent. Everything we could hope for."

"Except she's an outsider," I reiterated. "With no idea how things work here in Rock Creek Village."

"That could be an advantage," Dad said. "Objectivity. No emotional attachments to anyone. Maybe she'll be able to see things in ways none of us could."

I nodded. It was possible, I supposed.

Dad noticed my skepticism. "You need to keep an open mind, Sundance."

I leaned back in my chair as Mom placed the eggs and bacon on the table, along with fresh rolls and strawberry jelly. "You're right," I said. "I will."

"I'm glad you agree," Dad said. "Because Detective Clarke will be here at eight-thirty to interview you."

14

I sat on the edge of the bed, cursing under my breath. In the interest of expediency, I'd decided against a shower, but even so, the getting-ready process had turned into a Herculean feat that taxed my physical reserves. The Tylenol had provided a buffer against the pain, but my body felt exhausted from the effort of becoming presentable.

And now, this last step had me stymied. I couldn't figure out how to tie the sneakers on my feet.

Earlier, I'd refused Mom's offer of help and headed upstairs on my own. I'd shimmied into the yoga pants Mom had packed. A gray sweater with wide, batwing sleeves proved equally accessible. Easy breezy, I'd thought. I'd brushed my hair using my good hand, thankful I wore it in a simple layered style that was easy to manage.

But the shoes proved to be my Achilles heel. I tried one last time with the laces before surrendering to reality. My mommy would have to tie my shoes.

I walked back into the bathroom, careful not to trip on the trailing shoelaces. After some face powder and pale lip gloss, I studied my reflection in the bathroom mirror. *Not bad*, I thought. The highlights I'd added to my hair gave me a more mature, professional look. And despite my dad's joke about my gluttony, I'd lost a few pounds, giving my face a slimmer appearance that showcased my eyes. On the flip side, the loss of fat emphasized the crow's feet around my eyes and lips. So be it. As my mother said, lines on the face were evidence of a fully lived life.

Dad's voice calling up the stairs interrupted my self-appraisal. "Callie! Detective Clarke is here."

"On my way," I yelled back.

I flipped the bathroom light off and tramped down the stairs. My untied shoes flopped like a clown's. In the living room, I found Mom and Dad with a tall, slender, stylish woman who was crouching to pet Woody. The woman looked like a model. Her ash blond hair was styled in a long bob that highlighted sculptured cheekbones, full lips, and deep-set gray eyes. No evidence of a fully lived life marred *that* skin. Dressed in wide-legged plaid trousers and a long-sleeved, copper-colored blouse, her attire screamed runway rather than a police station.

Except for her main accessory: The gun holstered on her hip.

As she rose, I flopped into the room and extended my hand. "Callie Cassidy," I said in my best I'm-a-professional-too voice. On my approach, I tripped on a shoelace and stumbled into her. My hand trailed down her torso, from neck to waist, and she reached out to steady me, grasping whatever parts she could before finally getting hold of my armpits. It was quite a chummy moment.

My face burned. "I'm so sorry," I said. "How embarrassing."

"Nothing to be embarrassed about," my mother said, kneeling down to tie my shoes. "My fault. I should have packed slip-ons."

When Mom completed the task, I offered my hand again. "Shall we try this once more? I'm Callie Cassidy, though after that, I feel like we already know each other intimately."

Her grip on my hand was firm. "Detective Lynn Clarke," she said, offering a quick smile before turning all-business. She pointed at my cast. "How are you feeling? Are you up to talking?"

"Much better today, thank you. And yes, I'm happy to talk. Shall we sit?" I gestured to the taupe leather couch in my parents' living room.

Mom went to the kitchen and returned with a tray that held mugs of coffee, a pitcher of cream, and a bowl of sugar, which she placed on the coffee table. "I need to get downstairs and keep this business running," she said. "Nice meeting you, Detective Clarke."

"Likewise," she responded. She reached into her bag and pulled out a notebook and pen.

Dad settled into the chair across from us. "I'd like to sit in on the interview. I assume you have no objection, Detective?"

She cocked an eyebrow. I could tell Dad's presence wasn't part of her plan, but she nodded. "That's fine. Just…"

"Keep my mouth shut," Dad said, holding up a hand. "I know the routine."

She turned back to me, gesturing toward a small recorder she'd placed on the coffee table. "Do you mind if I record our conversation, Ms. Cassidy?"

"Not at all," I said, "but only if you'll call me Callie."

If I'd expected a reciprocal first-name offer, I was to be disappointed.

"Yes, well, let's get started," she said. After she'd recited the date, time, and circumstances for the record, she crossed her legs. My heart rate sped up. For some reason I had yet to deduce, she made me nervous.

"Why were you at the hockey rink yesterday morning, Callie?"

I considered her opening line and nodded appreciatively. A solid way to begin the interview. As a former journalist, I understood the effectiveness of starting with factual questions, asking people about simple, everyday events to put them at ease. Then, the interviewer could ease into the more emotionally laden questions. Now, I found the strategy working on me. I told Detective Clarke about my photography gig, setting up my equipment, lining up the players for team pictures.

Before I knew it, my nervousness had dissolved—just as the detective planned. Then, as predicted, she ratcheted things up a notch. "Now tell me about the moments surrounding Mr. Forte's fall. What did you see? Hear? Any detail, no matter how insignificant it may seem."

I took a deep breath, closed my eyes, and forced myself to

relive the terrifying experience. I told the detective about hearing the noises from above. Seeing the hockey stick hit the ice. Watching as Jeffrey's body pinwheeled toward me. The pain as he landed on me and the horror of seeing his dead body sprawled on top of me.

When I stopped talking and opened my eyes, Dad was bending forward with his elbows on his knees. His expression showed his sympathy, fear, and anger. His protective instincts toward me hadn't waned over the years.

I gave him a reassuring smile and refocused on Clarke. No sympathy on her face. No display of emotion at all, unless I counted impatience. She tapped her pen on her notebook, eager to get on with it, but well-trained enough to give me a moment.

I took a sip of coffee. "You can keep going. I'm ready."

She nodded. "You mentioned to officers at the scene that you'd witnessed Mr. Forte arguing with someone outside the rink. Did you see this person?"

"Not his face. But I know now it was his brother, Theo Clement."

"How did you arrive at that conclusion?"

"When I was on the gurney waiting to be transported to the hospital, I saw Theo run onto the ice, yelling. I identified him by his leather coat." I sipped my coffee again. "He confirmed who he was when we were in the ambulance."

Her eyebrows shot up. "You were together in the ambulance?" She scribbled a few lines in her notebook. "The two of you discussed the murder?"

"Not the murder exactly. More…the behind-the-scenes stuff. You know, background." I provided the details of our conversation, omitting the spike in Theo's heart rate toward the end.

"So Theo Clement believes Renata Sanchez is responsible for Jeffrey Forte's death?"

I winced, realizing too late that I just played into the Renata-as-main-suspect theory. "Well, he didn't exactly say that…"

"Witnesses have him pointing at Ms. Sanchez at the rink and

shouting—" She checked her notes. "She'll kill me too.'"

"I suppose, but—"

"Tell me about the altercation outside your studio yesterday morning."

The abrupt shift in topic threw me off balance. "What?"

"The altercation. Between Ms. Sanchez and her ex-husband. Detective Sanchez, her brother, was also involved, correct?"

I took a deep breath. "I wouldn't call it an altercation. More of a…disagreement. An awkward encounter."

Detective Clarke rummaged through her bag and came out with her phone. She tapped on the screen and handed it across to me. "Here's a video I'd like you to watch. Press play when you're ready."

Dad moved to the couch beside me so he could watch. I pressed the arrow on the screen. The video opened with Jeffrey insulting Renata. Then I appeared, asking him to move along. The amateur videographer took a moment to pan the crowd— mostly strangers, along with a couple of shop owners, such as David and Pamela. I noticed a familiar-looking bald man, too, though I couldn't quite identify him. I hit pause and squinted at the screen. Ah, yes, Mr. Pinkerton—Pinky, we called him—the man who'd run Pinkerton's Place, a small Mom-and-Pop store near the park, since I was in elementary school. His face was twisted into a scowl.

"What is it, Sundance?" Dad asked.

"Nothing. I hadn't realized Pinky was in the crowd. He looks mad."

Dad chuckled. "He was a grumpy old man thirty years ago. Now that he's in his seventies, he's perfected the image."

I hit the arrow, and the scene continued, paralleling my memory. The recording caught me looking concerned and then authoritative. It captured Jeffrey's performance as an arrogant bully and Raul's irate arrival on the scene. Renata appeared at first shocked, then hurt, and finally furious.

But it was Ethan's countenance that most astonished me. The hatred flashing across his face appeared so raw, so primal, that I caught my breath at the sight of it. Renata's hand on his arm seemed to be the only thing restraining him from lurching forward to pummel the man. I'd always known Ethan as an easy-going, peace-loving gentleman. This seemed out of character.

From that point on, the events on the screen moved as if on fast forward. Raul, not Ethan, lunged toward Jeffrey. Renata pushed him aside. When I saw her throw a palm into her ex-husband's nose, I understood why my characterization of the brawl as a mere disagreement had fallen flat.

Then the snowball fell on Jeffrey's head. A few more seconds of passionate conversation, and the recording ended with Jeffrey's angry departure. I stared at the blank screen for a moment before handing the phone back to Clarke. She studied me intently.

"Okay, things got a little more…heated than I remembered, I guess. Exes can get under each other's skin. It doesn't mean Renata killed him."

She responded by snapping her notebook shut and reaching across the table to turn off the recorder. Then she stowed her supplies in her bag and stood.

Dad got to his feet as well. Clarke extended a slender hand, and my father shook it. "Chief Cassidy, thank you for your time."

My father nodded as I struggled off the couch. Clarke shook my hand as well. "Ms. Cassidy, I'd appreciate it if you'd remain available for any follow-up questions."

"Of course," I said. "Whatever I can do to help."

She frowned. "As far as that goes, I've been told of your inclination to involve yourself in police matters. I'd advise you that the best way you can help is to steer clear of the investigation."

My tone turned defiant. "For your information, Detective Clarke, my past involvement in a few of this town's police matters has proven not only useful, but integral. Just ask Chief Laramie. Or Detective Sanchez…"

Dad placed a hand on my shoulder, whether in a show of solidarity or to shut me up, I wasn't sure. Detective Clarke slung her bag over her shoulder and headed toward the stairs. "Thank you again. I'll be in touch."

Woody trotted along beside her, and she reached down to pat his head. In that moment, her entire demeanor changed, and I heard her mumbling endearments to my dog. Then she stood, smoothed the crease in her slacks, and resumed her professional bearing, leaving without a backwards glance.

15

By early afternoon, I'd accomplished nothing productive except a call to Lars Eggars inquiring about my camera. He hadn't located it, but he promised to keep an eye out for it. After that, I'd eaten lunch, snuggled with the creatures, and played endless games of Candy Crush Saga, for which I'd shelled out more money than I cared to admit.

Now I was restless, eager to get back to my townhouse and my routine.

I sat on a stool next to my mother behind the lodge's front desk, trying to convince her that going home was a good idea. "I haven't needed a pain pill at all today. My ribs aren't achy, and my headache has all but disappeared."

"I heard 'all but' in that little speech," she said, shuffling through a stack of invoices. "When the disclaimer disappears, I'll be on board."

"Moooommm," I drawled, my teenage alter ego taking over.

A guest approached the desk and said the coffee urn was empty. Mom got up to take care of it. "Excuse me for a moment, darling. I need to tend to some grown-ups."

I sighed theatrically as she rounded the wooden countertop and bustled toward the Great Room, the huge rustic-style gathering area adjacent to the lobby. It was a warm, inviting area with an oversized fireplace and clusters of leather couches where guests could gather to chat, read, and sip coffee or mulled wine.

The floor-to-ceiling picture windows offered breathtaking views of the Rocky Mountains, including our own Mt. O'Connell, currently dotted with skiers and snowboarders.

With Valentine's Day only a couple of weeks away, the Great Room's decor included shiny red hearts dangling from the ceiling. Cupid cut outs lined the walls, and red cinnamon-scented candles flickered on the hearth and mantel. Even the nightly buffet offerings reflected the season of love. Delicate dishes such as lobster bisque, spinach and goat cheese crostini, heart-shaped mini lasagnas, and strawberry cheesecakes had found a place on the buffet over the past few days, all courtesy of Jamal Corban, the evening manager who was a final-year culinary student.

Mom returned from her barista duties. "Why don't you go upstairs for a nap, darling? Or you could curl up on the couch and watch a movie. Use your down time for something relaxing."

As I opened my mouth to argue, the lodge's glass entry door slid open. Tonya stepped inside, with her fiancé David hot on her heels.

She'd pulled her thick curls back from her face with a paisley silk headscarf. In black skinny pants, a maroon wool tunic that made her dark skin glow, and leopard print mini boots with chunky mid-sized heels, she appeared dressed to kill. Not literally, of course, though over our thirty-plus year friendship, I'd seen her mad enough to commit homicide plenty of times.

These days, though, the only fire smoldering in her was the flame of new love. Like me, Tonya was my age, and like me, she'd never married.

Though that was about to change.

In many ways, Tonya and David suited each other perfectly. Physically, they made a striking couple. His dark hair, slicked back with gel, and the laugh lines around his mouth gave him a middle-aged attractiveness that complemented Tonya's beauty. He also matched her in the style category, with his tailored black slacks and light gray pullover. And he'd been nothing but loving to Tonya and kind to me.

Still, there was just something about him that bothered me.

Maybe he just seemed too good to be true.

When I stepped around the counter to greet them, Tonya pulled me into a hug so tight I grimaced. "Hey, watch the ribs," I whispered.

Tonya stepped back and studied me, head to toe, as David swept past her and grasped my right hand in his. "*Buongiorno, cara amica*," he crooned. "We have been so worried about you."

I looked at Tonya. "Dear friend," she translated.

The man could pour on the charm. Not my thing, but who was I to judge? Still, judge I did.

Still clutching my hand, he leaned toward me and lowered his voice. "I see you—how do you say?—took one for the team."

My eyebrows lifted. "The team?"

He shook his head. "That Jeffrey Forte—a vile man. The world is a better place now, *cara amica*."

Tonya smacked his shoulder. "Enough. A man is dead. This isn't an appropriate time to dish the dirt."

"Dish the dirt?" He pretended not to understand, but a mischievous smile played on his lips.

Tonya ignored him and turned to me. "First question, how are you? Second: Can I sign your cast?"

I nudged her with my elbow. "I'm great. A hundred percent."

Behind us, Mom snorted, and I shot her a petulant look. "All right, ninety percent. I'm ready to go home, but my nurse here won't allow it."

"I can take her home," Tonya said. "My afternoon is open, so I volunteer as tribute."

"But your romantic weekend…" I said.

She looped an arm through David's and gazed up at him. "We had a lovely time, but he needs to get to the bookshop, anyway. So what do you say, Maggie? Do you trust me with your girl?"

Mom grinned. "Of course, my dear. Thank you. Now I won't have to listen to anymore whining. Will you be able to sleep over? I'd rather someone was close by at least one more night."

Tonya glanced at David. "Well, we have dinner plans…"

"No problem," I cut in. "I imagine I can talk Sam into staying over. Just let me run up and get my things together."

Tonya gestured to my cast. "You'd better let me give you a hand. Looks like you're down to one."

***

An hour later, Tonya and I sat on the couch in my living room, our feet resting on the coffee table and a wool throw across our outstretched legs. We sipped from mugs filled with fragrant hot chocolate. Flames crackled in the fireplace, and the creatures were curled up near the hearth. I'd taken more Tylenol, so I was pretty comfortable. It felt like a normal afternoon with my best friend—except for the topic of conversation.

After acquiring an off-the-record promise from my friend, the editor-in-chief of *The Rock Creek Gazette*, I filled her in on the events. When I finished the story, Tonya circled back to the beginning.

"He fell on top of you?" Tonya asked.

"Yup. I saw him coming but couldn't get out of the way."

"It's like you're a magnet. Trouble always lands on you."

"You know, I'm really tired of people saying that."

She smirked. "Can't argue with the truth, dollface. You're sure it's murder? He couldn't have fallen accidentally?"

"I suppose. That is, after he'd had his head accidentally bashed with a hockey stick."

"Ah yes. The hockey stick that belonged to Renata Sanchez, didn't you say?"

I took a long drink of the thick chocolate brew, suddenly exhausted with the subject of Jeffrey's death. "Enough of murder and mayhem. How are the wedding arrangements going?" Tonya and David had tentatively settled on a fall wedding, a long way off, but with her champagne tastes and perfectionistic tendencies, she'd require every minute of planning time.

Her face clouded. "It's not as easy as I'd hoped. You know I wanted a destination wedding—"

"Last I heard, you'd settled on Italy. David's old stomping grounds."

She shrugged. "I thought it would be romantic. Plus, I wanted to visit the place my future husband was born. But he nixed the idea. Said it was too far to ask people to travel, and he wanted us surrounded by family and friends on our special day."

"Hmmm. Well, you could honeymoon there."

"I suggested that, too," she said. "He said he'd rather travel in his new home, the United States."

It sounded reasonable, I guessed. Still, doubt scratched at the back door of my suspicious mind, demanding to be let in. *Why was David reluctant to take Tonya to his home? What was he hiding?*

I brushed aside my concerns. For now. "Have you decided on an alternate wedding destination?"

She rolled her eyes. "He's pushing for Vegas."

I'd been sipping from my mug, and I snorted, drawing froth into my sinuses. "Vegas?" I asked once I'd recovered. "Is he petitioning for a drive-through chapel? An Elvis impersonator to conduct the ceremony?"

"*Love me tender, love me sweet*," she crooned. "Some people love that scenario, you know. Anyway, Vegas isn't all seediness and cheap glitz. The city has some sophisticated venues, my skeptical friend." She tapped a long fingernail against her mug. "Besides, David's reasons are more personal. He said it would be easier for our Rock Creek friends to attend. There are multiple flights each day, or it's only a twelve-hour drive. Second, Vegas is a fun spot. Our guests would have lots of entertainment options and could even make a vacation of it. And then, of course, it's where Lydia lives."

Her voice trailed off, and I wrinkled my nose. I'd forgotten Tonya's mother, Lydia….what was her name now? Fredericks?…lived in Las Vegas. With her sixth husband, if I counted correctly. Assuming they hadn't already divorced.

Tonya and her mother hadn't been close since, well, as long as I could remember. The fact that Tonya referred to the woman by her name instead of her title made clear the distance between them. Lydia cared more about snagging the next man than being a mother. In fact, she'd divorced husband number three the day of our high school graduation. Two weeks later, she'd told Tonya she'd fulfilled her maternal contract, and she flew off to some distant locale to chase husband number four.

Surely, Tonya had told David about their tumultuous mother-daughter relationship. Was his suggestion of a Vegas wedding an effort to repair a bond that hadn't existed in decades? Or was he clueless about the nuances of emotional baggage?

More to the point, why did I possess so little trust for the man who was about to marry my best friend of over thirty years?

I indulged in one last gulp of chocolate heaven and glanced at Tonya over the rim of my cup. She gazed into the fireplace, her full mouth—adorned with her signature red lipstick—turned up in a serene smile. The woman was drop-dead gorgeous. But her heart was damaged by her past, leaving her vulnerable and yearning for love. Was David worthy of this enchanting woman? Or would he end up hurting her even more?

If it were to be the latter, I'd give him the fight of his life.

16

Are you sure you'll be all right?"

Tonya and I stood together in my foyer as my friend zipped up her hot pink parka. She'd gotten a call from Phil, her second-in-command at *The Rock Creek Gazette*, who needed her advice on a story. Duty called, but she was reluctant to abandon me.

I made a crossing motion over my heart. "I solemnly swear that I am in suitable condition to care for myself for the entire two hours until Sam arrives."

Her lips pursed, but she slipped on her gloves. "All right. But I'm only a phone call away."

"As is Sam. And Jessica. Mrs. Finney. My mother…"

She held up a finger. "Don't you dare tell Maggie I left you here by yourself. She'll skin me alive. Or worse, give me her I'm-so-disappointed look."

I chuckled, opened the door, and nudged her onto the porch. "Go on now. It's cold, and I can't afford to heat the great outdoors."

"Speaking of Maggie, you sound more like her every day." Tonya turned and headed down the sidewalk to her car.

"There are worse things," I called after her.

"So true," she responded.

I shut the door and stood with my back against it, cradling my casted wrist. To be honest, I was glad for some time alone. I was fading and just wanted to rest. It wasn't so much the pain—that was manageable. Mostly, I felt wrung out. Nothing curling up on the couch with a soft blanket wouldn't cure.

Stretching out on the sofa, I settled a pillow across my lap and propped my Kindle atop it. I read one paragraph, two…and the next thing I knew, Woody's barking startled me awake. The book dropped to the floor, and I shot up, on high alert. Nobody had ever accused Woody of being a guard dog—though, to his credit, he'd exhibited a few heroic moments. Still, it was unusual for him to engage in a sudden burst of barking.

I followed the sound down the hall and to the front door. Woody stood in the foyer, ears perked and tail stiff. I put my eye to the peephole. No one there. The blinds covering the sidelight window were closed, and I lifted a slat and peered through. Nothing. I opened the front door and stepped onto the porch, twisting my head up and down the sidewalk. The neighborhood was quiet. Clouds hung like hazy pink curtains across the setting sun. A gust of wind blew a flurry of pine needles across the yard.

I returned inside, closed and locked the door, and leaned down to scratch Woody's ears. "I get it," I told him. "It's a little eerie out there. More like Halloween than Valentine's Day. Nothing to worry about, though. I bet some dinner will cheer you up."

At the mention of food, he gave me his doggie grin and trotted off toward the kitchen. As I scooped kibble into his bowl, I heard a knock at the door. No barking this time—the pup was too intent on eating. Carl screeched and ran down the hall and up the stairs, his trademark sign that the visitor wore a familiar face.

I made my way back to the door. This time when I checked the peephole, I found Raul on my doorstep, clutching a bouquet of white roses. "Hey, were you just here?" I asked when I'd opened the door.

His eyes narrowed. "Just here? I'm here now. What are—?"

"Never mind." I stood aside so he could enter. Then I lifted my chin toward the flowers. "Are those for me?"

He thrust the roses at me and took off his coat. "Yeah. They're from Renata. She hopes you're feeling better."

Mr. Sentimental didn't offer his own well wishes, but his expression assured me he'd been worried too. I buried my nose in the flowers, inhaling their sweet scent. Raul hung his coat on the hook by the door and followed me into the kitchen.

"That's very thoughtful," I said, "especially considering her own current circumstances. How's she holding up?"

Raul snorted. "She went to a meditation class with Jessica. My sister has never let a little thing like a murder investigation intrude on something she wants to do."

I smiled. "I think it's a good idea. Meditation is calming. Don't knock it until you've tried it."

"I don't need meditation," he grumbled. "The only thing that'll adjust my attitude is finding Jeffrey Forte's killer."

I bent down to rummage for a vase beneath the sink. Raul saw me grappling with the task, nudged me aside, and found one that would do the job. He carried it to the sink, filled it with water, and arranged the flowers with the efficiency of a pro.

"Want a beer?" I asked. He nodded, and I grabbed one from the refrigerator and handed it to him. No alcohol for me, not when I might need a pain pill later. The two of us headed to the living room. I resumed my spot on the couch, and he dropped into the overstuffed armchair, popping the top on the beer and taking a long drink.

"How's the investigation going?" I asked.

He wiped foam from his lips. "How would I know? They've shuffled me off to Siberia. Frank tells me everything is under control, but he won't give me any details. And that detective…" He made a face. "She tells me to stay out of it. Acts like I'm only getting in her way."

I smothered a smile. Raul was getting a taste of his own medicine, though now wasn't the time to point that out. "I feel helpless," he said. He placed his beer on a coaster and studied me. "It's one of the reasons I'm here."

He paused. I could tell from his expression he was weighing his next words. He cleared his throat. "I know you, Callie. You're not going to sit on your hands…" He glanced at my cast. "What

I mean is, there's no way you'll stay out of this and let Frank and Clarke do all the sleuthing. It's not in your nature. Mine either, especially when my sister is involved. So I was hoping you and I could, you know, pool whatever information we find."

I batted my eyelashes. "Why, Raul, are you asking me to partner with you on a clandestine, off-the-books investigation? I've been told more than once it's quite improper for a civilian to get involved in police matters."

He sniffed. "Listen, Callie, are you in or out?"

"Don't worry, I'm in," I said. I got up and walked to my desk, returning with a legal pad and a pen, which I handed to Raul. "I'm injured, so you can do the honors."

He uncapped the pen and positioned the pad in his lap. "I assume we're making a suspect list?"

I nodded. "It's how I always begin."

He opened his mouth, and I expected a snide response. Instead, a pained expression flitted across his face. "Yeah, well, I guess we have to start with Renata. Can't clear someone's name if you don't acknowledge they're in the mix. And as much as I hate to say it, my sister has a powerful motive."

"Agreed," I said, though I didn't want her on the list either. "I doubt she told you this, but she asked to meet with me on Saturday morning. Wanted me to help her dig up some dirt on Jeffrey."

His eyes widened in surprise. "She did?"

"Yup. She believed he might be responsible for a few unusual incidents she'd been experiencing." He stiffened, and I held up a hand. "Nothing serious, just some unexplainable occurrences. Anyway, she blamed Jeffrey. She was angry that he'd shown up in the village, that he was invading her safe space. Toward the end of their marriage, she started to suspect Jeffrey was hiding something. If she could find out what it was, she figured she might be able to hold it over him and make him leave town. She asked me to reach out to my contacts at *The Sentinel*."

He shook his head. "I didn't know any of this. She never talks to me about him."

"Afraid of your reaction, I'm sure. And she wants to prove to her big brother that she can handle things on her own."

We sat in silence for a moment. Finally, I continued. "We agree that Renata's on the list, then. And her alibi—the one she gave me, anyway—is pretty flimsy. Said she was in the locker room by herself, getting ready for the game. I imagine Detective Clarke is looking for anyone who might have seen her—"

"I'm on it," Raul interrupted. He glanced at me, saw the concern on my face. "I'll be subtle, Callie."

"If you say so." I chewed the inside of my cheek. "Moving on, I'd add Jeffrey's brother Theo. On our way to the hospital, he told me Jeffrey was heir to their mother's estate. Money, family dynamics, resentment—he scratches off several of the top motives. And considering his past drug problems…" I shrugged.

Raul scribbled on the pad. "Leave Theo to me."

"What's your plan?"

"I don't have one yet, but I'll figure it out. In the meantime, I don't want you anywhere near him."

The paternal tone in his voice triggered my defiant streak. I opened my mouth to object, but glanced at my broken wrist and closed it. Maybe this was one of those times to step back and let someone else lead.

As if to punctuate the idea, my ribs began to throb. I looked at the clock—time for more Tylenol. I pushed myself off the couch, talking as I headed to the kitchen. "We should also include everyone involved in the scuffle outside my gallery yesterday morning."

I told him about the video Detective Clarke showed me. "I hate to say it, but I've never seen Ethan so mad. His whole body was shaking. And the twins said he left the gallery for a while later that morning." I filled a glass of water from the sink. "Honestly, I don't believe Ethan belongs on the list. He's not the type to commit murder."

Raul jotted Ethan's name on the page anyway. "Me either. But you never know what a person might do in the heat of the moment. Could be whoever killed Jeffrey had no intention of it.

Maybe the person just snapped. Happens all the time. Do you feel comfortable asking Ethan where he was yesterday morning? If he has an alibi, we can clear him fast."

"I can do that." I swallowed two tablets and returned to the couch. An image popped into my head. "You know who else in the crowd during the fight? Mr. Pinkerton—and he looked as angry as a storm cloud."

"Pinky?" Raul said. "The man must be in his late seventies. Hard to believe he'd be capable of throwing Jeffrey over the catwalk. Plus, what possible motive could he have?"

I pictured Pinky in my mind—built like a bulldog, even at his age. "If you'd seen his expression…But you're right, I suppose. It's a long shot."

"I'll add his name, but I won't expend much effort on him." He scanned the list. "This isn't much. I wish we had more."

"Well, I can think of one person we haven't included…"

I stared at him until he understood. "Do you mean me?"

I leaned forward, watching him with concern. "Raul, you know Detective Clarke will consider you a suspect. You should have seen yourself in that video—fists clenched, eyes bulging. Pinky looked like Gandhi compared to you. Then you disappeared all day. Frank couldn't get in touch with you. Neither could Renata."

I left the question unspoken. Raul turned to the fireplace, watching the flames. Then he sighed. "You want me to tell you where I was."

I lifted my good hand, palm up. "If we're going to work together on this, I should be in the loop."

"I'll tell you. But I want to keep it private. I don't want to read about it in *The Gazette* tomorrow."

I moved my hand to my heart. "Ouch. Is that how you see me—some Sophie Demler clone, running around dispersing gossip?"

He gave me a wry smile. "No, but…I'm not ready for Renata to hear about this. Or my mother."

My curiosity was piqued. What secret did Raul want to keep from his family?

He took a deep breath. "I was in Boulder, interviewing for a position as lead detective of their squad."

I snapped back, as if he'd hit me. "Boulder? Lead detective? Wait…you're…you're leaving us?"

"Don't get ahead of yourself. They haven't offered me the job. Even if they do, I haven't decided whether I'll accept. It's just an opportunity that fell into my lap. It seemed like I had to follow it."

Tears pooled in my eyes, and I turned away. "Well, you deserve it," I said softly. "There's no better detective in the state. They'd be lucky to have you."

The corner of his mouth turned up. "Thank you, Callie. But like I said, it's far from a done deal."

He tossed the legal pad on the coffee table, slapped his hands against his knees and rose. "Time for me to get going. I'll make a plan regarding Theo tonight. I'll also see if I can track down someone who might've seen Renata in the locker room at the time of Jeffrey's death."

I nodded. "I won't talk to Ethan until tomorrow. In the meantime, I'll contact Preston to see if he can help us with some research on Jeffrey."

"That'd be good, since I can't use police resources at this point."

Woody scrambled up from his post-dinner nap and accompanied us to the door. Carl made a cameo appearance on the stairs, meowing his goodbyes. Raul put on his coat and hat, and headed to his car.

Once he'd left, I leaned against the door and thought about his job interview in Boulder. Would this be our final collaboration?

17

Alone again, I spent a few minutes searching for my cell phone, finally locating it between two couch cushions. I dialed Preston's number, and the call went straight to voicemail. No surprise. As editor-in-chief of a major newspaper, he was a busy man. I left him a message telling him to check his email and get back to me as soon as possible.

Next, I took the legal pad and my laptop to the kitchen table. While the computer booted up, I microwaved a cup of hot chocolate and thought about Raul's job interview again. I didn't want to obsess over I, but I had to admit the idea made me a little sad. We'd only been friends for a year, but he felt like family to me. It'd be hard to see him go.

The microwave dinged, and I tossed a handful of mini marshmallows on top of the steaming liquid. If a girl couldn't indulge after a trip to the ER, when could she?

I sat at the table and typed an email to Preston, asking for his help with some research on Jeffrey Forte and Theo Clement. I didn't remind him that he owed me. He knew. I paused as an idea simmered in my brain. Making up my mind, I added David Parisi's name to the list. My finger hovered over the send button. Should I?

What the heck. It wouldn't hurt to ask. Right?

I heard a key turn in the front door lock. "Honey, I'm home," Sam called in a horrible Ricky Ricardo imitation. He walked into the kitchen, a broad smile on his face and the aroma of dinner wafting from the thermal bags he carried. Woody bounced on all four paws, his tail swishing fast enough to cool the room. In typical fashion, Carl darted past Sam and up the stairs.

Sam's eyes flitted around the room, taking in the flowers, the computer, the legal pad. His smile dissolved. "Looks like you're busy."

"Not really. Just finished sending an email. Now I'm all yours."

He set the bags on the counter and came over to kiss my cheek. "How are you?"

"Tiring out a bit," I admitted.

He gestured to the computer. "Maybe that's because you're jumping in to investigate when you should be letting your body heal."

"I'm not investigating," I said. "Raul and I are…"

I stopped mid-sentence, but it was too late. "Ah," Sam said. "Raul. He's roped you into helping him, hasn't he?"

"He hasn't roped me into anything." My irritation rose, and I tried to tamp it down. "He's frustrated. Frank won't let him work the case, and he's worried about his sister. I told him I'd contact Preston to see what we could uncover about Jeffrey and Theo that might help. That's all."

A minute lapsed. "Dinner smells fantastic," I ventured. "What is it?"

"Creamy parmesan chicken with sun-dried tomatoes. Rosemary potato wedges. Asparagus. Fresh garlic bread. Nothing fancy."

"Nothing fancy to you translates to gourmet fare for me."

He transferred the meal from containers to plates and brought them to the table. As we ate, Woody hovered at our feet, just in case.

"Mmm," I said. "This chicken is so tender. And the potatoes are to die for. Another masterpiece."

"Thank you."

After another beat, I leaned toward him. "Sam, tell me what's wrong. We have to communicate."

He put his fork on his plate. "All right, Callie. Here's the thing. You're at the top of my priority list, right next to my daughter. But I'm not sure where I fall on your priority list."

"Don't be silly," I said. "You're always number one."

"I wish that were true."

"Sam, I tell you all the time how much you mean to me."

"How can I explain this?" He ran a hand through his thick hair. Then he pulled his phone out of his pocket. "Here, let me show you."

He tapped Messages on the screen, pulled up our thread, and turned the phone toward me. "Six texts today from me to you, asking how you were doing, if there was anything you needed, what was going on with you."

I pointed at the screen. "Yes, and I responded to each one."

"Now show me the texts from you asking what I was up to. How my work was going. How last night's catering job went."

I stiffened. "But Sam, there was a murder. I was injured. This is an unusual circumstance."

"Is it?" He tucked the phone back in his pocket. "I won't scroll back through our texts over the past few weeks. Trust me when I say it's pretty one-sided. And then I come in, find you involving yourself in this case…"

I leaned back and crossed my arms, suddenly petulant. "I'm sorry I'm such a terrible girlfriend."

He threw up his hands. "Callie, I don't know what to do here. I hate that I sound whiny and needy. But you say you want to hear what I'm feeling. When I tell you, you get mad." He stood and carried his plate to the sink. "You know what? I don't want to talk about this right now. You've had a rough time, and I'm sorry for making it worse."

Tears welled in my eyes. I loved Sam—I knew that without a doubt—but I'd never been good at relationships. Was I too selfish? Too hardhearted? Or just too fearful of vulnerability? Whatever it was, I didn't want to lose this man over it.

"Sam, I'm sorry you feel this way."

He rinsed his plate and put it in the dishwasher. There was a long pause. "It'll pass," he said. "Let's change the subject."

***

We settled in the living room to have dessert—caramel cheesecake that melted in my mouth. The tension between us remained, and even the creatures were subdued. Woody curled up in a corner, uninterested in begging for scraps. Carl emerged from upstairs, glanced once at Woody, then glared at me, as if this were all my doing. Which I suppose it was.

Sam and I made small talk. The weather. His daughter's recent move to the dorm at her college. The town's Valentine's Day decorations.

"I think the village looks great," Sam said. "All those red hearts and Cupids."

"Valentine's Day is nothing more than a commercial venture by corporate America to get us to spend more money on their pointless junk."

"Wow, Callie, take it down a notch."

"Sorry. I've just never understood the appeal."

"I'm getting that idea."

Silence stretched out between us. I ran a finger across my plate and stuck the last few crumbs in my mouth as I tried to come up with a different topic. "Did you hear they're building a drive-in movie theater in Pine Haven? Everything old is new again."

His eyes lit up. "I love drive-ins. Remember seeing *Waterworld* at the one in Boulder when we were in high school? It was one of our first dates."

"Not the best movie ever made," I responded.

"True. But sitting there in the car, the speaker attached to the window, the warm breeze, my arm around you…"

"Why, Sam," I said, my voice teasing. "You're such a romantic. Next thing I know, you'll be writing poetry."

"Guess I'm just an old softie," he said, his voice wry.

I smiled and yawned, triggering an ache in my ribs. Sam noticed. He got up and took our dessert plates to the sink. "Time for you to get upstairs," he said. "Maybe take one of your pain pills tonight. Your mom said you're trying to stay off them, but it might help you get a good night's sleep."

I followed him into the kitchen and picked up my prescription bottle. "Good advice."

"Need any help?" he asked.

"No, I can handle it." I bit my lip. "Will you be up soon?"

He didn't meet my eyes. "I'm going to sleep down here tonight," he said. "You'll rest better without my snoring. Besides, I want to watch the hockey game. I'll be up to check on you every so often."

"All right," I said. I'd have preferred him next to me while I slept, but I wouldn't argue. "Sam, are we okay?"

He turned to me and kissed me lightly. "I hope so."

***

I trudged upstairs, with Woody trailing behind me. Carl, the wretched traitor, opted to remain in the living room with Sam.

After a challenging few minutes of twisting and tugging, I got out of my clothes and into my pajamas. During the struggle, I vacillated between guilt over not being a better girlfriend and irritation that Sam hadn't come up to help me. Then I remembered he'd asked, and I'd said I didn't need him. No wonder he was frustrated.

When I slipped between the sheets, Woody snuggled in beside me. Though my body was exhausted, my mind continued to spin. I pictured Sam sitting downstairs watching the game, his arm thrown over the back of the couch. Part of me wished I was down there next to him. I wondered why relationships were so hard for me and why I clung so stubbornly to my independence.

I thought of how joyful Tonya was at the prospect of joining her life with someone else's. Why couldn't I be more like her?

The thought of Tonya and David sent a fresh wave of guilt through me. Perhaps adding David to the list of names for Preston to research had been a mistake. Did I have the right to snoop into his personal business? I'd rationalized that I was trying to protect my best friend, but wasn't I, in some ways, overstepping? Treating her like a helpless child?

Beside me, Woody yawned. His eyes drooped closed, and just like that, he fell asleep. The effects of my painkiller took hold, and my eyelids grew heavy. I switched off the bedside lamp, snuggled beneath the comforter, and followed him to dreamland. The worries could wait until tomorrow.

18

I was vaguely aware of Sam checking on me a couple of times during the night, but the pain pill kept me from rising to full consciousness. It wasn't until five-thirty, when he kissed me on the cheek and asked if I needed anything before he left for work, that I woke enough to respond.

Even then, "Mmmph," was all I could manage. I felt Carl jump on the bed and Woody's tail thump against the covers.

Sam brushed the hair from my forehead. "I've left you breakfast in the microwave. Heating instructions on a Post-it. I've set coffee to brew in an hour. Your phone is on the nightstand. If you need anything, call me. I can be here in five minutes."

I tried to hold out my arms for a hug, but I'd forgotten about the cast. Only one arm rose. When he bent down and nuzzled his face against my neck, I pulled him tight. "I love you, Sam."

He went still for a moment. "Love you, too."

Guess it beat "ditto," but not by much.

This relationship might be in more danger than I'd realized. If I wanted to save it, I had some work to do.

But that wasn't going to happen right now. My eyelids were too heavy. Just because Sam had to be on the move before dawn didn't mean I needed to follow suit.

***

The jangle of the phone woke me, and I opened my eyelids to

a curtain of orange. At first, I thought it was the sun blazing through my bedroom window. Then I realized I was staring at Carl's furry tail. Not only was it draped across my eyes, but its tip had nestled between my lips.

"Pplttt," I said, pushing the cat off of my face. I glanced first at the clock—seven thirty—then at the caller ID. Preston.

I pressed accept and grumbled into the phone. "It's pretty early here."

"Good morning to you, too, Sunshine," he said, his voice entirely too cheerful. "If you're going to be grumpy, maybe you should find someone else to do your grunt work."

He had a point. "Sorry. I'm still groggy from the painkillers. Takes me a while to come out of the fog. I was injured the other day—"

"I heard," he said, cutting me off. "You forget I still have a source in your village."

"Mrs. Finney called you?"

"Bingo. She told me all about the human asteroid that nearly resulted in your extinction. From what I hear, your injuries aren't too serious. So I'd advise you to suck it up, Buttercup. That's what the Callahan Cassidy I knew would say."

Despite myself, I smiled. He was referencing the Callie of another era, albeit not that long ago. Back in my *Washington Sentinel* days, I was a tough, gritty investigative photojournalist who never allowed personal issues to deter her from the job.

Now, I'd apparently gone soft. The grittiest things about me these days were my eyeballs.

"You've made your point," I said, rubbing those eyes with my fingertips. "I will attempt to improve my attitude forthwith. So tell me, dear sir, what causes you to ring me up on a morning of such splendor and eternal sunshine? Have you uncovered some salacious details you're exhilarated about sharing with me?"

He laughed. "I'm going to attribute your blatant condescension and sarcasm to the lingering effects of a concussion. But to answer your question, nothing yet on your Forte brothers. Real world news occupies my researchers and thus interferes with my ability to grant personal favors. Tomorrow, I hope. But we did manage to turn up some details on David Parisi. Before I pass the info along, though, I have to ask: Are you sure you want it?"

I gritted my teeth. "Is it that bad?"

"Well, I don't know how to judge the information without context. But that's not what I'm talking about, anyway. This is the man who is engaged to Tonya Stephens, right?"

My eyebrows rose. Mrs. Finney really had kept him in the village loop. "It is," I said.

"Have you checked your motives? You're not a journalist anymore. This is personal. In my experience, possessing knowledge you have no genuine right to can be a double-edged sword. You can't unknow it."

"I didn't realize I'd signed up for a psychotherapy session." Defensive much? Preston had clearly hit a nerve.

He stayed silent, and I considered his question more seriously. Though I hesitated, there was never any doubt. "Just tell me, Preston."

"All right." He paused for dramatic effect. "It seems Signore Parisi is already married."

***

I processed the shocking news as quickly as I could, but digesting it fully would have to wait. Though today was Monday and the gallery was closed, a work-related appointment awaited— a podcast, of all things.

Last summer, two men had waltzed into Sundance Studio and promptly purchased five of my most expensive canvas photos. Unbeknownst to me at the time, Bradley and Tim's position as "social influencers" meant they'd amassed a wide online presence and many thousands of followers. When they gushed praise for me and my gallery, they catapulted Sundance Studio to stardom.

Okay, not exactly stardom, but business had definitely exploded.

Recently, Bradley and Tim had shifted into the podcast trend, and they'd invited me to be part of their Creative Entrepreneurs series. Much as I hated the idea of being on the interviewee side of the equation, I felt I owed them. Time to pay the piper.

I swung my legs around and put my feet on the floor, experiencing a wave of lightheadedness. When it passed, I took stock of my injured bits. Luckily, my head didn't hurt at all. The grade zero concussion seemed to have passed. I rotated my left forearm and experienced some mild throbbing in the healing wrist bone. Not too bad. The ache in my ribs was minimal. On a pain scale of one to ten, I landed at a three.

I made the trek downstairs. Woody headed out the doggie door to take care of business while Carl darted to his litter box in the laundry room. By the time I filled their food bowls, they'd both returned. I zapped the breakfast Sam had left me—a stack of blueberry pancakes and two thick sausage patties—poured a mug of coffee and chowed down.

A quick rinse of the dishes, then it was back upstairs for my first post-injury shower. The cast wasn't allowed to get wet, so I unboxed one of the waterproof cast protectors my father had purchased. The instructions made them look simple to use—stretch the plastic casing over my arm and pull the straps to tighten it—but my coordination skills did not rise to the expected standard. I spent five minutes tugging the straps with my teeth. When I finally got the casing secured, it was so tight I feared for my circulation.

All that was before I even stepped into the shower. My one-handed attempt at a shampoo must have resembled a slapstick comedy routine. I vowed never again to take my non-dominant hand for granted.

By the time I'd finished soaping and scrubbing, I felt exhausted, so I took a moment to rest beneath the shower head. As the soothing hot water pounded against my scalp, my thoughts scampered back to Jeffrey Forte's death. His murder.

When I remembered the moments before he fell, it was as if I were gazing through a sheer curtain at a hazy, indistinct memory. The hockey stick tumbled to the ice. Then I lifted my camera…

I'd wondered before, but now I was certain—I'd snapped a picture before the camera flew from my grasp.

No doubt in my mind. But I still didn't know if that image revealed Jeffrey's killer.

19

Despite my mother's protestations, I decided to chauffeur myself on today's errands. The doctor said I could drive when my symptoms subsided, and they had—at least, mostly.

I took it slow, starting with a couple of trips up and down my isolated street to get the hang of rotating the wheel with one wrist in a cast. I smiled to myself. All set.

My first stop was the police station. Parking was plentiful in front of the building that housed all the municipal services. Once inside, I stopped at the counter and waved at the department's administrative assistant, a slender, white-haired woman who'd been a fixture since my father's early detective days.

"Morning, Marilyn," I called.

She shoved her pencil into the poufy hair above her ear. "Well, hello, you. I'm surprised to see you. I heard you were on the wrong end of a missile Saturday." She dropped her voice to a whisper. "I assume you're looking into the murder?"

"No, of course not," I trilled, too loudly. "You know me better than that. I'm just here in search of the photography equipment I left behind at the ice rink. I was told I could pick it up here Monday morning."

She gave me a conspiratorial grin. "Just here for the equipment. Mmm hmm. Let me check on it."

Picking up her phone, she punched a few buttons, then held up a finger. As I waited, Frank walked into the reception area, accompanied by Detective Clarke, who was zipping her coat. I gave Marilyn a warning glance, and she made a "my lips are sealed" motion with her fingers.

Frank noticed the move and shot me a chiding look. "Seems your recovery is moving right along."

"Feeling better by the hour," I said.

He finally gave me a grin. "Takes more than a busted wrist to keep you down."

"Don't forget the concussion and the fractured ribs." I turned my attention to Detective Clarke. "Good morning, Detective Clarke. Any progress on the case?"

Her expression was inscrutable. "You must know I'm not at liberty to discuss an ongoing investigation."

I sighed. "I'm not the press, just an interested party. A victim. I'd like to know what's going on."

"We'll contact you when we have information we can share, Ms. Cassidy." She pulled on a pair of gloves. "Other than that, is there anything I can do for you?"

I bit my tongue. A snide retort at this point wouldn't earn me any points. More flies with honey, my mother always said. In my experience, though, that hadn't always been her own practice.

"Actually, I'm here to retrieve my camera and photo equipment. Sam and I tried to pick it up at the ice rink on Saturday, but Officer Tollison said it wasn't there, and I should check the station."

Clarke frowned. "I remember seeing a tripod and some other pieces, but I don't recall the camera. What about you, Chief?"

"No. I don't think it's here, Callie. Must've been left behind at the rink." He scratched his chin. "Though I can't imagine the crime scene techs just overlooking it…"

Clarke studied me. "Once the camera is located, we'll need to see it. If you find it before we do, you have to turn it over to us."

"I'll contact you when I have information to share," I said. So much for honey.

She ignored my sarcasm and turned to Frank. "Chief, I'm heading out now. I'll fill you in as soon as I have anything to share."

As soon as she was out of earshot, I leaned toward Frank. "She's not the sweetest apple in the pie, is she?"

Frank sighed. "And so it begins."

"What do you mean by that?"

"It's like watching the sequel to a movie. In case you haven't noticed, Lynn's approach to detective work is a carbon copy of Raul's."

"Oh, I noticed. Believe me."

"Which means the two of you are destined to butt heads. Just like you and Raul."

I looked at the floor. If he only knew about the alliance Raul and I had formed. My mind darted around for something to say, but I was saved when Raul himself rounded the corner, carrying a tote bag that belonged to me. His eyes darted from Frank to me, and I gave a slight shake of the head, trying to convey that I hadn't spilled the beans.

"Hey, Raul," I said, feigning casualness. "How is it going?"

He scowled. "There's one big case in this town, and I'm relegated to package delivery boy. How do you think it's going?"

Act mad to divert attention, I thought approvingly. *Good cover.*

"No whining, Detective," Frank said in a stern tone. "If you were in my shoes, you'd do the exact same thing. You'd never allow someone with your conflict of interest to work a case. There's plenty here to keep you busy."

"So, after I stow Ms. Cassidy's equipment in her truck, should I investigate the off-leash dog complaint?" Raul asked. "Shoo the elk off Mr. Pullman's yard? Or maybe I need to brew a fresh pot of coffee."

"No, honey, I'll take care of that," Marilyn called.

"You could track down my missing camera," I suggested.

"Excellent idea," Frank said. "I'll expect a report on your findings first thing tomorrow."

The chief strolled off, his lanky form receding down the

hallway toward his office. "You're in the doghouse," I whispered.

Raul waved me off. "I get where he's coming from, but he can't expect me to jump for joy while he's shoving me off to the sidelines. And this Clarke...I don't know if she has what it takes."

I put my hands on my hips. "Because she's female?"

"No. Because she seems fixated on Renata at the expense of pursuing other suspects."

"Sounds like someone else we know," I muttered.

He refused to take the bait. "Where's your car?"

"In the parking lot. Where do you think?"

He muttered something under his breath as we walked out the door. Once I'd popped the trunk and he'd stored my equipment inside, he turned to me. "What's the deal about this camera I'm now tasked with finding?"

I explained that crime scene techs had supposedly dropped off my Nikon DSLR at the station, but it wasn't here. He nodded. "I'll look into it. It's not like I have anything else to do."

I lowered my voice. "Have you made any progress with...the other things we discussed?"

He glanced over his shoulder. "I found out Theo moved into his brother's condo yesterday. Before that, he was in a long-term hotel outside of town."

"So he's moving up in the world," I mused. "Could be motive."

He shrugged. "What about you?"

I told him I'd been in touch with Preston and hoped to have some results from him tomorrow. "After my appointment today, I'll call Ethan and see if he has an alibi."

Raul slammed the trunk. "We're getting nowhere fast."

"Be patient," I said, touching his arm. "We'll get something. We always do."

20

Bradley and Tim's cabin was located on a spacious parcel of forested acreage about forty-five minutes north of Rock Creek Village. Living in Colorado, I was accustomed to gorgeous landscapes and mountain vistas, but once I turned off the main road, the scenery took my breath away. Rays of sunshine dappled through the pine canopy and glinted across patches of snow lining the road. Despite a temperature in the mid-thirties, I rolled my window down to inhale the fresh, evergreen-scented air. A place like this could whisk any lingering stress right out of a person's soul. I couldn't remember why I'd decided to move to the big city all those years ago, but I'd never make that mistake again.

I'd gone at least a half hour without spying another car, though I'd seen plenty of elk meandering through the forest and a herd of bighorn sheep rambling on a rocky outcropping. But the best sighting of the day came when I spotted some white-tailed ptarmigans nearly camouflaged against a snowy backdrop.

With about ten miles to go, I lost cell service and thus GPS. Bradley had instructed me to expect that, and I'd come armed with an old school map and printed directions. As I drew nearer to my destination, I glanced down at the map for a quick consult. When I lifted my eyes back to the road, I had to slam on the brakes, sending a jolt of pain through my ribs.

But when I realized what I was seeing, the ache seemed to

vanish. There, in the middle of the road, stood a gigantic Shiras bull moose—only the second time I'd ever spotted one in the wild. His black body must have measured nine feet from his nose to his rump. I'd guess seven hundred pounds easy. Broad, flat antlers stretched from the crown of his head. If I hadn't hit the brakes in time, the moose would have walked away uninjured, while my car would have been an accordion, and a broken wrist would have been the least of my worries.

Oh, how I longed for my missing Nikon. But I'd have to make do with my phone's camera. As I snapped picture after picture, the moose gazed at me with disinterest. Finally, I put the phone down and sat patiently behind the wheel. I was a visitor in the moose's home, and he'd move when he was ready. Nothing I could do but wait.

A minute later, he turned his head away and sauntered off the road and into the trees. I watched him for a few seconds before edging forward on the road, smiling to myself at the gift Nature had given me.

***

After only a single missed turn, I found Bradley and Tim's cabin and parked on the gravel driveway. My mouth dropped open at the sight of the place. It belonged in a magazine. Composed of three stories of glass and log and river rock, it seemed to sprout from the forest itself. The mountains rose behind it like glorious gods. To the side of the structure rested a satellite dish the size of a school bus. So that's how they achieved internet service in the boonies.

Tim opened the door, wearing a white cable-knit sweater, dark blue jeans, and brown chukka boots. "Callie, you made it. We were starting to worry."

"I got waylaid by a stubborn moose on the road. I'm not that late, am I?"

"Just a few minutes. But one never knows what obstacles visitors might face in this remote tundra of ours. We keep a close eye." He glanced at my cast. "Sweetheart. What happened?"

"Long story. Bottom line, an oversized body falling from the rafters crushed me."

He pursed his lip. "Oh, sweet girl. Always getting into scrapes. Let's go find Bradley. He'll want to hear the story too."

He ushered me inside and reached out a manicured hand to take my coat. My eyes scanned the place's stunning interior. "Your home is gorgeous."

He opened the door to a cedar closet and hung my coat inside. "Our little place in the woods. I'll give you the grand tour later. Right now, we're set up to begin the podcast. Please, follow me."

He led me past a glass encased living room with leather couches and a fireplace that spanned the height of the wall. Despite its rustic tone, the kitchen sported modern, upscale appliances. Tim retrieved a bamboo charcuterie board covered with mouth-watering goodies. "The wine is already breathing in the recording studio," he said.

Wine? Snacks? And I thought I'd come here to do *them* a favor.

We traipsed down a flight of stairs to the cabin's basement studio. I wasn't an electronics expert, but even I could tell this was a high-quality outfit. Acoustic tiles covered the walls and ceiling. A desktop computer and a sound board gleamed on a table near the wall. In the center of the room, a large round table, surrounded by executive chairs, held three independent microphones, along with headphones for each of us.

I'd known Bradley and Tim were well off, but wow. Next thing I knew, they'd be recording podcasts from their own personal spacecraft.

Tim positioned the snacks in the center of the table and went to a cupboard to retrieve china plates and cloth napkins. Bradley stepped into the room, carrying a bottle of wine in one hand and three slim crystal glasses in the other. Dressed in black and burgundy plaid chinos and a black sweater, he looked as if he'd stepped from the pages of a millennial fashion magazine. When he caught me staring at his burgundy loafers, he smiled and his eyes twinkled. "The shoes maketh the man, love. Never forget it."

He placed the bottle and glasses on the table and turned toward me, his eyes taking in my cast. He gasped. Tim put a hand on his shoulder. "Our dear friend had a run-in with a yeti," Tim told him. "Or some such."

"Do tell," Bradley said.

We took seats at the table, and he poured the wine as I told the story of the dead man and the photographer. When I finished, I popped a cube of pepper jack cheese in my mouth and held up a cautionary finger. "You can't ask me anything about it on this…this thing we're doing."

Bradley smirked. "Podcast, dear girl. When are you going to join the twenty-first century?" He cocked his head. "Truly, though, this story would make a tantalizing episode…"

"It's non-negotiable, guys. I can't jeopardize an ongoing investigation." I leaned over the tray and selected a piece of salami, along with a toasted cracker, washing them down with a sip of white wine. I smacked my lips.

Tim folded his arms. "If she can't, she can't, Bradley. Quit pressuring the poor woman."

Bradley pouted. "Very well. But Tim and I get dibs when you're prepared to go public. No argument."

"Well…"

"All right, that's settled," Tim said. "Let's get this show started."

I took a gulp of wine to settle my nerves. I was accustomed to being behind the lens of a camera, not a mic. But Bradley and Tim were so warm and easygoing that I relaxed into the conversation. We talked for a while about my prior career, and I shared a few anecdotes—some funny and some heart wrenching. But we spent the bulk of the podcast on Sundance Studio and my work as an artistic photographer and gallery owner.

When the interview portion concluded, they turned off my mic, and I was free to scarf down more meat and cheese and gulp the rest of the wine as they concluded the last ten minutes of the recording. Afterward, they explained all the whens, wheres, and hows of the podcast's release, and that was that.

A quick tour of their remarkable home, a pit-stop in the bathroom, and I was on the road again.

As I drove back toward the real world, I found my mind free to fret over a subject I'd earlier pushed to the back burner. *David, married?* I had to tell Tonya—didn't I? As Preston had predicted, the forbidden knowledge weighed on me.

I needed to run this by someone else, a person who possessed the wisdom and experience to help me see the situation clearly.

Next stop: Knotty Pine Resort, and a chat with my mother.

21

Mom and I sat at a card table in the study as she sorted through a pile of stickers, settling on a red, star-shaped one that proclaimed, "The Best!" Peeling off the back, she pressed it onto a page in the album that lay open in front of her.

"Voilà!" she said. "Now remember, darling, this project is top secret—a Valentine surprise for your father."

I smiled at her enthusiasm. My father and I referred to Mom as a hobby jumper. In the brief time since I'd moved back to Rock Creek Village, she'd tackled knitting and cake decorating, along with a brief stab at calligraphy. Now she'd thrown herself into scrapbooking. Her maiden voyage centered on an album commemorating my parents' early years together. Old photographs lay in stacks across the table, along with decorative cut outs and memories she'd handwritten on colorful paper.

And stickers. Piles and piles of stickers.

Like Valentine's Day itself, crafts weren't my thing, but more power to her. Sam would probably love the sentimental gesture as well. These days, even Tonya would be suckered in by the romance of it all.

The thought of Tonya reminded me of why I'd come. "Mom, I need a little advice."

She looked up from pasting a picture and raised a silver eyebrow. "Uh oh."

"What does that mean?"

"Well, darling, the last time you asked me for advice, you were nine. This must be serious."

"That's not true. I ask for your opinion all the time."

She chuckled. "If you say so. But tell me, dear, what's the issue?"

I hesitated, uneasy about revealing my snooping.

She paused her sticking and gave me her full attention. "Just dive in, Angelface. No sense prolonging the misery."

"Misery?"

"Of making yourself vulnerable."

I sighed. She knew me so well. "It's about David Parisi," I ventured.

She beamed. "Such a lovely young man. And Tonya seems so happy. There's nothing better than finding true love."

I pressed my lips tight. Mom wasn't making this any easier for me. "It's just that…well, I've come across some information about David."

"Come across?" She frowned. "Callahan Maureen Cassidy, don't you dare tell me you've been investigating that poor boy."

"Not exactly. Not me, anyway. Preston Garrison happened to send me some information."

She stared at me for a long moment, with that look I'd gotten all my life when I'd displeased her. "So you're telling me that, out of the blue, your former boss contacted you with eye-opening revelations about a man he's never met?"

I looked down guiltily. "I might have asked him to research David's background."

She threw up her hands, and I shrugged. "I had an instinct, Mom. You've always told me to follow my instincts."

"You're misconstruing my meaning." Her expression shifted to one of concern. "Did Preston discover something dangerous about David's past? Does he have a criminal record?"

"No, nothing like that. But it's serious."

"Well, I suppose you might as well tell me."

I cleared my throat. "Umm…David's married."

Her eyes widened. "Married? Do you mean, *was* married? As in, he's divorced?"

"Not according to the paperwork Preston's researcher found. David Parisi is currently married to a woman in Italy. The researcher didn't find divorce records, or even a filing."

Mom bit her lip as she processed the information, a gesture I must have come by genetically. Finally, she said, "What do you want to ask me?"

I couldn't read her reaction, so I plunged ahead. "Should I tell Tonya?"

"No."

I stared at her. "That's it? Care to elaborate?"

She reached for her cup of tea and took a long sip. "Darling, you came by this information through illicit means, and it's not yours to share. It's frankly none of your business. It's between Tonya and David."

"But what if David doesn't tell her? What if they go through with the wedding, and David becomes a bigamist? Tonya will be crushed."

"I doubt it'll come to that. It seems to me there's more to the story than a researcher could discover in a stack of paperwork. But if the worst happens, you will be there at her side, helping her pick up the pieces."

I wrung my hands the best I could, with only the fingers of the left one available for wringing. "How can you expect me to keep this information from my best friend?"

"I don't expect anything. You asked for my opinion, and I've given it. I'm not big on giving advice"—at that I smirked—"and you'll do as you see fit. You always have, darling. That's often a lovely quality, but it sometimes leads you into…recklessness."

I struggled to rein in my emotions, but I couldn't seem to view this situation rationally. "It's a horrible secret. How do I stay quiet about it? Keeping this from Tonya will cause me incredible stress."

"That's your burden to bear, I'm afraid. Your penance for seeking information to which you had no right. And I'd encourage you to consider Tonya's pain before your own."

Perhaps my mother was right. She usually was. But in this case, I wasn't sure. Wouldn't Tonya's pain be magnified if she found out too late about David's deception? Wouldn't it be better to face the terrible news now—and to hear it from a friend? I had a horrible image of David's Italian wife tearing down the aisle in the middle of Tonya's wedding screaming, "I object! I object!"

"How will Tonya forgive me if she finds out I had this information and said nothing?"

"How will she forgive you for digging into David's past in the first place?"

"But my intentions were good. She's my friend. I only want to protect her."

Mom put her hand on mine. "Well, darling, remember what they say about the road to hell."

"Paved with good intentions," I muttered.

"Yes. Take a moment to imagine if your places were reversed. If someone you trusted went behind your back to dig into your fiancé's personal life. Even if she did it to protect you, I suspect you'd be hurt and angry."

My head throbbed, but I thought about it. I hated being treated like a child in need of protection. If Tonya did what I'd done, I'd feel betrayed.

I gazed out the window, tears pricking my eyes. My head throbbed, but it wasn't from the concussion. "I hear what you're saying. And I promise, I'll think about it."

Mom turned back to her album, and from the corner of my eye, I saw her weighing her next words. "Not to change the subject, but are things all right between you and Sam?"

Now one of the pooled tears spilled over. The woman was prescient. "We're going through a rough patch," I said. "It'll blow over. All relationships have their challenges, don't they?"

"They do, Angelface, yes. But in the good relationships, the ones that weather the storms, people use the down times as an opportunity to turn toward one another rather than away. It's important that you and Sam talk through the rough patches. And more to the point, it's vital that you listen. Not just with your ears, but with your heart."

I sighed. "Listen with my heart? I don't even understand what that means, Mom. Sometimes I think the whole relationship thing is just too hard. I'm not good at it. I don't know how to make him happy."

She reached out and put a hand on my cheek. "He's not expecting you to make him happy, darling, just as you'd never hold him responsible for your own happiness. What both of you need is a partner who listens, who comforts, who holds your heart tenderly. Someone who considers your needs and your desires. That's what I mean about turning toward."

The tears fell in earnest now. "What if I don't I have that to give? What if I'm just not that…loving of a person?"

She smiled at me. "You are, believe me. The capacity is there, and insight will unlock it. Be aware. Take those small actions that will make him feel loved, treasured." She gestured at her album. "That's what this is about. Have a look, darling. Tell me what you think."

I wiped away my tears and flipped through the pages, smiling, chuckling, even welling up again at the photos she'd chosen and the words she'd written. She'd documented Dad's entire adulthood, from personal life to career. Here was a photo of a fresh-faced young police recruit, eager and hopeful. Next, I turned the page to find sepia-toned pictures of Butch and Maggie in their dating days. I couldn't believe they'd ever been that young. Then I read an article about my father saving a woman and her child after their car tumbled over the side of a mountain road. Humble as my father could be, it was a story I'd never heard.

The scrapbook concluded with a photo of the three of us grinning into the camera and holding up cupcakes on my forty-fourth birthday. When I closed the back cover, I stared at the book for a moment before turning to my mother.

"Mom, this is amazing. It's the most beautiful thing you've ever made."

She took my chin in her hand and gazed into my eyes. "Not by a long shot, darling."

***

In the spirit of my mom's relationship advice, I called Sam on my way home and asked if he wanted to come over. I said I'd even whip up something for dinner, which earned me a mocking retort. Given my legendary lack of culinary prowess, I supposed a meal wasn't the best incentive.

"That's a nice offer, but I'm planning to work late tonight. I'm experimenting with a few new recipes."

"Want a taste tester?"

He paused so long I wondered if our connection had broken. Then he said, "I appreciate the thought, Callie. But I could use a little time to myself."

"Oh. Okay." Tears threatened again. "Is there something…I should know? We're not breaking up, are we?"

"No," he said quickly. "I mean, you're not suggesting—"

"Not at all. I…you had me worried, that's all."

"I've just been stressed. Uptight. Time in the kitchen helps. That's all."

"I understand. I'll give you whatever space you need, but sometime…well, I'd like to hear what's stressing you out."

"You would?"

The surprise in his voice hurt my heart. I hadn't been paying attention, not nearly enough. "Yes, Sam. I want to know everything. Maybe tomorrow we can have dinner and talk?"

"I'd like that," he said, then took a breath. "Are you feeling all right? Will you be okay on your own tonight?"

"I'm good. Healing fast. But I'll miss you."

"Absence makes the heart—"

"I don't think my heart could be any fonder of you. Now go experiment with your food. I'll talk to you tomorrow."

"Sounds like a plan." There was a moment's silence. "Callie? My heart's pretty fond of you, too."

22

It was only four-thirty when I pulled into the driveway behind my townhome, but dusk stretched across the sky like a soft cashmere sweater. When I unlocked the back door, Woody ran toward me at warp speed, skidding to a halt when he remembered my cast. He snuggled his wet nose into my outstretched hand instead.

I rewarded him by plunking cross-legged onto the floor and letting him climb in my lap. I'd had my golden retriever—full name Woodward, after one of my all-time favorite journalists—for six years, but sometimes he still acted like a puppy.

After a couple of minutes, just long enough to display his indifference, Carl sauntered into the room. He graced me with a rub against my knee, an arched back, and a deep purr at my touch. My tabby cat, a former stray whom Woody had adopted as his brother soon after my return to Rock Creek Village, bore the name of Bob Woodward's partner, Carl Bernstein. For the cat, the name was even more fitting. His intelligent, curious nature had provided a tremendous help solving some recent crimes in the village. If Carl could talk, though, I was certain he'd say I was the one assisting him.

After a few minutes of mutual lovefest, I struggled to my feet with an oomph. Woody raced out the pet door to the backyard, and Carl trotted beside me into the kitchen, studying me with inquisitive eyes. "Nothing new to report," I told him. "Raul says the new detective has Renata in her crosshairs, but that's about it."

He swished his tail and gave a discontented meow before sashaying into the laundry room to visit his litterbox.

I pulled my phone out of my purse. No texts or missed calls. The well-wishers who had inundated my message box for the past two days had dwindled. I texted Tonya to invite her over for pizza and wine—if she agreed to supply the pizza. Maybe her presence would help me decide: *to tell or not to tell. That was the question.* Three dots blinked on my phone as she composed a response.

Sorry, not tonight, sugarplum. Hot date with a handsome Italian.

Does David know? I responded.

Two laughing emojis, followed by, *Feeling okay?*

All good. Have fun.

Talk tomorrow, followed by two heart emojis. The woman embraced her emojis.

I tossed my phone onto the counter and brooded over my mother's advice. Thinking about David only soured my mood, so I decided not to. As Scarlett O'Hara said, "Fiddle dee dee. After all, tomorrow is another day."

I sighed. With Sam and Tonya otherwise occupied, a long evening alone loomed. Usually, I was satisfied with my own company—rather liked it, in fact. I'd just gotten unaccustomed to it lately. My disposition brightened when I realized alone time meant early pajama time. I hurried upstairs to change.

After wrenching myself out of my daytime attire, I slipped into a pair of flannel pajama pants. I pulled one of Sam's t-shirts over my head and completed the ensemble with a woolen shawl my mother had created during her knitting phase. I wouldn't win any fashion prizes, but I was oh-so comfortable.

Back in the kitchen, I opened the fridge. No leftovers from one of Sam's delicious meals, so a frozen dinner would have to do. I debated whether red or white wine would pair best with frozen lasagna and barbecue chips, settled on red, and poured myself a healthy serving. As I sipped, I zapped the Lean Cuisine and reached into the bag of Lays for a handful.

The microwave dinged, and I removed the container, pulled off the plastic, and watched the steam rise. I didn't bother to sit at the table, just grabbed a fork and plunged in. Strings of melted cheese stretched from my mouth to the container. Chips crumbled as I crunched. All the while, Woody stood at attention at my feet, anticipating falling tidbits. The tableau hearkened back to my days on the newspaper beat, when I was less civilized and more rushed. I didn't miss those days. Not much, anyway.

When I'd scraped up the last bite of lasagna, I placed the container on the floor and watched Woody lick it clean as Carl looked on impassively. I polished off the wine in my glass and refilled it. Tidying up the kitchen took all of ten seconds. Then I grabbed a pen and the list Raul and I had made and moved to the couch.

Bradley and Tim's podcast had forced me to put the murder investigation aside for the afternoon. Now it was time to dig in again.

***

One by one, I considered each suspect on the list, starting with Renata. I didn't believe she'd murdered Jeffrey, but I had to admit, her motive was compelling. Her ex-husband had arrived in her village and thrown her life into chaos. He'd been harassing her, and she wanted him out of her life. Her alibi wasn't fabulous, either—in the locker room by herself. Then I thought of her bloodied hockey stick, by far the most problematic concern.

I imagined the scene as it might have happened: Renata follows Jeffrey up the stairs. During a heated exchange, she bashes him with her hockey stick, which then skids over the side of the catwalk. Realizing she's killed him, she tosses his body over the railing, hurries down the stairs, and races into the locker room.

The fictional scenario, feasible though it might be, left me with several unanswered questions. Why was Jeffrey on the catwalk? Was Renata strong enough to lift his dead weight? And what was the purpose of throwing him over?

Still, unless Raul tracked down someone to confirm her flimsy alibi, I worried Renata was in serious jeopardy.

Next on the list: Theo Clement. He'd seemed sketchy to me from the get-go. Yes, he and Jeffrey were brothers, but history recorded ample instances of fratricide, all the way back to Cain and Abel. And hadn't I witnessed Theo and Jeffrey arguing less than an hour before the murder?

From the little I'd learned of Theo, he'd been a troubled soul since his teenage years. The addictions, the years in rehab, the sense of never measuring up—all of it must have taken a toll. And when his mother died and left everything to his big brother—well, it might have been the proverbial straw that broke little brother's back. Did Theo stand to inherit Jeffrey's money? That would give him a huge motive. I made a note to find out whatever I could about Jeffrey's will.

As far as an alibi, Theo said he'd been walking in the park when Jeffrey was killed, but had anyone verified that? Again, I tried to picture the scene. Theo, already angry from their prior argument, confronts Jeffrey on the catwalk, kills him, throws him to the ice below.

But how would he have gotten Renata's hockey stick? Also, Theo appeared fairly scrawny. Did he have the strength to commit the deed? Again, I had more questions than answers.

Ethan's name followed Theo's. My mind almost refused to even consider him. I just couldn't picture him as a killer. He'd always been so kind, mild-mannered, and thoughtful. But when I called to mind the video and the rage on his face, I knew I had to keep his name on the list. Even a docile creature could turn murderous in defense of a loved one.

As with the others, I closed my eyes and pictured Ethan carrying out the crime. He runs up the steps to the catwalk, strikes Jeffrey down, throws him over the edge. I'd seen Ethan haul hefty packages of canvases, so I knew he had the muscle to pull it off. But why would he use his girlfriend's hockey stick? It didn't make sense.

Technically, his alibi should have been me—or Banner and

Braden, at any rate. But as I'd later discovered, he'd flown off the radar for a while, leaving the shop in the care of the twins. I sighed. I'd told Raul I'd ask Ethan for a more specific accounting of his time. If he'd stopped at Rocky Mountain High for coffee or The Fudge Factory for a treat, I could eliminate his name. I'd call him as soon as I was through going over the list.

The last name, written lightly as if Raul hadn't even wanted to waste the ink, was Pinky. I shook my head. I couldn't come up with a single motive, nor could I visualize him hoisting Jeffrey over the guardrail. Still, it wouldn't hurt to find out where he'd been at the time of the murder.

I scanned the anemic list one last time. There had to be something—someone—we were missing. I tossed the pad onto the coffee table in frustration and reached for my phone. Time to call Ethan and hopefully make the list one person shorter.

23

As the phone rang, Woody jumped up and scrambled down the hall. At the sound of a knock on the front door, I disconnected and followed behind him. I looked through the peephole and smiled. Then I glanced down at myself, all jammied up before six-thirty. I pulled the shawl tighter around myself and opened the door.

Ethan held up his phone. "You rang?"

"Now that's what I call response time," I said.

Beside him, Renata grinned. I saw Terror tucked into the crook of her arm and felt Woody at my thigh trembling with excitement at the thought of an unexpected playdate.

Renata's gaze traveled from my shawl to my flannel pajama pants. "Looks like you're ready for bed. We won't stay. Just wanted to stop by and check on you."

"No, please come in," I said, glad for the company. "Pardon my attire. I craved comfy clothes. You'd better put Terror down before Woody knocks us all over like bowling pins."

She stooped to release the dog, who dashed toward the living room with Woody hot on the chase. A yowl from Carl telegraphed his displeasure.

We laughed. "How about a glass of wine?" I asked.

As they hung up their coats, I trotted off to the kitchen, making a quick pit stop in the living room to grab my glass. Catching sight of the legal pad, I flipped it face down. I wasn't

Miss Manners, but displaying your guests' names as potential murder suspects didn't seem like proper etiquette.

By the time I'd pulled two more wine glasses from the cabinet, Ethan and Renata had joined me at the kitchen island. "Let me," Ethan said. "You're the patient."

"I'm not terribly adept at that role, turns out."

"Doesn't take a psychologist to figure that out," he said, opening the refrigerator. "Looks like we have a choice between white and red."

We all decided on red. As he poured, I nodded to the flowers. "Thank you, Renata. That was such a thoughtful gesture."

"They're from me, too," Ethan protested.

"Whatever." Renata gave me a grin. "Men. Always trying to take credit for women's efforts."

We carried our glasses to the living room. I took the armchair so the lovebirds could sit side by side on the couch. Ethan asked me about the podcast, and I summarized. "You should see that cabin," I said. "It makes this place look like a backyard storage shed."

He chuckled. "I've done some research on Bradley and Tim. Believe me, they can afford it. We should prepare for another surge in sales once the podcast airs."

I smiled and held up my cast. "Hope I can keep up with demand."

"Braden can help you in the darkroom. You might consider displaying some of his photography in the gallery, too. I've seen his work. He's quite talented."

We sipped our wine in silence for a moment, watching the two pups wrestle on the rug. Carl swatted their noses if they came near him, but they didn't care. Ethan and Renata exchanged glances, and I deduced there was more to this visit than idle chit chat.

"Something you want to talk to me about?"

Renata's face scrunched up. "Actually, yes. Raul told me the two of you are looking into Jeffrey's murder, trying to figure out who did it. So I'm here,"—Ethan nudged her with his elbow—

"*we're* here to, well, to reassure you it wasn't me."

I held up my hands. "Listen, you guys, I'm not a cop. It's Detective Clarke you should talk to."

Renata grunted. "I *have* talked to her. It's obvious she thinks I'm guilty."

"I'm worried," Ethan said. "That detective seems fixated on Renata. She wants her to come in tomorrow for more questioning."

I hadn't heard that news, but it didn't surprise me. I figured Ethan would be summoned to the interrogation room before long, too.

"Well, I'm worried for both of you," I said.

Ethan didn't flinch at my words, but Renata appeared shocked. "*What?* You mean Ethan, too?" she demanded.

"Did Clarke show you the video of the altercation outside the studio? There was a shot of Ethan's face, just before you smacked Jeffrey in the nose. If looks could kill, as they say…"

She waved dismissively. "Oh, please. Everyone who crossed paths with Jeffrey looked at him like that eventually. If hateful expressions make someone a suspect, you'll find a thousand would-be killers out there."

I looked at Ethan. "The problem is, you don't have an alibi for the time of the murder. At least, not as far as anyone knows. You weren't at the studio as scheduled. If I've found out about that, you can bet Detective Clarke will, too. So let's get ahead of it. Where were you when Jeffrey was killed?"

He glanced at Renata, and her eyes widened in realization. "Oh no! You came to the arena," she said. "You were there just before…"

He sighed, then nodded. "You remember that Renata and I had a…misunderstanding that morning?"

"It wasn't a misunderstanding," she cut in. "You were being a Neanderthal. I'm capable of—"

"Maybe we can table that discussion for now," I said. "Let's focus on keeping the two of you out of jail."

Ethan took a deep breath. "Well, I couldn't stand the thought of that argument hanging between us. I knew the twins could handle the gallery. So I walked over to The Ice Zone to find her and make things right."

They looked at each other with lovey dovey eyes, and I almost told them to get a room. After a moment, I cleared my throat. "You found her, I assume?"

Renata continued gazing at him. "He brought me coffee from Rocky Mountain High," she said, as though he'd presented her with the Hope Diamond.

"How lovely," I said. "But back to the matter at hand. How long were you at the arena, Ethan? Can anyone—besides Renata—vouch for you?"

Ethan rolled his shoulders. "Once I got inside, it took me a few minutes to locate Renata. There were people in the stands, but I doubt any of them paid much attention to me walking by. I spotted you on the ice, Callie, but I kind of turned my back so you wouldn't see me. I didn't want to explain why I'd left the gallery." He snapped his fingers. "Lars saw me. I asked him where Renata might be."

"That's good," I said. "Did you go to the locker room?"

"No, Renata came out then. She had her hockey stick! We walked toward the front entrance and into the alcove to talk."

"That's right," Renata said. "I rested the stick against the wall to…"

They both blushed, and I envisioned an apology followed by a passionate embrace of forgiveness. "I don't remember picking it up again after that," she went on. "I must have left it there in the alcove."

I felt a burst of excitement. This explained how someone else had access to the murder weapon.

"Okay, good," I said. "Did you leave right after that, Ethan?"

He nodded. "I walked back to Sundance Studio."

"Did you talk to anyone on the way? Someone who might verify the time?"

He shook his head. "Not that I recall."

I turned to Renata. "What about you? Where did you go?"

128

"Back to the locker room to get my skates on," she said.

"Do you have any idea how much time elapsed until Jeffrey fell?"

She shrugged. "I'd guess about ten minutes, but I can't be sure."

I felt deflated. We still had no definitive alibi for either of them—except each other. "One last question," I said. "Did either of you see Jeffrey or Theo during that time frame?"

"I didn't," Renata said. "I would have remembered that for sure."

Ethan thought for a few seconds. "I didn't see Jeffrey. But Theo…" He stroked his chin. "There was a man outside the door. I only noticed him because of the black leather coat—not too common in Rock Creek Village. I've never seen Theo, so I can't be positive..."

"It was him." My pulse quickened. "I'm certain of it. What was he doing?"

"Just standing there. As I said, I didn't pay much attention to him." He looked at me quizzically. "Is it relevant?"

"Could be," I said. "He told detectives he was in the park. You've placed him just outside the arena door. Now, if we could only pinpoint the exact time."

"Why is Theo being there so important?" Renata asked.

I held up the legal pad. "Because besides you two, he's the only viable suspect we have."

24

Once Ethan and Renata left, with Terror in tow, the weight of the day fell over me like a heavy blanket. My brain simply couldn't process another iota of information, so I curled up on the couch to watch some mindless TV. I must've dozed off, because when the phone rang, the cooking competition I'd tuned into had given way to a couple flipping a house.

I read the screen but didn't recognize the number. "Hello?" I said, expecting a robo voice warning me of the looming expiration of my car's warranty.

Instead, it was a deep voice with a Swedish accent. "Ms. Cassidy? Zees is Lars Eggars. I manage Ze Ice Zone."

"Yes, hello, Lars. Please, call me Callie."

"Zank you, Callie. I vanted to share vith you some good news. I have located your camera."

I squealed in delight. "Oh, Lars, that's wonderful. Where was it?"

"She vas in ze stands, pushed far beneath a bleacher seat. I do not know cameras, but to my eye, she looks vell."

"When can I pick it up?"

"Ve open for Early Skate at five-thirty is ze morning. I vill be here any time after that."

I thanked him again. When we hung up, I sent Raul a text.

Lars found my camera. Want to go with me to pick it up tomorrow a.m.?

He responded right away. *I'll pick you up at seven-thirty. Don't keep me waiting.*

***

My alarm chirped at six-forty-five, before even the sun had decided to get up. I picked up my phone, and with a jab not quite forceful enough to break the screen, I shut it off. Then I noticed a text from an hour earlier. What kind of fool would text me at that hour of the morning?

Preston, of course. Eastern Standard Time was two hours ahead of Mountain Standard Time. And unlike me, Preston was one of those early-to-bed, early-to-rise people.

I pulled myself to a sitting position, jostling Woody, whose eyes didn't open even a smidge. Playtime with Terror had worn him out.

Preston's text was brief. *Sent you an email. Didn't want to risk waking the sleeping bear again with a phone call.*

I clicked on my Google account and scanned the document he had sent. I read through it a second time, studying it more closely.

Preston's researcher had uncovered some interesting information about Jeffrey Forte, and I couldn't wait to share it with Raul.

***

Forty-five minutes later, a short beep from the curb alerted me that he'd arrived. I threw on my coat, grabbed my bag, and dashed down the sidewalk to the Explorer. The heated seat felt nice on a frosty morning.

"Glad you could make it," he said sarcastically.

"What do you mean? It's seven-twenty-eight, and here I am. By the way, I doubt my neighbors appreciate you honking at this hour. They'll probably file complaints with the police department."

"Well, those complaints will land on my desk. That's the kind of work I'm doing these days."

"This little pity party doesn't suit you," I said, flinching as I heard my mother's voice emerge from my mouth.

The corner of his mouth quirked. "Point taken."

"Anyway, I have lots of news to share. First off, Ethan and your sister paid me a visit last night." I filled him in on the details.

He rubbed a hand over the stylish scruff on his chin. "The information about her hockey stick is good to know," he said. "But we still don't have an alibi for either of them at the time of Jeffrey's murder."

"Okay, Debbie Downer," I said. "Maybe this will cheer you up. Preston emailed me this morning with some research results on Jeffrey and Theo."

"Anything of substance?"

"Concerning Theo, nothing much. Drug problems dating back to his high school days, which we already knew. Several stints in rehab—again, old news. But there is one thing: Last year, Theo filed paperwork to challenge their mother's will. He later withdrew the lawsuit. I'm guessing they came to some sort of settlement, but Preston's researcher couldn't access the confidential documents."

Raul nodded. "That could be important. I'll dig up the name of Jeffrey's attorney and get in touch with him. He might talk to a cop." He put on his blinker and waited to turn. "What did Preston say about Jeffrey?"

"Financial trouble out the wazoo, at least until his mother died. A couple of bankruptcies. Several failed businesses. He tried hard to make it as an entrepreneur but never achieved any success. Screwed over any number of people in the process. As soon as he got his hands on his mother's money, he dove feet first into a new venture." I summarized the researcher's findings, which centered on Jeffrey's participation in a group lobbying the state legislature for legalized gambling. Jeffrey had poured a lot of time and a good deal of cash into that pursuit, so there had to be a money-making scheme involved. I couldn't unravel it yet, but I would.

We stopped at a light, and Raul thought for a minute. "The other day, when Jeffrey was being such a jerk to Renata, wasn't he coming from upstairs?"

"Yes. From Willie's office."

"Wonder what he was doing in a realtor's office," he said.

I considered his question. Suddenly, the information clicked into place. Renata had mentioned that Jeffrey came to town for business. In the ambulance, Theo told me Jeffrey was pursuing a "business venture" in the village. And now we heard from Preston's source that Jeffrey had been lobbying for legalized gambling. Put that together with his visit to Willie, and the conclusion was clear.

"I bet Jeffrey was planning to build a casino." I wrinkled my nose at the thought. "Can you even imagine a casino in Rock Creek Village?"

Raul frowned. "We love our tourists, but this town doesn't really give off a gambling mecca vibe."

"Exactly. If any of the locals discovered his plan, they'd have been up in arms. Dad told me about the angry protests when that big box store came sniffing around a few years back."

He nodded. "I remember that. But I don't think anyone was mad enough to kill."

I shrugged. "You never know. After the twins come in to work, I'll run upstairs and ask Willie about it."

We arrived at the rink just as Early Skate let out. A line of cars driven by bleary-eyed parents snaked out of the lot as we pulled in. We parked near the door, went inside, and found Lars driving a beat-up old Zamboni across the ice. He wore black polyester athletic pants, the same jacket with the red tubing, and clashing powder blue sneakers. When he caught sight of us, he shut off the machine and met us at the boards.

"Morning, Detective," he said. He turned to me. "And Ms. Cassidy. Callie. I am pleased to see you up and around. I vas quite vorried over you. But you seem fresh as a vildflower in spring."

I grinned. "Oh, Lars. When you say such things in that fabulous accent, it makes me a little weak in the knees."

He threw back his head and laughed. "Vell, stand strong. Ve can't have you falling to ze ice. Not again." With a tilt of his chin, he indicated my cast. "How long must you vear zis?"

"Several weeks," I told him. "But it's not too bad. I can still drive—and hopefully operate a camera. Speaking of…"

"Ah, yes. You come for your baby. I lock her safely in ze office."

We followed him down the hall, past a locker room, two changing areas, bathrooms, and a small kitchen. He unlocked the office door, and the three of us entered. The small space smelled like feet, an odor someone had tried to cover with a pine scent. An upscale ergonomic chair rested behind a battered wooden desk. Two plastic guest chairs faced the desk, and Lars gestured for us to sit. He unlocked a metal file cabinet and removed my camera, cradling it as if it were the holy grail. Which it was, to me.

Lars settled the camera into my hands, and I ran my hands over it. No dings or dents. I examined the lens, took off the cap, and checked the glass. My finger hovered above the power button, but something made me hesitate. I glanced at Raul, who gave a small shake of his head. We'd wait on that part until we got to the car.

I looked at Lars gratefully. "The camera looks pristine. Thank you for taking such good care of it."

"You feel about her as I do about my rink," he said. "More zan an object, yes? Almost a living, breathing thing. Part of ze family." Raul squirmed in his seat. Lars noticed, and his fair skin tinted pink. "Please excuse. I become…emotional."

"I get it," I said. "It's the same with my cameras, my darkroom, my gallery. When you are passionate about what you do, you can't separate yourself from the objects that make it possible."

Lars nodded, his blue eyes sparkling. "Yes. Zat is it exactly. And I am passionate about my rink." He sighed. "Zat is why this…this tragedy hurt me so. Nothing bad should happen in zis space."

My thoughts flitted to the body I'd found in my darkroom several months ago. It had taken weeks for me to recover the sense of safety and joy I'd always experienced in my happy place. But then, one day, I'd walked through that revolving door and discovered the simmering anxiety had disappeared. Once again, the darkroom filled me with peace. I was certain the same thing would happen for Lars.

"The memory will fade," I assured him. "After a few days of watching the kids skate and hearing their excited voices, you'll find the shroud has lifted."

Raul rose, having tolerated the spiritual talk as long as he could stand it. He reached across the desk and shook hands with Lars. "We need to be going. Thanks for your help."

Lars walked with us past the bleachers and toward the door. Raul stopped at the staircase leading from the alcove to the catwalk. "Quick question, Lars. Where were you when Jeffrey fell? I'm wondering if you noticed anyone hanging around in this part of the arena."

"Detective Clarke asks me ze same question. I notice no one. I vas here in ze office, and I hear shouting. I rush out to the rink to see Callie pinned beneath ze man." He paused and looked at me, his eyes shining. "I vish I could have done more to help."

I patted his arm. "You did plenty. You got him off me and brought me a blanket. I appreciate your kindness."

Raul and I left the arena. Outside, the cold air nipped at my cheeks and lips. Raul strode across the parking lot and opened my car door. Juggling my camera and my cast, I managed to wedge myself into the passenger seat. Once he'd rounded the car and gotten inside, I held up the camera. "Okay, let's see what we have."

I pressed the power button, my heart pounding. If I'd captured a photo of the killer, this could all be over right now. I mentally crossed my fingers.

The screen was black. I pressed one button after another and scrolled through black, empty spaces. Nothing. Not even the team photos I'd shot. Then I opened the door that held the memory card, finding it intact. "Blank," I muttered.

"Damaged in the fall?"

I shook my head. "The camera looks fine. I think the memory card was erased."

"Could that have been done accidentally? When the camera was being jostled around?"

"Unlikely," I said. "Erasing a memory card requires several steps. If the card was erased, I suspect it was on purpose."

"Can you get the photos back?"

I thought about it. "Depends. If someone reformatted the card, it'd be tough. Retrieval software exists, but I don't own any."

Raul pounded the steering wheel in frustration. "This morning has been a total bust."

"Not necessarily," I said. "Give me a little time. If the solution is buried in a digital graveyard, I might be able to dig it up."

25

I pulled my Civic into my designated spot behind the gallery. Raul had dropped me off at home on the way back from the rink, and the creatures convinced me it was Bring Your Pets to work day—just like most days. They were gallery animals, accustomed to prowling the studio during off hours and content to snooze on their cozy pet beds in my office when customers showed up.

When I opened the car's back door, Woody jumped out and ran through the alley to the gallery. I awkwardly lifted Carl's backpack carrier from the back seat, earning a yowl of protest at the jostling. "Listen, cat, I'm doing the best I can one-handed," I said. "How about cutting me some slack?"

Once inside the studio, I released Carl from captivity, filled food and water bowls, and checked to make sure the litterbox was clean. "Hold down the fort for a while, guys," I said. "I need a good cup of coffee."

I exited through the front, locking the door behind me, and took a moment to breathe in the fresh mountain air. The sun gleamed, suspended like a ripe peach against the clear, blue sky. I turned my gaze to Mt. O'Connell and watched as two skiers, tiny in the distance, swooshed down the east slope.

Right now, they were the only humans in sight. It was nine o'clock, and like Sundance Studio, most shops didn't open until ten—some even later during slow months. Though the Chamber marketed Rock Creek Village as a year-round tourist destination, February rarely drew throngs of visitors. We stayed busy enough with skiers and other outdoor enthusiasts, many of them day trippers from surrounding towns, but the crowds picked up in March when schools let out for spring break.

I strolled down the sidewalk toward Rocky Mountain High. The door flung open as I reached for it. Then a hand reached out, took me by the elbow, and yanked me inside.

I had the sudden sense a heavenly spirit had captured me. A second glance, though, assured me this was no angel—not even close. It was Tonya, and except for a pair of bright red boots, she was clad in pure white, from her wool coat to her stockings to her gloves—one of which clutched a paper coffee cup and a pastry bag. Atop her black curls rested a white fedora designed for fashion rather than warmth. Beneath its brim, Tonya's makeup was flawless, as always, with her trademark red lipstick providing a perfect complement to the boots. Her skin glowed. Love had made her even more beautiful, if that was possible.

She closed the door and began to scold. "It's people like you, letting in the winter cold, who drive up poor Mrs. Finney's heating bill. Show some consideration." She leaned towards me, her voice taking on a confidential tone. "I'm glad I ran into you, sweetpea. Would you be available to meet for drinks tonight? There's something I need to discuss with you."

Uh-oh. Had Tonya found out about David's wife all on her own? Was she going to say she was calling off the wedding? Would I be relieved of the burden of secret knowledge?

"Of course," I said. "Can you give me a hint?"

She glanced around the coffee shop. A few customers sat around bistro tables, chatting amiably or swiping at their phones. "Not now. Meet me at the lodge? Free mulled wine, and those hors d'oeuvres of Jamal's—mmm. Six o'clock?"

"It's a date," I said.

Tonya kissed my cheek and sashayed out the door. Feeling a little shell-shocked, I made my way to Mrs. Finney.

"Any idea what that's about?" I asked, jerking a thumb over

my shoulder. Despite Tonya's cloak-and-dagger behavior, I knew Mrs. Finney had overheard our conversation. The former CIA agent knew everything that went on in her coffee shop. She either had the hearing of a bat, or she'd installed listening devices in every corner.

She shrugged. "Wedding planning, perhaps?"

My face screwed into a frown. If Tonya planned to bombard me with talk of wedding dresses and flowers, I didn't think I'd have the strength to keep my secret. When I looked at Mrs. Finney, she was studying me through narrowed eyes.

"Callie, dear, it's not my place to offer advice—"

I smothered a chuckle. My friend spurted advice as if she were a malfunctioning sprinkler head.

She stared at me for a moment, then turned to fill a cup with house brew, adding a squirt of vanilla and a shake of cinnamon, just as I liked it.

While I sipped, she crossed her arms. "My dear, it has come to my attention that you've gotten hold of some information about Tonya's young man."

I felt the blood rush to my face. *Darn you, Preston Garrison.* My request for information had not been intended for Mrs. Finney's ears.

"Mrs. Finney, I only want to protect—"

She held up a hand. "Your motives are not my concern," she said. Her fake British accent always became more pronounced during lectures. "My interest lies with what you intend to do with the knowledge. I'd urge you to think long and hard before you share potentially damaging information with your friend."

I sighed. "That's what Mom said."

She lifted a bushy eyebrow. "Well, dear, you'd be wise to listen to her. But I know you are sometimes—how do I say this delicately?—prone to acting impulsively."

Humph. No one seemed willing to acknowledge that I was an adult on the cusp of middle age. I'd navigated a challenging career in the field. I now managed a semi-lucrative business. I'd even solved a couple of crimes in this very village. Yet everyone apparently viewed me as a hasty creature.

"You're pouting," Mrs. Finney observed.

I caught myself. "Am not."

She smiled. "Just know this: Sometimes our best intentions create our worst outcomes."

"Another phrase for your coffee cups?"

"Ah, good idea." She reached under the counter and pulled out a pad of paper, jotting down the axiom. "To the matter at hand, dear, I encourage you to keep your ill-gained knowledge to yourself, at least for now."

I nodded. "Duly noted."

She reached across the counter and touched my cast. "How is your recovery progressing? Are your injuries causing you a great deal of agony?"

"Actually, I'm feeling much better. I'm a fast healer, and I've always been told I have a high pain tolerance."

"Good to hear. And what about your emotional resilience? A body landing on you might give even the most stalwart person the heebie jeebies."

I tilted my head. "I haven't even really thought about it," I said. "I guess that means I'm fine."

She studied me for a moment. "Well, I'd urge you to keep an eye out for signs of PTSD, dear. Drinking too much, depressive thoughts, snappishness. Perhaps a visit to your therapist would be in order."

From anyone else, even my mother, such a suggestion might have made me prickly. But from Mrs. Finney, with her knowledge and background, I took it to heart. "I'll call her and set something up. In the meantime, could I get a coffee to go…" I pointed at the glass dome on the counter. "And maybe one of those irresistible creations, too."

Her eyes brightened as she lifted the cover and used a pair of tongs to remove a flaky work of art. "As you know, I've been experimenting with international pastries. Today, I've chosen Austrian cuisine: A cherry cream cheese streusel. Morello cherries give it a hint of tartness. It's gotten rave reviews from this morning's customers. I believe you'll like it."

"Probably too much," I said, patting my stomach.

She tucked the streusel into a bag and handed it across the counter, along with a fresh cup of coffee. "Everything in moderation, my dear. Except sweets, I think."

26

offee and pastry bag in hand, I left Rocky Mountain High and began the short walk back to Sundance Studio. Traffic along Evergreen Way had increased, both vehicular and pedestrian, as shop owners made their way to work and tourists window-shopped. I strolled down the sidewalk, pondering my upcoming date with Tonya, so lost in thought that I didn't see Theo until he came up from behind and laid a hand on my shoulder.

I gasped, and the pastry bag fell from my hand. Theo picked it up and held it out to me. "Sorry, Ms. Cassidy. Didn't mean to scare you. Just wanted to see how you're doing." He pointed at my cast. "I feel bad you got hurt, especially since it was my brother who…" His voice cracked, and he dropped his eyes. The skeptic in me wondered whether his grief was sincere.

After a beat of silence, I decided to err on the side of compassion. Besides, maybe if we talked for a while, he'd end up revealing some detail that would help clear Renata. "I'm sorry for your loss," I said. "You said you were in town helping your brother with that business he was pursuing. The two of you must have been close."

When he looked up, I saw a brief flash of contempt in his eyes. He blinked, and it disappeared. "We were as close as two brothers can be," he said, his tone mournful. "More than ever these past few weeks. I…well, I got my act together. I've been clean and sober eight months now."

"Congratulations. That's an enormous achievement."

"That's what Jeffrey said. He was proud of me and wanted to give me a second chance—even offered me a position in the business he was starting." He shook his head. "But now it's too late."

By now, I was convinced Theo was faking his anguish, but if he could manufacture emotion, I could, too. I put a hand on his arm. "Jeffrey's death must have come as a terrible shock to you, especially since I've heard it may not have been an accident."

He clenched his jaw. "Someone killed him, no doubt about it. I know it, and the police know it, too. Detective Clarke says they're getting close to making an arrest. I've been talking to her a lot, giving her background information and stuff."

My brain whirred. Background information? What did that mean? "I'm sure she's grateful. I know the police can use all the help they can get. What have you told her?"

"Oh, you know. How much his ex-wife hated Jeffrey. Her brother Raul couldn't stand him either. Those two are psychos. They threatened Jeffrey so many times…You even witnessed one incident, didn't you? The morning Jeffrey died."

"I saw a confrontation," I said. "I'm not sure I'd characterize it as a threat, though."

"It was a threat, all right. And it wasn't the only time the two of them attacked my brother. They were constantly harassing him. One night, Jeffrey and I were eating dinner at the condo he was renting until he could find a permanent place. I'm staying there now, getting his affairs in order." He squared his shoulders self-importantly. "Anyway, that night…someone started pounding on the door. When Jeffrey opened it, Renata and Raul started screaming at him, saying he'd cheated her out of the money from our mother's inheritance. Raul said he'd better get his sister the cash she deserved. Then he put his hand on the gun in his holster. Like I told Detective Clarke, in that moment, I feared for my brother's safety." He shook his head. "And now Jeffrey is dead."

His story was so absurd I could barely restrain an eye roll. The man was obviously an opportunistic liar with an agenda of his own. After all, if anyone had reason to feel bitter over money, it was Theo, whose own mother had left him out of her will.

He was studying me intently. "Oh, I forgot. You're friends with Raul, aren't you? Hope I didn't upset you. But you should know the truth."

I forced a grim smile. "No worries. And you're right—the truth is always what I'm after. It has a way of turning up, even if it takes a little time." I looked at Theo hard. "I'm sure whoever committed this terrible crime will be caught. Your brother will get the justice he's due."

He visibly blanched, but then nodded. "I hope you're right."

"I am. Well, nice running into you, but I need to get to the gallery. I'm sure we'll talk again soon."

When he reached out to shake my hand, his eyes were cold. "Yes, Callie. I'm sure we will."

As he turned away, a chill crept up my spine—one that had nothing to do with the temperature.

***

The time until opening passed quickly at the gallery. First, I reveled in my streusel. Mrs. Finney was right. It was delicious. Then I sat in my office, calculating last week's sales and organizing the invoices on my desk. Finally, I turned the sign in the door to Open and raised the blinds. A young couple strolled inside seconds later, scanning the canvases on the wall before settling on a few inexpensive landscape postcards from the rack by the door.

The next two hours passed with a small but steady stream of shoppers—mostly browsers, with only a few minor purchases. Not enough to keep me in the black, but too many to allow me time to research digital data retrieval software for my erased camera card.

For thirty minutes, a lone customer examined each photo on the wall, then flipped through the smaller, matted offerings, then strolled around the perimeter of the gallery a second time. She finally left without buying anything, and the studio was empty. But just as I sat at the computer to start my search, a buzzing at the back door alerted me to the delivery I'd been expecting— twenty large canvases featuring original Callahan Cassidy photos. Five of them I'd have the twins hang in spots vacated due to last week's purchases. The rest I'd put into storage, awaiting the surge that would hopefully come after the podcast aired Thursday afternoon. I signed for the pieces and instructed the delivery person to leave them in the back hall.

Just after the delivery, Banner and Braden come in the back door, smiles on their identical faces. "Hey, Callie," Braden said. "Been this slow all morning?"

I nodded. "Eh. A few small sales, but nothing worth writing home about."

Banner nodded and jerked a thumb toward the hall. "I saw we got a delivery. You want the unwrapped ones hung in the empty spots?"

"Yes, and the rest can go in the storage room. If you'll be all right on your own, I thought I'd grab lunch at the Chow. I'll be happy to bring you guys something. My treat."

"I never say no to food," Braden said. "Especially free food. Maybe a BLT? And an order of snow fries?"

I could have predicted his order, especially the snow fries. Though French fries coated with olive oil and powdery white cheddar cheese held little appeal for me, they were popular among the younger crowd. Sam told me he sold them by the truckload.

"I'll have the same," Banner said. "Thanks, boss."

"Sure thing." I started toward the office, talking over my shoulder. "Woody and Carl are camping out here today. I'll take Woody for a quick bathroom break before I head out."

I put on my coat and opened the office door. Carl lay on his bed. He swished his tail but otherwise didn't budge. Woody scrambled to his feet and gave me his "I've gotta go bad" whine.

"Oh, please," I said, as I snapped on his leash. "You have the bladder the size of Mt. O'Connell. You'd be fine until midnight."

He dragged me out the back door and down a slight slope to a spot near the ravine. A light layer of snow covered the ground, and I was glad to be wearing boots with heavy tread.

Woody took care of business—thankfully not the kind that required one of the baggies tucked in my coat pocket. As we climbed back up the hill, I noticed Willie Wright's silver Mercedes parked in his spot. I'd told Raul I'd speak to the realtor about Jeffrey's visit to him. Now seemed as good a time as any. Lunch could wait.

27

Once I'd settled Woody back into the office, I headed upstairs to Willie's office. The bell jingled when I walked through the door, and Willie looked up from his desk wearing his customer-greeting smile. When he saw it was me, the smile faded. Our relationship had improved after a contentious period last summer—during which I may have accused him of a crime—but I was pretty sure Willie still didn't consider me his BFF. Whatever. I wasn't crazy about him, either, though my opinion of him had elevated after the snowball-on-Jeffrey's-head episode.

"Good morning to my favorite real estate agent," I sang out.

He shot me a rueful look. "What do you want, Callie?"

"Must I want something? Maybe I'm here paying a neighborly visit."

He straightened a stack of papers on his desk. "If you're here to discuss the death at The Ice Zone on Saturday, I assure you I had nothing to do with it. I'm not one iota involved."

I slouched into the chair across the desk from him. "Of course you're not involved. But as Chamber of Commerce president, I'm sure you want to do everything in your power to get this crime solved."

He heaved a sigh of resignation. "Just ask your questions."

I smiled. "Jeffrey Forte was here Saturday morning."

He nodded but otherwise didn't reply. I shook my head in

frustration. Like pulling teeth with this one. "Willie, what did Jeffrey want?"

"Detective Clarke already asked me this, Callie. I told her everything I know." He tapped his pencil on the desk blotter. "I'm sure she wouldn't appreciate me talking about it with you."

I straightened in my chair, undeterred. "Listen, Willie, Detective Sanchez asked me to talk to you. As you know, he and Chief Laramie have found my skills useful in the past."

"I was told Sanchez isn't on the case." He paused before throwing up his hands. "But I know how this dance plays out. You'll keep haranguing me, and I'll end up telling you what you want to know. Might as well just cut to the chase."

My thoughts precisely.

He leaned back and folded his hands across his stomach. "I'm afraid I have little pertinent information to share, anyway. Mr. Forte wanted to research large-acreage properties in the area. He had some fantastical notion that the state would legalize gambling soon, and he was interested in buying land on which to build a casino."

Aha. Just as Raul and I suspected. "Why do you say the idea is fantastical?"

Willie shrugged. "I suppose it's not outside the realm of possibility. The legislature appears to be moving closer to approval. But bureaucracy moves at a snail's pace. I think it'll be years until they vote to legalize."

"Did you tell Jeffrey that?"

"Sure. It didn't dissuade him, so he and I looked through the available local properties. I'm always happy to broker a sale, even if the buyer ultimately can't use the land as intended. Caveat emptor."

It sounded like Jeffrey and Willie were a perfect match. "What properties did you show him?"

Willie got up, and I followed him to an oversized county map hanging on the far wall. He pointed at a spot in the lower village. "Ten acres for sale here, behind the Safeway. Not a pristine view, but sufficient space." Shifting his finger, he indicated another location. "Over here, about ten miles outside the village, we have a substantial plot of land available. But Jeffrey said he didn't want his casino that far from town."

Then Willie signaled a third area, this one near the foot of Mt. O'Connell, less than half a mile from my parents' resort. "This was Jeffrey's top choice. Close to the mountain, the lake, lodging. Unfortunately, the property on the market wasn't large enough to suit Jeffrey. But then I mentioned that the adjacent land belongs to a conglomerate out of Denver who might consider selling, if the price was right."

Ugh. I couldn't imagine a gaudy, neon-covered casino at the foot of the mountain, marring the landscape's natural beauty.

"What's on that land right now?"

"A small apartment building. The Ski Shop, which is only open during winter months. The ice rink. Pinkerton's Place."

Huh. I thought about Pinky. Could he have found out about this? What about the other shop owners whose properties would be taken?

But it wasn't just those particular shop owners who'd be affected. A casino would damage the views of numerous residents and shops—including the Knotty Pine Resort. Jeffrey's casino would have hurt so many people. I was certain the proposal would have generated large-scale protests.

"Wouldn't the Chamber of Commerce need to approve such a purchase? It doesn't seem like Jeffrey would get much support."

He shrugged. "As long as the business met requirements concerning easements, building materials, and such, we'd have no legal grounds to intercede. To be honest, though, I don't understand why Mr. Forte chose Rock Creek Village to begin with. A casino would be much more lucrative closer to a big city."

Willie was right. That kind of business would be more likely to flourish near a major hub with an airport, big hotels, fancy restaurants. But I completely understood why Jeffrey Forte wanted our town. Renata.

Even more than he wanted profits, he wanted to win. Bringing his casino here would not only ensure their constant contact, but it would also forever change the low-key village Renata called home. It was a form of revenge she couldn't combat.

From what Raul said, Detective Clarke had focused on Renata as the prime suspect from the start. She must have viewed this information as a validation of her theory.

But from my perspective, Jeffrey's casino scheme—and its potential damage to the village—created a whole new pool of suspects. People here were willing to fight to preserve their business, their way of life.

I wondered if any of them would kill for it.

***

When I left Willie's office and headed to the cafe, I resolved to push thoughts of murder and revenge aside for the time being so I could focus on Sam. I wanted to show him I was serious about making him a priority.

Today, customers filled about a third of the tables and booths at Snow Plow Chow, and they all seemed to have their meals in front of them. Dan, Sam's "main man," as he called himself, greeted me as I came in.

"Hey, Cal, how's it hangin'?" He stroked a hand across his thinning hair and puffed out his chest as usual.

"It's hangin' just fine, Dan. How about you?"

I squirmed out of my coat, and he stared at my cast. "Heard that jerk Forte fell on you."

"That he did," I said. "But why do you call him a jerk?"

He carried my coat to the rack and hung it up. "Just how he struck me. All high on himself, bossin' me around like he owned the place. Didn't do much to…what would you say? Endear himself to me."

I smiled. Dan was an acquired taste, but I'd acquired it. I liked him—and he'd proven himself an exemplary employee and loyal friend to Sam. "Well, Jeffrey suffered substantially more damage than I did," I said. "I suppose we shouldn't speak ill of the dead."

He looked contrite. "Spose you're right." He held onto his reverence for a full three seconds. "Anyways, you want a table, or you going to the kitchen?"

"I'll sit." He led me to a booth, and I scooted in.

"Know what you want?" he asked, pulling out an order pad.

"I'll need two BLTs and two snow fries to go for the twins. Oh, add two orders of Beary Special Cobbler. As for my own lunch, have Sam surprise me. Do you think he'll be able to join me for a bit?"

Dan glanced around the cafe's interior. "Don't see why not. I'll send him out in a few. Diet Coke while you wait?"

I nodded, and he walked through the swinging door that led to the kitchen, returning to set the drink in front of me. "Sam said to tell you he's on it, and he'll be out in a minute."

As I sipped my Diet Coke, I studied the cafe's interior. The red vinyl booths gave the cafe a retro look, but the wooden flooring and the seating area near the fireplace provided an inviting rustic warmth—a nice balance. The walls were lined with Callie Cassidy photos, all sporting discreet price tags. I noted with satisfaction two empty spaces, indicating sales. I'd need to get the twins to deliver replacement canvases, and I had just the ones in mind.

The silver door to the kitchen swung open, and Sam came through it, wiping his hands on a towel. His hair swept back from his face, except for a single strand that fell across his forehead. His plaid flannel shirt and jeans, a working uniform of sorts, fit him just right. The sight of him still took my breath away—kind of surprising since we'd been together a year now. Nearly thirty, if I counted back to our first date.

When he caught sight of me, his eyes lit up, and my heart fluttered. I scooted over, and he squeezed in next to me. He put an arm around me and pulled me close. When I turned to him, he kissed me on the lips.

"Pleasant surprise," he said.

"I've been missing you. I hope I'm not too late. You haven't eaten, I mean."

"Nope. And I'm starved." His lips nuzzled my ear.

I smiled. Perhaps, as my mother said, we'd weathered our

recent storm and were emerging stronger as a couple. "What's for lunch?" I asked.

"You said to surprise you, so I'm not telling. Rodger is whipping it up right now." He reached over and grabbed my glass, taking a sip through the straw. The gesture felt so intimate that it filled me with a burst of joy.

"Been slow all morning?" I asked.

"Not bad, for February. How about the gallery?"

"Same." I pointed out the empty spaces on his walls and said I had a couple of pieces in this morning's delivery that would work. He told me about some new recipes he'd experimented with last night. I asked how Elyse's stay in Boulder was going. Our conversation, probably mundane to other ears, felt comfortable and…right.

Soon, Dan emerged from the kitchen brandishing two plates. He placed them in front of us, and I clapped in delight—as best I could, considering the cast. "ChipMunch. My favorite!"

"First thing you ever ate at Snow Plow Chow. Sometimes, a reboot is the best thing in the world." He smiled at me.

I dug into the strange but savory concoction: Potato chips covered in a queso meat sauce, garnished with sour cream, green onions, and cheddar cheese—nachos on chips. An unlikely combination, but tasty. We made more small talk as we ate. Sam mentioned the drive-in theater we'd talked about the other night. "I Googled it," he said. "Construction doesn't begin until next month, so it won't open until summer." He looked disappointed.

"I didn't realize you were so into it."

"I loved the old place. Can't wait to go to this new one. My favorite memory of our high school years together."

If I were being honest, it hadn't made quite the same impression on me. In fact, I barely remembered that date. No need to mention that, though. I was fast learning that, in a relationship, not everything I thought needed to find its way through my vocal cords. Instead, I told him I looked forward to going with him this summer. To my surprise, I realized I was telling the truth.

He laced his fingers through mine. "This is nice," he said. "Just a quiet moment to ourselves, no distractions. It makes me—"

Behind us, the door burst open. We swiveled around to see Raul stride inside. Sam let go of my hand and frowned. "And the moment's over."

28

"Maybe he's just here for lunch," I told Sam.

Nope. As soon as he spotted us, Raul headed toward our table, ignoring Dan's greeting.

He slid into the seat across from us and stared at me. "I need to talk to you."

"*Hello, Callie and Sam,*" I said, sarcasm dripping in my tone. "*How was your lunch? I don't mean to bother you…*"

Raul took a breath. "Yeah, right. Sorry." He looked at Sam and lifted his chin. "Doing all right, Sam?"

I rolled my eyes. "Sam and I are having lunch. Can't this wait?"

Raul looked at my plate, all but licked clean.

Sam scooted out of the booth and rose. "It's okay. You two go ahead. I need to get back to work, anyway."

"Call me later?" I asked.

"Sure." He grabbed our plates and walked off to the kitchen.

Raul watched him retreat. "Trouble in paradise?"

"You interrupting our lunch doesn't help."

"Sorry, but your love life isn't the top thing on my mind right now. My sister is. Things are looking worse for her."

Now he had my attention. "What happened?"

"I overheard Clarke talking to the chief. She's pushing for an arrest."

"Oh, no. What did Frank say?"

"He told her she didn't have enough evidence yet, so now she's on the hunt again. If she comes up with one more thing, even circumstantial, I think Frank'll have to back her. They'll take Renata into custody." The worry lines etched his forehead. "I'm glad Mom is out of town and doesn't have to go through this. Not yet, anyway."

I wanted to comfort him, but the only consolation I could provide was to help solve the case. "Clarke has gotten some of her information from Theo," I said, relaying my earlier conversation with Jeffrey's brother. "He's one shady character. It wouldn't surprise me if he killed Jeffrey himself."

"Especially if he stands to inherit Jeffrey's estate," Raul said. "Money is a powerful motive. But right now, there's not a shred of evidence to support it. I can't even get Jeffrey's lawyer to return my calls."

I sighed. All the evidence we'd heard pointed to Renata. Until we could prove unequivocally that someone else wanted Jeffrey dead…

I snapped my fingers. "I talked to Willie earlier. He confirmed Jeffrey was looking at property. Specifically, he had his eye on a parcel of land near the foot of Mt. O'Connell, across from the park. If he succeeded in acquiring it, he planned to build his casino there. Can you imagine? It would destroy the scenic views for residents and business owners alike."

Dan approached and set another Diet Coke in front of me. "Want anything?" he asked Raul.

Raul shook his head, and Dan slouched off. I looked at Raul. "Plus, you know whose store sits on the property Jeffrey wanted to buy? Pinky. Have you talked to him about an alibi?"

"Not yet. I'll head over as soon as we're done here. But I have to tell you, I'm not inclined to believe that old man killed Jeffrey over the threat of ruining his store. I don't think anyone around here even realized all this was in the works. And I'm sure Clarke won't buy it. She has her bird in the hand. She won't listen to some vague theory for which there's no other evidence."

"Then I guess it's time for us to find some."

***

Raul headed out with renewed vigor, but despite what I'd said, I didn't feel the same optimism. I put on my coat, gathered the to-go bags, and peeked through the kitchen door's window. I didn't see Sam there. He must have gone upstairs to his office. I decided to leave him be for a while. We'd hit another pothole in our rocky road. Would the path ever run smooth for us?

There were still no customers in the gallery, so the twins pounced on their meals. Now I understood what Mom meant when she said I ate with gusto. These two acted like they'd been fasting on a desert island for a week.

A tapping sound on the front bay window made us turn to look. Two hefty boys about the twins' age, dressed in shirt sleeves despite the cold, wiggled their fingers in greeting. Then they ripped off their shirts and began twirling the garments above their heads as they gyrated their hips. The bizarre dance ended with their substantial bellies smooshed flat against the glass.

Banner's hand, curled around a bunch of snow fries, stalled halfway to his open mouth. Braden put down his sandwich and stomped out the door. "Get out of here, you—" He stopped, realizing I could hear every word he said. "—you morons."

Banner looked at his lunch and made a gagging noise. "Gross. The sight of those stomachs made me lose my appetite."

I grabbed a couple of his snow fries and shoved them into my mouth. They were really pretty good after all. "Friends of yours?"

"Yeah, old football buddies. They're a little…"

"Exuberant?" I offered.

"Yup. They're not bad guys—just idiots. Pascal, the one on the left, says he's going to law school someday. Wants to be a judge."

"Heaven help us," I said.

My cell phone chirped in my hand. Preston—just the man I wanted to talk to. I headed toward my office to take the call, glancing back at Banner. "Tell your idiot buddies to keep their flesh off my glass. And one of you needs to get out there with some Windex and clean up the disgusting smudges they left behind."

I clicked the accept button as I closed the office door behind me. Woody and Carl, napping on their beds, barely acknowledged my presence. "Hi, Preston. I was about to call you. Did Mrs. Finney fill you in on my coffee and streusel this morning?"

"She didn't need to. The strategically placed surveillance cameras revealed your decadence."

I grinned. I didn't regret leaving the newspaper business, but sometimes I dearly missed my boss.

"Did the info on Jeffrey and Theo help at all?" he asked.

"Jury's still out. I'd hoped to have a Jessica Fletcher moment and solve the entire case when I recovered my camera this morning, but it was not to be."

I explained my theory about snapping the shutter before Jeffrey fell. "But when I got my hands on the Nikon, the memory card was empty. Either the camera was damaged during impact, or someone erased the contents."

"Do you have retrieval software?" Preston asked.

"No, I don't, and that's what I wanted to talk to you about. Can you hook me up?"

"Sure. *The Sentinel* bought a bunch of licenses from a new company a few months ago. Good stuff. Expensive, but it's been money well spent. This software works, I'd say, ninety percent of the time." He paused, and I heard the clicking of fingers on a keyboard. "We have a few unused licenses. Want me to send you one? On the house."

I felt a surge of excitement. This could be the solution Raul and I were looking for. "Is it hard to use?"

"There's a learning curve, but I'm sure you're up to the challenge. I'll need to clear it with Finance first. You know accountants. I'll email you the link as soon as I can. Sometime tomorrow, I'd guess."

I thanked him effusively. After we hung up, I went to the metal cabinet in the corner, unlocked it, and took out my Nikon. Placing it on the desk, I opened the tiny door on the side and removed the SD card, tucking it into a zippered pocket in my purse. With any luck, I'd soon be probing its amnesiac depths.

Perhaps the answer I found there would be enough to prove Renata's innocence—and to reveal the guilty party.

***

I'd just settled behind my desk when a knock came at the office door. "Enter," I called. Banner opened the door a crack and popped his head in. "A Detective Clarke is here to see you."

The last thing I wanted right now was to joust with the detective, but I could hardly avoid her. "Send her in," I said.

When Lynn Clarke entered the office, you would have thought from Woody's reaction she was a beloved family friend he hadn't seen in months. He padded toward her, his entire back end wiggling out of control. Clarke crouched down and ruffled his fur, smiling. Then, back to business, she took a seat and crossed her legs. Woody rested his head in her lap, and she stroked his ears.

"Good afternoon, Detective," I said. Carl jumped on the desk and watched the detective with haughty eyes.

She nodded. "I was hoping we could talk, Ms. Cassidy."

"Certainly. But I insist you call me Callie."

"All right. Callie. I'd like to follow up regarding the morning of Saturday, February first."

"The morning of the murder."

"Correct. We've already discussed the confrontation outside Sundance Studio—"

"Disagreement," I said.

"What's that?"

"You insist on characterizing it as a confrontation. I believe that's a little excessive."

She sighed. "I want to know about the moments leading up to the... disagreement. It's come to my attention that you met Ms. Sanchez at Rocky Mountain High beforehand. Can you tell me what the two of you discussed?"

I carefully straightened a stack of papers on my desk for no other reason than to buy some time to think. Who had told Detective Clarke about my meeting with Renata? Did she already know what we'd talked about? Was she trying to trap me somehow? If I told her about Jeffrey's harassment, would it further implicate Renata?

All these thoughts whipped through my mind in seconds. Finally, I decided that telling the truth could only benefit my friend.

"Renata asked for my help with some… intrusive behavior on her ex-husband's part."

"Intrusive behavior. Can you elaborate?"

"She had the idea that Jeffrey was spying on her. He entered her apartment without permission when she wasn't home. Took pictures of her and her boyfriend through the living room window. Things of that nature. She wanted me to help her prove Jeffrey was behind the incidents so she could make him go away."

I told the detective about the moved car, the photo, the filled dog bowl. When I finished, Carl meowed, and I leaned back in my chair. "So, you see, Renata wanted to pursue peaceful means of stopping Jeffrey's behavior. She didn't want to kill him."

Detective Clarke nodded. "I see. Well, thank you for the information, Ms. Cassidy. I believe that's all I need." She nudged Woody's head off her lap and stood. "I'll need to get a formal statement at some point. Please remain available."

My mouth opened, but before I could respond, the detective swept out of my office. A moment later, I heard the bell jingle above the front door.

Woody stood at the door and whined after her. Carl curled his tail around himself and stared at me. As I replayed my conversation with the detective in my head, a sense of foreboding skittered down my spine. *I believe that's all I need*, Detective Clarke had said.

The question was, all she needed for *what*?

29

A steady swarm of customers throughout the afternoon kept me from dwelling on Detective Clarke's visit. We sold two large canvases, as well as ten smaller matted prints and quite a few postcards. I told Braden I'd need him in the darkroom tomorrow to help replenish our supply, and he beamed in delight.

At five o'clock, I hustled the boys out of the gallery and completed the closing ritual on my own, shutting off computers, locking doors, lowering blinds. Then I herded the creatures into the car. On the short drive to the lodge, I fretted as to what Tonya might want to talk to me about. In a way, I hoped she'd found out about David's marriage. If she hadn't and only wanted to gush about wedding plans, I wasn't sure what I'd do with the information I was keeping from her.

I hurried upstairs to drop off Woody and Carl. Mom was making roasted turkey breast, sweet potatoes, and creamed spinach for dinner. Stomach-growling aromas filled the kitchen. "You're welcome to stay," she said. "Tonya can join us, too. I've made plenty."

"As always," Dad teased.

Despite the desires of my palate, I declined. I needed to be alone with Tonya. I headed downstairs and was in the lobby ten minutes before our arranged meeting time. I waved at Jamal and glanced around the Great Room, but my friend hadn't arrived.

At the buffet, a couple finished filling their plates with hors d'oeuvres. I watched them walk to a loveseat near the floor-to-ceiling window, and I envied their easy intimacy. On a couch by the fireplace, three men devoured snacks and gulped mulled wine after a day on the slopes. Aside from these few guests, it seemed Tonya and I would have the place to ourselves.

I went to the buffet and selected a few treats of my own. Months ago, Jamal had taken over the planning and execution of the daily fare, even designing fancy tented signs to place in front of each offering. Tonight, I loaded my plate with pear and prosciutto bruschetta, bacon-wrapped dates with bleu cheese, and Chinese egg rolls. Then I used a silver ladle to scoop steaming mulled wine into a mug, adding a slice of orange and a cinnamon stick. I took my treasures to one of the two large armchairs in the far corner of the lobby, where Tonya and I could find some privacy.

As I ate and waited, I watched the cuddly couple on the loveseat. My thoughts drifted to Sam. We'd been on an emotional roller coaster the past few days, and I wanted off. Not that I wanted out of the relationship—not at all. I wanted to rediscover the peace and contentment we'd experienced prior to this rough patch. I sensed the ball was in my court, and he was waiting for some romantic gesture on my part to prove my devotion.

Something akin to the album Mom was making for Dad.

I thought of the drive-in theater he'd been reminiscing about, and an idea began brewing. But before I could give it much thought, the lobby's glass entry door slid open. Behind the counter, Jamal flushed with pleasure as Tonya made her grand entrance. She whipped off her coat and hung it on the rack, and I noticed she'd changed outfits from this morning. The woman was a clothes horse. Now, she wore high-waisted tweed trousers and a lacy cream-colored blouse—still a vision. She glided to the front desk on brown stilettos and spoke to Jamal, who'd been smitten with her since the first time he'd laid eyes on her. She was old enough to be his mother, of course, but hormones were hormones.

I tried to evaluate her mood—depressed over a pending breakup?—but she was so adept at the flirtatious facade that I couldn't get a read on her. After she'd smiled and laughed and lightly touched Jamal's arm, he pointed in my direction. She held up a finger to me and made a pit stop at the buffet, where she filled two mugs with hot wine.

As she reached the chair next to mine, she took a huge gulp from one mug, then set them both on the coffee table. She leaned down and gave me a hug and a wine-laced kiss on the cheek. After slipping off her heels, she curled up in the chair, tucking her legs beneath her.

"So, you must be wondering why I asked you here."

"It's crossed my mind." I bit my lip.

She assessed me, tilting her head. "Why so glum?"

"Two-handed drinker." At her confused expression, I pointed at the mugs on the coffee table. "Seems like you need a double dose of liquid courage."

Her smile widened, her teeth extra-white against the red lipstick. For the hundredth time, I reminded myself to ask her for her dentist's name.

She lifted a mug and cradled it in her hands. "One's for you, sugarplum. I'm hoping we'll have something to toast, and I wanted to make certain you were well-supplied."

So much for her uncovering the dire news.

Her eyes shimmered. "It seems I'm attending a wedding this fall. And it's mine. Can you believe it?"

Despite my reservations, I smiled at her excitement. Maybe my mother and Mrs. Finney were right, and I should keep my ill-gotten information to myself. It could all work out. Couldn't it?

"This isn't breaking news, Tonya. Everyone in town knows you're engaged. You haven't kept it a secret."

She took a moment to admire the rock sparkling on her left ring finger, twisting it to catch the light. Then she dropped her hand into her lap and locked eyes with me. "True. But what people don't know—even you—is that David and I have decided to go the traditional route: White dress, tux, flowers, music, the whole kit and caboodle." She paused. "And that means attendants."

I finally realized where this was headed. "Tonya, I—"

"Hush. Let me do this the way I rehearsed. Callie, sugarplum, heart of my heart, soul of my soul, for the past thirty years, you've been there for me through thick and thin…"

"This sounds like a proposal," I said.

"It is, in a way. You've always had my back. There is no one else I'd want standing up for me at the most important event of my life. I can't stand the phrase maid of honor, so I'm asking you this: Will you be my Grande Dame?"

Her eyes shone with tears. Mine did too, but for a different reason. I stammered but couldn't put together three coherent words. Tonya's expression shifted from excitement to concern. "I mean, we could go with Best Woman if Grande Dame sounds too ancient…"

I was torn. Part of me wanted to squeal with joy and accept the honor without hesitation. But what was she asking me, really? I thought being her best friend meant more than just standing beside her wearing a ridiculous dress as she took her vows. To properly fulfill my title, whatever it was, I had to protect her.

I believed that meant telling her everything I'd discovered about David.

I took a deep breath, held it, and exhaled. "Tonya, I love you with my whole heart. You're more than my friend. You're my sister. Nothing would give me greater pleasure than to stand beside you when you marry the man of your dreams."

She clapped. "Good. That's settled. And I promise you won't have to wear some pink taffeta monstrosity. I have a highly evolved fashion sense, after all."

I stared at her. She paused, and her smile faded. "Why do I feel like a shoe is about to drop?"

"I…I came across some information the other day. Something you should know. Something that might change everything."

Her brow furrowed. "Okay, out with it."

I realized however I approached it, my words were going to

cause her pain, so I did it fast, ripping off the proverbial bandage. "Honey, David is already married."

She sat back as if I'd tossed my wine in her face. Then she turned toward the fireplace. I watched the flames reflect in her clouded brown eyes. Seconds ticked past. A minute. Her fingers kneaded the arm of the chair. I stayed quiet, giving her the time she needed to process the news.

When she turned her gaze to me, the pain on her face stole my breath. "How exactly did you come across this information?" she asked.

"I, well…I've had some misgivings about David. A weird vibe. So I…um…Tonya, I asked Preston to look into David's background."

She nodded, her lips pressed thin. "You sneaked around behind my back, behind David's back, to snoop into his past."

Heat rose from my neck to my cheeks. "I only wanted to protect you. Anyway, it turns out I was right."

Unfurling her legs, Tonya perched on the edge of her chair and placed her empty mug on the table with a restrained thump. "Callie, I already know about David's marriage. He told me months ago. If I'd thought it was any of your business, I'd have told you myself. But, unlike some people, I value the privacy of the people I care about."

My mind reeled. Tonya knew David was married, and she'd accepted his proposal anyway? "But Tonya, how can you—?"

"The divorce is being handled. Annulment, actually." She stared at me. "It was a marriage in name only. The woman he married—six years ago, since you're so keen on details—was a Libyan refugee facing deportation and possibly execution. He'd met her through a humanitarian agency he volunteered with. They never shared a life, a home, a bed. In fact, he hasn't even seen her in five years. Since the time of the marriage, she's gained Italian citizenship and, at David's request, is seeking the annulment." She sighed. "I guess Preston didn't dig up that part of the story."

My heart clattered and skipped a beat, trying to keep up with this revelation. "Tonya, that's wonderful news. I'm so sorry, I should've…"

"You should've trusted me to make my own decisions," she snapped. "To choose well and wisely for myself."

I held up a calming hand. "I understand why you're angry. If I were in your place, I would be too. But I hope you'll try to understand my intentions."

"I'm not mad, Callie. I'm hurt. I expect I'll get over it eventually and forgive you. But right now, I need some time. And as for standing up for me at my wedding, I'll need to think about that. Especially now that I know you have—what was it you said?—*misgivings* about the man I love."

She stood and slipped her feet back into her shoes. I scrambled to my feet as well. Reaching out, I grasped her arm, feeling the tears trickle down my cheeks. "Tonya, wait. Don't leave like this. Let's talk."

Gently, she disengaged my fingers. "We will. But not right now. Give me some space, Callie. This needs to be on my timeline, not yours."

I bit my lip, but nodded. The only thing I could do now was wait and hope we could mend the gash I'd torn in our friendship.

As Tonya walked away, the glass doors whooshed open again. Ethan hurried inside, looking as frazzled as I'd ever seen him. His eyes darted frantically around the room, skimming over Jamal and Tonya, finally landing on me. He sprinted across the Great Room. Tonya turned and followed him.

"What's happened?" I asked.

"Callie, Detective Clarke and a couple of officers showed up at Renata's apartment. They've taken her to the station." Ethan's blue eyes were round with fear. "I don't know what to do. Please, will you help us?"

30

My brain struggled to process the news. They couldn't arrest Renata. She was innocent. I was sure of it. I sprang into action. "Wait here," I said. "I'm going upstairs to get Dad."

Clarke wouldn't have arrested Renata without Frank's approval. If anyone could succeed in getting to the bottom of things, it was Frank's best friend, Butch Cassidy.

Tonya looped her arm through Ethan's. "I'll stay with him until you come back. Then I'm going to the station too."

I looked at her gratefully. "Thank you. Will you also text our friends? We need a show of support. There's power in numbers."

She pulled out her phone and started tapping a message. "Raul, too?"

Ethan said, "I already tried calling him. No answer. I left a message telling him to get to the station as soon as he could."

I hoped we got there before he did. He'd be so riled up, he'd likely do more harm than good.

Darting through the lobby, I rushed up the stairs to my parents' condo. About halfway up, I stumbled, sending a spark of pain through my ribs. Wrapping an arm around my torso, I slowed my pace.

At the top of the stairs, I gave a quick knock and opened the condo door, hustling into the kitchen. Woody smiled at me and wagged his tail. Carl leapt onto the counter, his gaze inquisitive.

Dad held up his phone. "Just heard," he said. "Let me grab my coat."

"I'm coming too," Mom said, drying her hands on a towel.

Within two minutes, we were down the stairs.

***

It was just past seven when we arrived at the municipal building. Except for the police and fire stations, open twenty-four seven, the village offices closed at five, so the parking lot was nearly empty. We'd taken two cars, Tonya and I riding with Ethan, and Mom and Dad in the truck. As we pulled in, I spotted a black SUV pulling out. I couldn't be certain, but I thought it looked like Theo behind the wheel. I wondered if he'd been involved in orchestrating the arrest.

The second we lurched to a stop, Ethan leapt out from behind the wheel and started running to the door.

"Ethan, wait!" I yelled.

He stopped, but bounced on the balls of his feet impatiently. "Callie, I have to get inside."

"Just wait a second. We need to make a plan."

A series of headlights appeared down the road, reminiscent of the scene in *Field of Dreams*. "People will come," I murmured.

Three cars pulled into the lot, one after the other, and our friends stepped from their vehicles. Jessica and Summer emerged from Jessica's Jeep. Sam got out of his CR-V. Mrs. Finney stood tall beside her sporty Mazda. Then a fourth car arrived, a Fiat driven by David Parisi.

I couldn't help but feel overwhelmed with emotion. These people had dropped everything to rush across town without even knowing the details of why they'd been summoned. In my previous career, I'd lived in big cities all around the country. I'd had friends. But I could count on one hand the number of people who would have rushed to my aid in similar circumstances. Here in Rock Creek Village? A few texts and the troops assembled.

The reinforcements helped quell my fear. Even Ethan seemed calmer. We gathered in a circle. Sam stood beside me, his arm tight around my shoulder. David gripped Tonya's hand. Ethan summarized the series of events culminating in Renata being loaded into the back of Clarke's car. When he finished, everyone looked at my father.

"Was she handcuffed?" Dad asked.

"No. Detective Clarke said she needed to come with her, so Renata did. It was...civil, but it was obvious she shouldn't refuse."

Dad nodded. Then his gaze traveled around the circle. "I don't want anyone's expectations too high," he cautioned. "If they've arrested Renata, they won't let us see her. And she won't be released tonight." Ethan flinched, and Dad put a hand on his shoulder. "We're here as a show of support. To let Detective Clarke and Chief Laramie know we believe in Renata's innocence. So stay cool. Leave it to me to get whatever information I can."

Everyone nodded their agreement. Dad stroked his chin. "In fact, maybe it'd be best if you all stayed in your cars and let me handle this. I'll come out and tell you—"

The sounds of harrumphs and snorts echoed around the circle. No way that was going to happen. Dad sighed in resignation—and, I thought, a bit of pride—and led the group into the police station.

It was after hours, so Marilyn wasn't behind the desk. Officer Tollison occupied the spot, and she tapped at the computer's keyboard. Next to her stood Detective Clarke, reading over her shoulder. When we entered, both women looked up and seemed startled to see so many of us.

Dad approached the desk, his demeanor calm and his attitude friendly. "Evening, Officer. Evening, Detective. Heard you brought in Renata Sanchez. I was hoping to get some information on her situation."

Clarke kept her face noncommittal, but her body language told a different story. She stood rigid, arms at her sides. "Chief, we don't discuss ongoing investigations with civilians. And you're a civilian now."

It was my father's turn to stiffen. He wasn't accustomed to his questions going unanswered. My mother moved beside him and put a hand on his arm. "Very well," he said. "We'll just take a seat here until someone gives us some answers."

The detective's mouth opened and closed. Tollison shifted from one foot to the other. Dad turned and led us to the seating area against the wall. There weren't enough chairs for all of us, so some sat while the rest of us leaned against the wall. Dad gazed at Clarke. "One thing the law does require you to tell me—does Ms. Sanchez have a lawyer present? Even us civilians know she has that constitutional right."

Clarke's face flushed. "Not yet."

"I will contact her attorney right away," Dad said. "Do not question her until representation arrives."

Before she could respond, the station's door crashed open, slamming hard against the wall. Raul stormed inside, eyes blazing. "Where's my sister?"

Down the hall, the door to the interrogation room opened and Frank exited. He walked quickly toward the lobby. Raul pushed past my father and stood toe to toe with Frank. "You need to release my sister," he said.

Frank's face hardened. When he spoke, his voice was firm. "Take a step back, Detective."

Raul hesitated, but he did as he was told. His tone shifted from anger to desperation. "Frank, Renata didn't do this. You know she didn't."

"I understand your desire to protect your sister, son, but we have to follow the leads where they take us. New information Detective Clarke has uncovered means we need to talk to Renata again. But we will treat her fairly and respectfully. You have my word."

New information? My pulse raced as I recalled my earlier conversation with the detective. I'd told her about Jeffrey's harassment, assuming it would help clear Renata. Had my disclosure led to the opposite result? Had I provided Detective Clarke with the last piece of evidence she needed to arrest Renata?

I rushed over to the group and planted myself next to Dad. "Frank, what I told Detective Clarke about Jeffrey and Renata doesn't implicate her. It absolves her."

Raul's head snapped toward me. "What did you tell her?"

As I began stammering out my explanation, Dad leaned toward me. "It's best if you stop talking," he whispered.

Raul squeezed his eyes shut. Clarke frowned at Frank. "Chief, we shouldn't be having this conversation."

Then Raul held up a hand. "None of it matters. Renata is innocent."

"You can't know that," Detective Clarke said sharply.

"I know," he said. "Because I did it. I'm the one who killed Jeffrey Forte."

31

I t felt as if the air had been sucked from the room. I reached out my hand and saw it tremble. "Raul, you know that's not true," I said. "Don't do this. There's another way."

He ignored me and held out his wrists. "I've confessed. Take me into custody. You have no reason to hold Renata any longer."

Frank put his hands in his pockets and locked eyes with Raul. "Son, I appreciate that you are trying to protect your sister. But remember, we've already confirmed your alibi. You were in Boulder at the time of the murder."

The room was silent—until Ethan stepped forward. "It was me," he said. "I hit Jeffrey with a hockey stick and pushed him off the catwalk."

I looked over my shoulder at the rest of the group. Were we having a *Spartacus* moment here? Was everyone in the room going to confess, one by one?

I saw Clarke reach for the handcuffs on her belt, but a stern glance from Frank stilled her hand. Frank looked at the floor for a moment and rocked back on his heels. Then he turned to Ethan. "You're wasting our time here—time we could spend figuring out the truth." Now he looked at the rest of us, and his gaze lingered on Dad. "Go home. Let us do our job."

Dad nodded, then turned to face Renata's friends. "The chief is right. We're only impeding their progress." Then he put a hand on Raul's shoulder. "It's time for us to go."

For a long moment, Raul didn't budge. At last, he turned on his heel and marched through the door without uttering another word. A moment later, we heard an engine start outside and the sounds of a car receding into the distance.

Frank headed back toward the interview room. As Dad began ushering the group through the door, Ethan planted himself in a chair and crossed his arms. Dad paused inside the door, with Sam at his side.

Officer Tollison rested her fists on the counter and stared at him. "You heard the chief. Everyone out."

"I'm not leaving," Ethan said. "Not without Renata."

I crouched beside him, hoping I could reason with him. "Ethan, Renata will be fine. You need to trust the process. Besides, someone needs to take care of Terror."

He dug in his pocket and pulled out a key. "This is for Renata's apartment. You take Terror for the night. I'm not going anywhere."

I glanced at Officer Tollison. She shrugged, unwilling to escalate the tense situation. I held out my hand, and Ethan dropped the key into my palm. He looked so much like a scared little boy that I wanted to cry. "She'll be all right, Ethan. I promise."

When I stood, Detective Clarke gestured to me to join her at the side of the room. Surprised, I nodded and held up a finger for her to give me a second. I joined Dad and Sam at the door.

"Dad, can you and Mom pick up Terror at Renata's place? I'll call you as soon as I'm through here." He gave me a long stare, but then took the key and left.

I turned to Sam. "Do you mind waiting for me in the car? I rode with Ethan, and it looks like I'm going to need a ride home."

Sam wore a concerned expression, but he nodded and followed Dad out the door.

I took a breath and walked toward Detective Clarke. She hesitated, and I saw her wrestling with a decision. When she spoke, she wouldn't meet my eyes. "I know you feel guilty, Callie. Like what you told me earlier makes you responsible for all this.

But I want you to know there's more to it—much more. We've come across additional information. I can't tell you anything else. As it is, I've already said more than I should, but I wanted you to know this isn't on you."

Then she strode down the hall, leaving me perplexed.

***

The next morning, I awoke to a dim light filtering through the curtains. The clock read six-thirty. I lifted my hand to the top of my head, surprised at Carl's absence. But then I looked over and saw Sam sprawled on the bed beside me, and the memories of last night flooded back to me. My conversation with Tonya, gone oh-so-wrong. Ethan's panicked arrival at the lodge. Renata's detainment. Raul's confrontation with Frank. Two confessions.

I grabbed my phone from the nightstand and sent a text to Ethan. When several minutes passed without a response, I gave up and pulled the covers back around my shoulders.

My pets had slept over at Mom and Dad's, along with Terror. Sam had driven me home from the station. On the way, he'd contacted Rodger and asked him to cover the early morning shift at Snow Plow Chow. By unspoken agreement, we'd put aside the tension between us and snuggled in front of the fire with a bottle of wine. When he massaged my shoulders, the stress of the day melted away. He'd stayed over, this time foregoing the couch for the comforts of the bed.

Now, as I watched him sleeping, the dregs of my bad dream drifted away. He twitched in his sleep, and I nestled next to him, reveling in his warmth. As I smoothed the hair from his forehead, I experienced an overwhelming wave of affection. No, more than that. *Love.* I knew I loved this man. So why did I keep pushing him away, whether through action or neglect? In my working life, I'd always been so competent and self-assured. I'd navigated so many complicated situations with ease. Why was this so difficult?

A topic for my therapist, I concluded. For now, I needed an action plan. I thought again of my mother's album, created as an act of love for my father. What could I do to let Sam know how much I cared for him? The idea that had germinated at the lodge yesterday—my romantic gesture—wriggled back into my mind.

Then it disappeared again as my thoughts turned to another damaged relationship. I winced as I recalled the pain and betrayal on Tonya's face when I told her what I'd done. I'd told myself I'd only taken those actions to protect her.

Right?

I did what Preston had urged days earlier and forced myself to examine my motives. If David had been a friend of mine, would I still have pried into his personal business? Would I have done the same to Jessica? Summer? Tonya herself? The answer was no. I would have respected their privacy. At the very least, I would have discussed my concerns with them face to face.

Tonya had asked how I'd feel if the roles were reversed. The answer was simple. I only had to remember the many times I'd told the people in my life to quit interfering with my decisions. My parents. My former boss. Sam.

I had treated Tonya as if she needed saving, as if she was incapable of making her own choices. I'd undermined her power and her autonomy.

At the very least, I owed her a heartfelt apology. Even more important, I owed one to David.

Sam stirred, and his eyes fluttered open. He smiled sleepily and pulled me close. I pressed my lips against his neck. Maybe everything would turn out all right.

***

"Not even a single egg?" Sam stood at my open refrigerator and grunted. "No milk? Callie, how do you manage to stay alive?"

I moved behind him and wrapped my arms around his waist. "I have people for that."

He shut the door. "Personal chefs, you mean, like me and your mother."

"Now, now. You're exaggerating. In fact, today I'm providing your morning sustenance." With a flourish, I poured him a cup of coffee and pulled a box of frosted strawberry Pop Tarts from the pantry. "You must admit, it doesn't get much better than this."

He rolled his eyes and snatched a silver bag from the box, tearing it open and sinking his teeth into a processed pastry.

"For extra added flavor, consider toasting it," I said.

"If only you owned a toaster," he said.

I grinned. This was the type of banter our relationship thrived on. It seemed like we might be edging back to normal, but I didn't want to take that for granted. Though I hadn't settled on the details, I still meant to plan a romantic evening for us.

"So tell me, handsome, what's on your agenda a week from Friday night?"

He raised his eyebrows. "Sounds to me like you already have my agenda planned."

"Would you be able to take off a Friday night from the cafe?"

An inscrutable expression crossed his face. "I think that's doable. What do you have in mind?"

I raised a finger to my lips. "You'll find out when it's time. But until then, here's your invitation: I request your presence at Sundance Studio at seven o'clock on the evening of Friday, February fourteenth."

He narrowed his eyes. "That's Valentine's Day."

"You are a calendar savant," I responded. "Dress casually."

"But you hate Valentine's Day."

"I never said I hated it, just that it was commercial." I gave him a coy smile. "Besides, a girl can change. Now, will you be there or not?"

"Intriguing," he said, flipping the last of the Pop Tart into his mouth. "I wouldn't miss it for all the Pop Tarts in Rock Creek Village."

32

Once I'd reassured Sam I didn't need a ride to Pine Haven for my doctor's appointment that afternoon, he dropped me off at the lodge to retrieve my car and my pets. My mind wandered back to Renata's situation. I'd tucked my list of suspects into my bag for further scrutiny. In the meantime, I hoped Dad had gleaned some information from Frank.

I found my father behind the front desk, flipping through the newspaper. "Morning, Sundance," he said. "Been thinking about you. Feeling okay?"

"Sure, Dad. Except for this stupid cast and a few aches, I'm good. Why do you ask?"

"All this stress can't be good for healing."

"I'm managing. They'll do follow-up X-rays this afternoon, but I think all is well." I walked behind the desk and gave him a one-armed hug. "Any word on Renata? I tried contacting Ethan but didn't get a response."

"I'd guess the two of them are still sleeping. Renata's lawyer got her released late last night—or rather, early this morning. She's still the top person of interest, no getting around that, and they told her not to leave town. But at least they let her go home."

I breathed a sigh of relief. "That's good news. Who's her lawyer?"

"Betsy Pelletier at the moment, but not for long. Betsy's not a criminal lawyer. She's lining up someone from Boulder, I'm told."

"That should have happened already," I grumbled. "Renata's been on the detective's radar for days. I'm surprised Raul didn't insist on a criminal attorney before now."

"I think everyone believed, naively perhaps, that the evidence would lead the case in a different direction. Didn't work out that way."

"Speaking of evidence," I said, "last night, Detective Clarke told me she didn't bring Renata in solely because of the information I gave her. Clarke hinted that she'd uncovered something in addition. Did Frank tell you what it was?"

Dad's eyes slid away from my face, and I tapped his knee with my fist. "Don't even consider keeping this from me."

He sighed. "I suppose it'll be public knowledge by the end of the day, anyway. Detective Clarke interviewed Jeffrey Forte's attorney yesterday. The man handled all Jeffrey's legal business. He told Clarke that Jeffrey never changed his will."

It took me a second to comprehend the significance. "Are you saying Renata is Jeffrey's beneficiary?"

Dad nodded. "The lawyer said it was Jeffrey's intention to reconcile with his ex-wife, so he saw no point in changing things."

I processed the information. The reconciliation part was no surprise—Theo had said as much to me in the ambulance on Saturday. But the money... That seemed like a game changer, though I wasn't sure exactly how. "So let me get this straight. The theory is that Renata killed Jeffrey to get her hands on his estate?"

Dad shrugged, and I shook my head. "It doesn't make sense. It assumes she knew about the contents of the will. There's no proof that's true. But supposing she did, and supposing even further that she hatched a plot to kill Jeffrey so she'd inherit, why on earth would she kill him at the ice rink? A place she was so associated with? And why would she use her own hockey stick?"

"Well, Sundance, as you well know, most criminals get caught because of some stupid mistake. If I were working the case, I'd argue Renata didn't plan to kill Jeffrey where and how she did. That the opportunity presented itself, and she took it, without considering all the ripple effects."

I thought about it and shook my head. "I'm not buying it."

"Whether you buy it or not, that's the supposition Frank and Detective Clarke are likely running with. And I'm afraid, faced with the evidence, things look rough for Renata. To tell the truth, I'm surprised Frank let her out of jail. If I'd still been chief, I doubt I would have."

My gut clenched as thoughts spun in my head. Money. Revenge. Loss. Desire. Fear. Then my mind focused an image of Theo in his black leather coat.

"Dad, I saw Theo arguing with Jeffrey outside the arena the morning of the murder. Later, in the ambulance, Theo told me he'd been afraid Renata and his brother would get back together. What if Theo killed Jeffrey before that could happen, not realizing he wouldn't be the one to inherit?"

My father rubbed a palm across his cheek, considering the idea. "It's a valid premise," he said. "I haven't heard any proof—not yet, anyway—but it's worth pursuing."

I began tapping my foot, and he narrowed his eyes. "What I mean by that is, I'll call Frank and mention it to him. You need to stay out of it, Sundance."

"Of course I will, Dad. You know me."

***

After enduring yet another of Dad's stern looks, I went upstairs to collect the creatures. When I got inside, Terror whipped by me in a blur, with Woody on her heels. It took me a minute to corral him and to track down Carl, who was hiding out behind the refrigerator. Mom said Renata had called and would be by soon to pick up Terror.

With my creatures in tow, I drove to the gallery and got the place ready for opening with an hour to spare. When I sat at my desk and tried to tally sales, my conversation with Dad kept creeping into my thoughts, and I found it difficult to concentrate. Maybe a jolt of caffeine would help me focus. I left my sleeping pets in the office and headed to Rocky Mountain High.

The coffee shop was crowded for a Wednesday, and I scanned the place to see if I recognized anyone. Mostly out-of-towners, it appeared, but then my gaze landed on two familiar faces at a table in the corner: Lars and Pinky. An interesting duo. I hadn't realized the two of them were acquainted.

After a brief chat with Mrs. Finney, I carried my coffee cup over to their table. Both men rose when they saw me approach. "Please, sit down," I said. "I just wanted to say good morning."

The two of them took their seats. "Vould you care to join us?" Lars asked, and I slid into a chair beside his. "Ve vere just talking about Renata."

Pinky's face clouded. "She's a good kid. She don't deserve this."

Lars nodded his head glumly. "Vill she end up in prison?"

"I hope not," I said simply.

Pinky grunted. "I hear things. Don't look good for her."

"Not at the moment, maybe," I said. "But we need to stay positive. I'm certain she didn't kill her ex-husband, and I'm doing everything in my power to find out who did. And I'm not alone. A lot of people are working to exonerate her."

The three of us fell silent and sipped our coffee. Over the rim of my cup, I studied Pinky, remembering the anger on his face Saturday morning outside Sundance Studio. "Mr. Pinkerton," I began.

"None of that, missy. I'm Pinky. Always have been, always will be."

He ran a hand through his thin, gray hair. I smiled at him. "All right, Pinky. I noticed you were in the crowd Saturday during the disagreement outside my studio."

"Disagreement? All-out brawl, more like." Pinky snorted.

I sighed. "Anyway, Detective Clarke showed me a video of the incident. The way you were looking at him—well, it didn't seem as if you thought too highly of him."

Pinky shrugged a meaty shoulder. I imagined the decades of loading crates and moving product that had gone into creating the still-firm muscles of his arms and chest. He gripped his paper cup so hard I feared it would collapse. "I didn't like the guy. He got what was comin' to him."

I lifted my eyebrows. "What happened between the two of you?"

"Nothin' particular. He was a horse's…" He dropped his eyes as his old-school manners kicked in. No cussing in front of a lady. "Like I said, I hear things."

He rose abruptly. "Gotta get back to the store. Nice to see ya."

As Pinky left, Lars gave me a wry smile. "Ze man has a vay vith vords."

"That he does," I said.

Lars chewed the last bite of his pastry. When he swallowed, he said, "All is vell with your camera?"

I nodded. "Yes. Thank you again."

"Is good. I vas hoping to get a copy of ze Rockets' team photo you shot. I vould like to display in the locker room."

"Unfortunately, the photos aren't available," I said. "The card must have gotten damaged somehow. I'm hoping I can figure out how to retrieve the photos, though. I'm working on it."

He smiled. "Zat is good. If you do, please send one to me." He took a last gulp of coffee and stood. "I must get back. But if there is anything I can do to help Renata, I hope you vill let me know. She's a lovely girl, and I feel vorried."

His eyes glistened. On impulse, I hugged him. My head barely reached his shoulder, and my arms wouldn't stretch fully around his broad waist, but I gave it my best shot. He looked surprised, but then returned the hug.

"It'll be all right," I said into his chest. "We'll make sure of it."

33

I stayed busy at the studio all morning, leaving me no time to ponder suspects and motives. The twins arrived just after eleven, early on account of a canceled class. I greeted them with enthusiasm and hurried off for a much-needed bathroom break.

Feeling a headache coming on, I spent a few quiet minutes sitting on the floor in my office with my back against the wall, engaging in pet therapy. Woody crammed as much of himself as possible in my lap, and Carl perched on my shoulder, his claws digging through my sweater. I let my mind go blank.

After a few minutes, Carl meowed in my ear, and I looked at him. "Got any ideas about this case, O Shrewd One?"

He leapt from my shoulder to the concrete floor and began licking his paw. "I'm not sure if I'm supposed to interpret some deep meaning from your self-grooming. If so, I'm not getting it."

A knock had Woody scrambling to the door. Carl responded by darting under the desk, and I saw his green eyes glowing in the darkness. With all the grace of a hippo in quicksand, I pulled myself to my feet and opened the door to find Renata and Ethan standing there.

I pressed my palm to my heart at the sight of them, especially Renata. When I hugged her, the bag slung over her shoulder rippled. A yap sounded from its depths. Renata pulled from my grasp and opened the bag, revealing a wriggling shih tzu.

Woody whined in excitement, as if he hadn't just seen his friend a few hours ago. Renata lifted Terror from the bag and set her on the ground. The two dogs spent a few seconds tail sniffing and then happy dancing. From beneath the desk, Carl hissed a warning.

I gave Ethan a quick hug. "You're not in school today."

"We took personal days," he said. "We didn't leave the police station until after two this morning. No way we could face a herd of wild teenagers on only a couple of hours' sleep."

I moved behind my desk and sat, while the two of them took seats across from me. I studied Renata's face. Bags beneath her bloodshot eyes showed her exhaustion, and creases on her forehead revealed her worry. Still, she looked strong, resolved. "I'm glad you got to spend last night in your own bed," I said.

"Thanks to a little help from my friends." She put a hand on Ethan's arm. "Especially this guy. He's stood beside me through it all. I don't know how I'd cope without him."

He laced his fingers through hers, and I smiled. Sometimes, trauma severed relationships, especially those in their early stages. Here, though, it seemed to draw the two of them even closer.

I lifted my chin toward Ethan. "He did more than that, you know. He tried to confess. Right after Raul did. For a hot minute, I thought everyone in the station would step up and take the blame. You have a lot of good friends here in Rock Creek Village."

Renata looked at Ethan with surprise. But beneath the surprise lay another emotion, one I couldn't quite get a handle on. Concern, perhaps? "You did it?" she asked, her voice low.

My breath quickened, and Ethan drew back in shock. Renata shook her head, as if coming out of a fog. "I mean, you did it for me?"

His cheeks tinged pink. "Not because I don't think you can take care of yourself. But the short answer is yes. I'd do almost anything for you."

Anything? I wondered. I thought back to a few months ago, when Sundance Studio was being vandalized. I'd witnessed

182

firsthand Ethan's protective instincts come into play. And that was nothing compared to this. How far would Ethan go to defend the woman he loved?

But I didn't want to go down that road, so I pushed aside my worries and addressed Renata. "No sense dancing around the elephant in the room," I said. "I'm sure Detective Clark told you about Jeffrey's will. Sounds as if you are about to become a wealthy woman."

She blew out a breath. "I heard. I admit I'm a bit stunned. Jeffrey despised me, yet he left me his money? It boggles the mind. If this were some Agatha Christie story, we'd discover he killed himself just to frame me for his murder."

"Wouldn't that be an ironic twist?" I said.

Renata tucked a strand of hair behind her ear. "The truth is, I don't even want Jeffrey's money. If Theo didn't have a monkey clinging to his back, I'd renounce my claim. The problem is, if Theo gets hold of that kind of money, it might push him back into a self-destructive lifestyle."

"You mean drugs?"

"Yes. He says he's been clean for a while, but who knows? Even if that's true, a sudden windfall might be too much of a temptation."

I nodded. I'd interviewed enough doctors, psychologists, and even junkies to understand how difficult overcoming addiction could be. I thought about what Theo might do if he got his hands on Jeffrey's money. "I wonder if Theo would follow through with his brother's plans to build a casino," I mused.

Renata and Ethan looked at each other. "Callie, what are you talking about?" Renata asked.

"No one told you? Jeffrey joined a group of lobbyists intent on legalizing gambling in Colorado. That's why he was in Rock Creek Village—scouting properties for his own casino."

Ethan's face tightened. "A casino? Think of how that would damage the village's charm."

"Not to mention that a lot of people could suffer, too," I said. "A casino in town might encourage even more developers to build here: Box stores, entertainment venues, fancy hotel chains. Small business owners would take a huge financial hit."

Renata winced. "How did I ever get mixed up with that man?"

"We're all guilty of misjudging people," I said. "But the point is, this could widen our suspect pool considerably."

"I doubt anyone would kill over it, though," Renata said.

I shrugged. "People have killed for less. Much less."

"I guess you're right," Renata said. "And that makes what I'm about to tell you even more important. It's time for you to back off, Callie. I appreciate everything you've done for me, but I don't want to see you in any more danger. This isn't a battle my friends need to fight. I'm confident the police will figure this out. And now I have a shiny new lawyer to protect my interests."

I opened my mouth to object, but she held up a hand. "I dragged you into this mess, and I couldn't live with myself if you got hurt any more than you already have."

There was a moment's silence. Then the dogs raced three quick circles around Renata and Ethan's chairs before sliding into the wall. Terror yipped in surprise, and Woody shook his head, dazed. The three of us laughed, and the tension broke.

Ethan glanced at his watch and stood up. "We should get going. I need a nap before my meeting tonight at school."

"I thought you took the day off," I said.

"Yeah, but there's no way to get out of the regional business teachers' meeting. They scheduled it months ago."

Renata scooped up Terror and put her back in the bag. We walked to the door, and Renata hugged me again. "I mean it, Callie," she whispered in my ear. "You've done all you can. And it's enough."

34

Once Renata and Ethan left the gallery, I filled the pets' food bowls, then lured Carl from beneath the desk with a taste of tuna. I stroked his back and set him next to his scratching post. I kissed Woody's head and picked up my bag. "Time to get to my doctor's appointment," I told them. "You two be good. The twins will take care of you."

In the gallery, Braden was conferring with a customer, so I pulled Banner aside to speak to him. "My appointment's at three, but you know how it is at the doctor's office. I doubt I'll be back before closing. If you wouldn't mind taking Woody out, I'd appreciate it. Then you can lock up at five."

From the corner of my eye, I saw David Parisi stroll past the front window carrying a takeout bag from Snow Plow Chow. I glanced at my watch and did a quick calculation. If I stopped at a drive-through for lunch instead of the cafe, I'd have just enough time for a chat with David. Much as I dreaded facing up to what I'd done, I owed him an apology. Procrastinating would only prolong my misery—and my rift with Tonya. No time like the present.

I hurried back to my office, surprising the creatures mid-snooze. Shuffling through a stack of photos on my desk, I found the one I was looking for—a candid shot of Tonya and David I'd taken in the park last summer. In it, Tonya was laughing. One hand held a floppy hat onto her head, while the other cupped

David's cheek. He'd wrapped his arm around her waist, and his gaze was one of pure adoration. Anyone who looked at a woman that way clearly had her best interests at heart. Why hadn't I seen that sooner?

I selected a rustic gray frame from the cabinet in the corner and taped the photo in place. Then I rushed out of the gallery.

When I entered A Likely Story, David looked up from behind the sales counter, a sandwich halfway to his lips. I steeled myself for an angry reaction and was astonished when his mouth curved into a warm smile. Perhaps Tonya hadn't mentioned my snooping...

"Ah, *cara amica*, what a pleasant surprise. I thought perhaps you might be reluctant to speak with me."

So he did know.

He laid his sandwich on a napkin, stepped around the counter, and took my hands in his, gentle with my casted arm. Then he kissed my cheek. "Please, do not fret. As I told *mi amore*, she is fortunate to have such a dear friend looking out for her."

Of all the scenarios I'd imagined, this one hadn't even made the list. "But David, you haven't even let me apologize yet."

He squeezed my hands. "No need. Your presence is apology enough. If I were—how do Americans say it?" He glanced down at my feet. "Ah, yes. If I were in your shoes, I'd have done exactly as you. But I fear I would not have had the courage to make it right. I am hoping Tonya explained my situation to your satisfaction. The marriage, it was...well, Simone and I were never *together*. I hope you understand."

"Tonya explained everything, even though none of it is any of my business. I'm sorry I butted my nose in where it didn't belong. Will you accept my apology?"

"Callahan, I accepted your apology before you made it. Did you forget? Tonya, too, will forgive your...what did she call it? Your meddling. She enjoys wearing her anger like a tight garment, but before you know it, she's ready to change into more comfortable attire. I suspect all will be normal between you two soon. She loves you."

I smiled. "I hope you're right. Because I love her, too. I can't imagine my life without her in it."

He lifted my hand to his lips, kissed it, and returned to his seat. "Nor can I, *cara amica*. Now, may I offer you half my sandwich? Your Sam sculpts creations large enough for two."

"No, thank you," I said, though the sight of the roast beef and provolone on rye made me regret the drive-through decision. "I was wrong about you, David, and I'm glad I was. You're perfect for her, and I'm thrilled the two of you found each other."

"That in itself makes this ordeal worthwhile." He took a bite of sandwich, chewed, and swallowed. "Perhaps now we can enjoy a, a..." He snapped his fingers. "Double date!"

"I'd like that," I said. "Before I go, though, I have something for you. A token of my appreciation for your forgiveness."

I reached into my bag and drew out the framed picture and set it upright on the counter. David wiped his fingers on a napkin and lifted the photo. When he looked at it, the tenderness in his eyes smothered any residual doubt I might have harbored. This man was deeply, madly, devotedly in love.

***

I hummed to myself as I left the bookstore, joyful and relieved that I'd made my apology—and that David had accepted it. I was completely caught off-guard when a passerby jostled me with enough force to send me stumbling back against the wall. A flash of déjà vu sent me back to the morning of the murder, when Jeffrey had bumped into me at the coffee shop.

This couldn't be Jeffrey, though I quickly noticed it was close. I regained my balance and stared at the offender. His back was to me, but from the black leather coat and stringy hair, I recognized him at once. "Theo!" I said. "You almost knocked me over."

He whirled on me. His face, his body language, everything about him radiated a high-strung edginess. His red, swollen eyes protruded from his gaunt face, making him look as if he hadn't slept in days.

Or worse yet, as if he'd fallen off the wagon.

He leaned toward me, his face just inches from mine. When he exhaled, frost poured from his nostrils, and a sour odor oozed from his mouth and pores. I restrained the urge to gag. "If you don't want to get knocked over, stay out of my way," he snarled.

Experience had taught me there was a time to fight and a time to retreat. This was definitely the latter. I put my hands up in a gesture of peace. "It's okay. No big deal."

He stared at me for a moment, and my breath quickened. Finally, he took a step back. "Whatever," he said curtly, then turned and staggered off.

I shuddered and gave him a few seconds to depart. Then I darted through the studio, out the back door, and into the haven of my car.

***

An hour later, I'd scarfed down a dry burger and greasy fries and made it to my doctor appointment with five minutes to spare. After I tackled the requisite pile of paperwork, a radiologist X-rayed my wrist through its fiberglass cast. Then he sent me back to the lobby to wait for the doctor.

The encounter with Theo weighed on me. I sensed the man was on the brink of losing it. I made a mental note to call Raul on my way home from the doctor to talk to him about it.

In the meantime, I took out my legal pad and pen and went through my scrawny list of suspects. *Renata, Theo, Ethan, Pinky.* Knowing what I now did about Jeffrey's business dealings, I scribbled a few vague additions. *Disgruntled Villagers. Scam Victims. Swindled Partners.*

I tapped the pen against the pad as my frustration grew. Obsessing over potential suspects wasn't getting me anywhere, so I started a new list, titled Facts of the Case. This might be what I needed to jostle the pieces of the puzzle into place.

1. Renata threatened. Stalked by Jeffrey?
2. Fight outside gallery: Renata, Raul, Ethan, Jeffrey, Pinky
3. Jeffrey and Theo argued outside the rink.
4. Jeffrey killed (Renata's hockey stick). Body falls from

188

catwalk (onto me!)

5. Ethan at the arena. Saw Theo outside when he left.

7. Jeffrey lobbied for gambling. Scouted property for a casino.

8. Renata beneficiary of Jeffrey's will. (Did she know beforehand? Did Theo?)

9. Raul and Ethan confess to Jeffrey's murder. No one believes them.

10. Theo…

Before I could make additional entries, a nurse appeared at the door and called my name. I tucked my pad and pen into my bag, feeling as if I'd made no progress at all.

35

Twenty minutes later, my doctor still hadn't appeared. I sat in a too-warm exam room and tried to coax my blood pressure into normal range, but my patience was wearing thin.

At long last, the door opened and a pudgy, silver-haired man in a white coat entered the room carrying a manila folder.

"I was just about to send for search and rescue," I said, not even trying to hide my annoyance.

"Sorry to keep you waiting, Ms. Cassidy. I was consulting with the surgeon about when to schedule the amputation."

My mouth dropped open. "Wait, what?"

Then I noticed his eyes twinkling mischievously. He pointed at me. "Gotcha," he said, a jovial grin lighting up his face.

He stepped toward my chair and held out a hand. "I'm Dr. Graves—pardon the unfortunate name—and I'm happy to inform you that amputation won't be necessary."

I shook his hand, my head spinning. After my experience with Dr. Foster in the ER, I couldn't quite wrap my mind around a medical person with a sense of humor. But despite the moment of panic he'd caused, I decided it was a refreshing change of pace.

Dr. Graves laid the folder on a nearby table and removed an X-ray, which he wedged into the light box on the wall. When he pressed the button, the box brightened, and my skeletal arm and hand appeared. He pointed at a part of the wrist joint that looked slightly off kilter. "It's healing well. A few more weeks in the cast, followed by six months of PT, and your wrist should be good as new."

I scrunched up my face. Was he joking again? "I need physical therapy?"

"Yes, of course. You've broken a bone in a major joint. Physical therapy is the only path to regaining full function." He tapped my cast with his pencil. "When this comes off, your wrist will be weak. It'll take persistent effort on your part to return it to normal."

He perched on a stool and looked at me over the top of his glasses. "On the plus side, our physical therapist is almost as funny as me. It'll be like having your appointments at a comedy club. We'll leave you laughing."

Despite my displeasure at the prospect of half a year of recovery—*after* I'd gotten free of the cast—I found myself smiling. I'd never met a doctor like this one. How on earth did he end up on the stoic Dr. Foster's referral list?

Dr. Graves took a piece of paper from the folder and handed it to me. "Here is a list of low-key exercises you can begin now. The sooner the better, as far as rehab goes."

I scanned the illustrations of finger stretches and hand motions. "I was expecting rubber chickens would be required," I said.

He snapped his fingers. "Now there's an idea. I'll get my nurse on that right away."

We chatted a few more minutes, and he walked me to the billing desk. Once I'd handed my credit card to the bookkeeper and amassed a small debt, she released me.

***

On the drive home, I turned on the radio and found a classic rock station. My mood was upbeat—a strange result of a doctor's visit, I thought. A light snow fell. Tiny flakes sparkled in the glow of headlights and melted on the windshield as soon as they landed. It was past five o'clock, and the day had given way to dusk. The journey from Pine Haven to Rock Creek Village wound through the mountains at a decent altitude, and the rocky terrain combined with the low, snow-laden clouds to create the sensation of being nested beneath a soft comforter.

Ahead, a herd of elk decided it was the perfect time to descend from the mountains for a night in the valley. Cars halted in both directions as the huge animals strolled across the pavement. The beasts moved at a leisurely pace, pausing to turn their large brown eyes toward the humans trapped inside the machines. I felt as if I were in a zoo, and they had paid admission to study me.

On the slope, I noticed a long queue of them waiting their turn. I put the car in park, found my cell and called Raul.

He answered after three rings. "Hey, Callie, I'm in the car, about to hit a spot where I'm likely to lose service. Can I call you later?"

"Where are you?"

"On the way home from Boulder."

"Boulder? Is this about that job interview?"

Just as the last elk hopped over the guardrail and the road was clear, I heard a brief crackling noise on the line, and the connection dropped. I tossed my phone into the passenger seat, shifted into drive, and touched the accelerator with my foot.

A second trip to Boulder probably meant a call-back interview—good news for Raul's job quest, I supposed. Still, I felt my cheerful mood trickling away as I contemplated life in Rock Creek Village without Raul around as detective—and friend.

A short time later, I turned into the alley behind Sundance Studio and parked the car. The snow shower had followed me from Pine Haven, heavier now. Shivering, I hurried to the back door, key in hand. Inside, the hallway lay in shadow.

Woody whined from behind the office door, and I pictured him quivering in excitement at my imminent arrival. I doubted Carl trembled with anticipation, but I knew he'd secretly be pleased at my presence. I opened the door and flipped on the light.

In the office, a pine scent floated just beneath the ever-present chemical smell from the darkroom. Ethan's cologne, perhaps? Or did it belong to the twins? Was it the cleaning crew's detergent? I'd never noticed it in here before…

Woody pressed his wet nose into my outstretched palm. I crouched down and buried my face in his fur. "Well, the pleasant aroma certainly isn't you," I said. "You need a bath."

My gaze flitted around the office until I found Carl standing to the side of the room. He let out a short yowl, directing my attention to the metal storage cabinet in the corner. Its door stood slightly ajar.

I felt a twitch of unease. The cabinet housed my most expensive possessions, so I was careful to keep it locked. Ethan had a key, of course, and since Braden had started doing some darkroom work for me, I'd given him a copy as well. Had he needed to get something out of the cabinet and neglected to relock it?

I pulled the door all the way open and studied its contents. I owned three DSLRs—all present and accounted for. Two Canon film cameras also occupied their spots. Tripods, flashes, and lighting equipment were in place. Nothing appeared to be missing.

I dug my phone from my pocket and dialed Braden's number. He answered on the first ring. "Hey, Callie. What's up?"

"Did you get something out of the equipment cabinet, by any chance? When I came in to pick up Woody and Carl, I found it unlocked."

"No, the only time I went in the office was to walk Woody and check on Carl," he said.

I bit my lip, thinking. "No one else came back here, did they?"

"Not that I noticed. We had a steady flow of customers, but I didn't notice anyone walk into the hall."

I thanked Braden, told him I'd see him tomorrow, and hung up. I tapped a finger against my chin as I tried to recollect when I'd last accessed the cabinet. Ah, yes. I'd opened it to select a frame for David's photo. I'd been in a rush. Had I forgotten to lock the cabinet door? I couldn't remember.

I glanced at the creatures and shrugged. "Who knows, guys?" Then I closed the cabinet door firmly and locked it, tugging on the handle to double-check.

***

Once I'd loaded Woody and Carl into the back seat of the Honda, I drove down an almost deserted Evergreen Way. The incident at the gallery had put me on edge, and the tussling going on behind me wasn't helping to steady my nerves. In the rearview mirror, I saw Carl leaping across Woody's back, clearly wound up. My usually patient golden retriever seemed irritated as well as he nipped at the cat's ears.

"Stop it, you two," I scolded. "You're worse than a couple of toddlers. Don't make me pull this car over."

Woody panted at my reflection, the image of the innocent sibling. Carl glared at me but ceased pouncing.

After I'd passed the Knotty Pine Resort, I turned onto the road leading past the lake and toward my townhouse. A malfunctioning streetlight emitted a strobe effect, painting the road with an eerie red glow. In one sudden leap, Carl screeched and jumped across the seat, landing on my shoulder and snagging his claws into my neck.

"Ouch!" I squealed. I tapped the brake lightly and continued coasting forward, gripping the steering wheel with the fingers of my left hand and using my good hand to extricate the cat. I took my eyes off the road for a moment as I deposited the cat in the passenger seat. When I looked back at the road, a white blur dashed in front of the car. I slammed on the brakes.

Carl hopped onto the dashboard and stared through the windshield. In the back seat, Woody pressed his nose to the side window. My heart beat furiously.

I leaned forward and identified the white blur as a dog semi-camouflaged near a snow-covered bush. A familiar dog, I realized. It was Terror, wet and bedraggled.

How had Renata's little shih tzu ended up out here, alone in the snow? I craned my neck, but there was no sign of Renata—or any other human. I eased the car onto the side of the road, switched off the ignition, and unbuckled my seatbelt. "You two stay here," I told Woody and Carl.

Popping the trunk, I grabbed a towel and edged toward the frightened pup. "It's okay, Terror," I said in a soothing tone. "Remember me? I'm Callie, a friend of your mom's. Let's get you in the car and warm you up."

I heard a bark from inside the car and looked over my shoulder. Woody scratched lightly at the window and barked once more. Terror saw him and started wagging her tail. I wrapped the towel around her and gently placed her next to Woody. Carl jumped into the back seat, too, and sniffed Terror's fur.

Back behind the wheel, I restarted the car and pulled onto the road, turning down the side street that led to Renata's building. I parked and hopped out, leaving the animals in the car. At the top of the stairs, I located my friend's apartment and knocked. No answer. The blinds were drawn, so I couldn't see inside, but dim light filtered through the slats. I leaned my ear against the door but heard nothing from inside.

After a moment's hesitation, I reached out to turn the knob. The door was unlocked, and I nudged it open. "Renata?" I called out. Still no response.

Cautiously, I stepped inside.

36

The first thing I noticed was the sour odor—one I'd been subjected to just a few hours earlier.

I knew then that Theo had been in this apartment.

A scan of the living room and kitchen areas proved inconclusive. Someone, probably Renata, had scooted a chair away from the kitchen table, as if she'd gotten up in a hurry, but that didn't warrant much concern. Loose-leaf papers piled on the table indicated she'd been working on lesson plans for a chemistry class. In the kitchen, I found Terror's food bowl upended and nuggets of kibble strewn across the floor.

An unlocked door, a scooted chair, dog food on the floor. Out of context, none of these checked the "urgent" box. But together with finding Terror on the road and the smell in the apartment, they left me with the powerful sensation that something bad had occurred here—and that Theo was involved.

***

I hurried back to the car, grabbed my phone, and pressed Renata's number. The call went straight to voicemail. As I started to dial Raul, the phone rang in my hand. Renata's name appeared on the screen, and I breathed a sigh of relief.

"Renata," I said. "Thank goodness. Where—"

Her voice filtered across the line as if through a layer of snow. It was apparent she wasn't speaking to me. Was this a simple butt dial, or was she in trouble and reaching out for help?

The answer came quickly, in the form of a question. "Where are you taking me?" She tried to project a forceful tone, but anxiety lurked beneath the surface.

For a moment, the only noise was the rumbling of a car engine. My stomach tightened as the picture in my mind came into focus. Theo had taken Renata from her apartment against her will, and Terror had escaped in the struggle.

The silence stretched for thirty seconds, a minute. I sat in Renata's parking lot, wracking my brain, feeling helpless. I couldn't just start driving around to search for her. Though I had a hazy memory of Theo driving a black SUV, there had to be dozens of black SUVs in Rock Creek Village. Trying to locate the right one, especially in the dark, would be a fool's errand.

The most obvious course of action would be to call for help—Raul, Dad, 9-1-1. But my tech skills weren't that savvy, and I couldn't risk losing my only connection to Renata. *Give me something*, I pleaded. *Help me get to you.*

Then I heard her muffled voice again and realized the phone must be in her pocket, or wedged beneath her leg. "Theo, what do you want from me?"

Theo. I'd been right.

At the sound of fear in Renata's voice, Terror lifted her furry paws onto the center console and barked. I scrambled for the mute button.

"What was that?" Theo's voice boomed.

"What was what?"

"That noise. It sounded like…like a dog."

"It's your guilty conscience torturing you for turning poor Terror loose in the street, you brute. What if she's hit by a car? Or freezes to death?"

"If anything happens to that stupid mutt, it's on you," he growled. "If you'd just come with me willingly, she'd be safe and sound in your apartment right now. Someone would have found her there. Eventually."

Another prolonged silence. "Eventually. You mean I'm never

going back?" Renata's single question was heart-wrenching.

My hand shook so hard I almost dropped the phone. I made out a crunching sound and speculated that Theo's car had turned onto gravel. "Why are we going to the Event Center?" Renata asked.

Good girl. I shifted the car into drive and peeled out of the parking lot, making a U-turn and heading toward Evergreen Way. I could be in the Event Center parking lot in five minutes.

But what then?

I pondered again whether to hang up on Renata and call Raul, but with an injured arm and at my current excessive speed of travel, I couldn't risk it.

Taking the corner too fast, my tires skidded on the snow, and the animals protested as they tumbled across the back seat. The seat belt bit into my sore ribs. I eased up on the accelerator. I'd be of no use to Renata if I rolled the Honda.

Through the line, I heard a car door open, followed by a series of grunts. Then Renata's voice called out. "Let me go! You're not—" Mid-shout, her voice muffled. Theo must have put a hand over her mouth or gagged her. I gritted my teeth and bent over the steering wheel.

Thankfully, Evergreen Way was devoid of traffic. I glanced at the clock on the dashboard—almost eight o'clock. Light spilled from the window of Snow Plow Chow, but I didn't risk a glance inside.

Down the street, past a public parking area and a small park with benches and a gazebo, I spotted the Event Center. Haloed in the dim light of a single streetlamp, it appeared as dark and spectral as a haunted house. There were no cars in the facility's lot. My heart sank. Had I misheard Renata? Then I remembered the staff parking area on the far side of the building. I bet Theo had pulled in there, out of sight of anyone who happened by.

I pulled to a stop at the edge of the park and turned off my headlights. Snow drifted over the park. A thunk and a groan came from Renata's phone, then a smothered shout. I couldn't wait another minute. I had to act.

In the back seat, Terror yapped. Beside her, Woody whined, and Carl arched his back and hissed. I twisted in my seat and gave the creatures a stern look. "That's enough," I said. "The best way you can help her is to stay here and keep quiet."

The three of them huddled together and stared at me. I got the feeling they understood. "Good," I whispered. "Now wish me luck."

I lowered the volume on my phone so if Theo or Renata talked, they wouldn't detect the echoes of their own voices as I approached. Then I stepped out of the car and slowly, quietly eased the door closed. As I made my way toward the Event Center, I was hyperaware of the crunching sounds my feet made in the snow.

When I rounded the side of the building, I noticed a lone vehicle in the far corner of the staff parking lot—a black SUV. The passenger door stood open, but there was no sign of Theo or Renata inside.

Scuffling sounds came from behind the building. I tried to picture the layout of the area. I'd only been back there once, over a year ago, but I could visualize the ravine where Rock Creek cut through the mountains. A wooden footbridge crossed it.

That had to be where he'd taken her.

I tiptoed through the parking lot, past the SUV, and around the back of the Event Center, squeezing into the shadow of a green dumpster. Twenty yards away, I saw the bridge. Two silhouetted figures stood in the center.

With his left hand, Theo gripped Renata's upper arm. Though he wore a thick coat and boots, Renata was clad only in a long-sleeved shirt and yoga pants. She had to be freezing. She squirmed in his grasp, but not as fiercely as I would have expected from such an athletic person.

Beneath the bridge, Rock Creek gushed. Though its name implied a mellow trickle of water, the creek behaved more like a river in this part of town, rushing deep enough in some places that a person would find herself submerged. Elk used it as a water source, but even those huge beasts exercised caution when crossing in this spot. Patches of ice lined the banks, but the current never subsided enough to allow the creek to freeze into a solid sheet.

I reached for my phone and disconnected the open line to Renata before quickly scrolling my contacts. Raul? 9-1-1? Maybe Sam? If he was still at the cafe, he could be here in a heartbeat. But a call would require me to speak, and I didn't want to alert Theo to my presence.

I started tapping out a text, intending to send it to Raul and Sam. *Need help. Behind Event Center. Ren—*

Before I could send the message, a scream from the bridge told me I'd run out of time. I looked up to see Theo shoving Renata toward the bridge rail.

In a loud hiss, he said, "Don't make this any harder than it has to be."

When I moved from the cover of the dumpster, my hand bumped against the hard metal edge, knocking my phone to the ground. I left it and sprinted toward the bridge. "Let her go!" I yelled.

He startled at the sound of my voice, and his grip on Renata's arm loosened. Still, she didn't move. I knew she was stronger than Theo, more agile. *Why wasn't she trying to escape?*

"Renata, run!" I screamed.

She looked at me with pleading eyes. "Get out of here, Callie. Now."

Theo grabbed her arm again and shifted his stance. Then I saw the glint of metal clutched in his right hand and understood.

Theo had a gun, and now he was pointing it at me.

37

S top right there!" Theo yelled.

I halted and put my hands up.

We stood there for a moment, at an apparent stalemate. Except he had a gun. Advantage Theo.

"Theo," I said, forcing a reasonable tone into my voice. "Put the gun away. Don't make things worse for yourself."

"How could it get worse? My brother is dead, and I'm dead broke." He turned the gun toward Renata. "And it's all because of her."

"That's not true!" Renata wrenched against Theo, but he forced his elbow into her back, bending her precariously over the side of the bridge. I had a flashback to Jeffrey plunging over the catwalk guardrail.

Renata stopped struggling. A sob escaped her lips. "Theo, I swear to you, I didn't kill Jeffrey."

Theo smirked. "Don't worry about it, Sis. I don't blame you a bit. I wanted that arrogant jerk dead, too. You saved me the effort."

He eased the pressure on Renata's back but kept the gun trained on her. "Everything would be fine if it wasn't for that stupid will. Jeffrey told me he'd changed it to cut you out and make me his heir. Like a fool, I believed him." He barked a bitter laugh and looked at me with crazed eyes. "He screwed me over again. Story of my life. Well, I'm tired of it. It ends here."

"Theo, you have a right to be upset," I said. "I get that. But think logically. Killing Renata won't get you any closer to that money. You'll go to jail."

He took a deep breath. "I've got a plan that might work. But even if it doesn't, I don't much care anymore."

He sounded so lost. Maybe the best tool in my arsenal—the only tool, really—was empathy. *But could it stop a bullet?* I caught Renata's eye, transmitting a silent plea for patience. "It's been rough on you," I said to Theo. "The people who were supposed to care about you abandoned you. First your mother—"

His nostrils flared. "If you can even call her a mother. She never wanted me—I was just a way of keeping her claws sunk into my father. Didn't work, though. He left and she was stuck with me, a stupid kid who only got in her way. When I started using drugs, she gave up. Tossed me out like garbage, even though it was her fault I'm so messed up."

"Oh, Theo. I'm so sorry for everything that's happened to you."

He looked at me sharply, as if evaluating my sincerity. I kept my expression sympathetic. Renata didn't move. Theo's eyes glistened. "First it was my mother, the woman who was supposed to love me no matter what. Then it was my brother, who should've protected me."

"Jeffrey hurt you, too?"

Theo shifted his weight, and the gun dropped an inch. My heart raced a little faster. *Could this end peacefully, after all?* "Jeffrey was ten when I was born," he continued. "Never had much interest in me. He was out of the house by the time my real problems started. But he knew. He saw how much I was struggling, saw how our mother treated me. He didn't lift a finger to help me."

"That's terrible," I said, stalling in the slim hope that help would arrive. "But Theo, if you resented Jeffrey so much, why did you follow him to Rock Creek Village?"

Theo gazed off into the distance. The seconds ticked by. I took a step toward the bridge, very carefully, trying not to draw attention to myself. Then another, and one more. I still wasn't sure what I'd do when I got there.

Finally, Theo turned back to me, and I froze. Lost in his memories, he didn't seem to notice I'd moved closer. "I wanted what was mine. I thought the only way to get it was to convince my big brother I'd changed. If I did, he'd bring me into his business. I even fantasized he'd make me his partner."

"Is that what you were talking about Saturday morning? I saw the two of you outside the arena."

"Jeffrey was there to scout the property. He said the spot was exactly what he was looking for." Theo snorted. "His stupid casino plan. Gambling isn't even legal in Colorado, and he couldn't be sure it ever would be. I told him it didn't make sense to risk so much capital before that happened. He got so mad. He said I'd never understand the scope of his power and influence."

Theo's jaw clenched. "I said I believed him and that I only wanted to help him. When I asked him to make me part of the business, he laughed and called me an idiot. Then he said..."

He dropped his eyes, and a greasy strand of hair fell across his face. "He said I had my father's brains, which meant no brains at all. He said he wished I'd never been born."

Genuine sympathy filled me. No one deserved to be treated that way, especially by his own family. Then I took another look at the gun, and at Renata pressed against the side of the bridge, her face constricted in fear. Any tender feelings on my part immediately faded.

Still, I maintained my sorrowful tone. If he believed I was on his side, Renata and I might find a way out of this.

"Your brother was wrong, Theo. He should have given you a chance. You have value. He should have appreciated you."

He removed his hand from Renata's back to wipe the tears that trickled down his cheeks. I saw Renata stiffen and prepare to spring away. Theo felt it, too, and jammed the gun against her neck.

"Theo!" I yelled. "Hurting Renata won't solve anything!"

When he looked at me again, a cold emptiness had replaced

the pain in his eyes. "I never planned to kill her, you know. If only she'd left Jeffrey alone after the divorce, everything would have been fine. He would have changed his will and welcomed me into his life. I was his brother. His only family. I would have gotten what I was due. But she wouldn't let go of him. She convinced him they were getting back together and ruined my life all over again."

I knew that was a fantasy, one Theo had probably replayed in his mind so many times he'd convinced himself of its truth.

Renata twisted her head, trying to catch his eye. "Theo, you're wrong. Jeffrey wasn't here to get back together with me. He was here to hurt me, just like he hurt you."

Theo grunted. "Your lies won't work on me. You coerced him into keeping you in the will. Otherwise, he would have left everything to me."

I lifted my hands in a calming gesture. "I think I understand, Theo. You brought Renata here to teach her a lesson, right? Or maybe to talk some sense into her, so she'd release her claim on the money."

"Don't be stupid. I brought her here to kill her."

Renata's body went still. Theo shook his head. "Like I said, it wasn't my original plan. I figured Renata would go to jail for Jeffrey's murder, like she deserved. Then the money would come to me. There's nobody left. But those morons let her go, and I finally understood. Her brother is a detective here, and the two of them had duped the entire town. She'd never be found guilty. So I had to find another way."

"But Theo, this way won't work," I pointed out. "If you kill Renata, you'll be the one in jail. You won't get the money. You'll ruin your own life, too."

"If my plan had worked, no one would have known I killed her," he said. "I'd throw her over the bridge, and she'd be so scared, like my brother must have been when she bashed in his skull. Sweet justice in that. And when she landed in the water, the current would carry her off. Maybe they'd find her body, or maybe they wouldn't. If they did, I figured they'd think she jumped, tormented by her conscience. One way or the other, they'd never be able to tie it to me."

He turned the gun in my direction. "But you showed up and ruined everything."

38

I gulped. Theo's tone made it very clear that both Renata and I were in big trouble.

Then I saw Renata's expression transform from fear to determination. Without hesitating, she pushed backwards against her captor's elbow and tried to tear out of his clasp. Theo responded with a forceful thrust that knocked her stomach hard against the railing. The breath whooshed out of her.

"Theo, stop this madness!" I shouted. "If you really didn't kill Jeffrey, you can still get out of this. You need to talk to the police. I'll vouch for you and make sure you get the help you need."

"I'm done with help. I've been to rehab three times and talked to doctors and shrinks until I was blue in the face. I've taken their meds, worked their twelve steps. What's it gotten me? Well, no more. I'm going to get what's coming to me."

At that moment, a sound like a caterwaul burst from behind us—barking, yelping, yowling that I recognized instantly. Theo squinted toward the sound. I turned to see two dogs and a cat racing like wild animals around the corner of the Event Center, careening toward the bridge. How had they…? I remembered closing the car door so gently and realized it must not have latched.

Woody took the lead, followed by Carl. Scrambling behind on short, furry legs, Terror kept pace. As they passed, I swiveled my head in time to see Theo point the gun toward the approaching trio. Renata saw it, too. She hurled an elbow into Theo's gut. When he jackknifed from the impact, Terror sprang past Woody and Carl and sank her teeth into Theo's calf.

Theo cried out. Still clutching the gun in his right hand, he reached down and yanked the dog off his leg. He straightened up scrambled away from Renata, toward the side of the bridge, holding the dog by the scruff of the neck. I inhaled sharply.

"No!" Renata cried. "She's just a puppy!"

Terror writhed and snapped in a futile attempt to bite Theo's hand. He swung his arm toward the edge. Carl screeched, and Woody bolted onto the wooden boards of the bridge.

At the sight of Woody's bared teeth, Theo took a step back, and Renata jumped into action. In one quick move, she pivoted, wrestled Terror from Theo's grasp, and swung her foot sideways, swiping Theo's legs out from under him. He fell forward, landing on his stomach. His head cracked against the wooden boards of the bridge, a sequel to several days earlier when he slipped on the ice. The man's skull was taking a beating.

As he fell, the gun pitched from his hand and landed a few feet away. Carl swatted it, and the gun tumbled over the edge of the bridge into the rushing water.

Calmly, Woody settled his furry body onto Theo's back. The dazed man barely struggled. When I ran onto the bridge, Renata held Terror out to me. Then Renata nudged Woody off Theo and dropped onto his back, her knee grinding into his kidneys.

I ran back to the dumpster and snatched up my phone, relieved that it appeared undamaged. I pressed speed dial on my phone. Raul answered on the first ring. "Hey, Callie, I was just about to call—"

"Stop talking and listen," I said. "I'm at the bridge behind the Event Center with Renata and Theo. Theo tried to…Never mind. I'll fill you in when you get here. We're okay, but come quick. And bring backup."

***

As soon as I hung up with Raul, I called Sam. He ran straight over from the cafe, carrying the requested set of zip ties from his kitchen. He bent over Theo and secured the man's hands behind his back.

Renata still wouldn't relinquish her position. After some excessive whining and fidgeting, Terror persuaded me to put her down. Now she stood guard near Theo's face. Woody remained close by, growling every time the man so much as took a deep breath. Only Carl stood apart, watching the scene with keen interest.

A short time later, we heard sirens approaching. Flashing lights reflected off the falling snow as three police vehicles squealed into the Event Center parking lot. An ambulance appeared in their wake, but it was Raul who made it to the bridge first, with Detective Clarke close behind.

Sam and I corralled the animals and backed away to give the police room to do their thing. Clarke kept her gun on Theo as Raul hoisted Renata off her former brother-in-law. Officers Laherty and Tollison rushed onto the scene to cover Theo while Detective Clarke crouched down and read him his rights.

Maddie and Roland, the paramedics who had treated Theo and me at the rink, took over. After a preliminary examination, they determined that, though the bump on Theo's head was probably no cause for concern, they'd take him to the hospital as a precaution. They cut off the zip ties, strapped him onto a gurney, and handcuffed his wrist to a side rail. While Roland pushed Theo toward the ambulance, Maddie assessed Renata and pronounced her injury-free. A few minutes later, the ambulance screeched away.

I looked at Renata, who was squatting over Terror, inspecting every inch of the little dog for injuries. "You naughty puppy," she scolded gently. "What were you thinking?"

An argument broke out behind us in the parking lot, and Detective Clarke jogged over to check it out. She returned with Ethan, who'd risked arrest in his determination to get to Renata. He ran to her and pulled his girlfriend—and a squirming Terror—into a tight embrace.

Woody approached Detective Clarke and began sniffing her coat. She chuckled, reached into her pocket, and produced treats—one for each animal. She caught my expression of surprise and shrugged. "I have two daughters at home, and we all love animals. Our menagerie consists of two dogs, two cats, a hamster, and a turtle. Oh, and I almost forgot the poor goldfish."

"I'm assuming you have fish food pellets in that pocket as well?" I asked.

She grinned. "I'll never tell."

After a brief conference, Detective Clarke and Raul agreed that Sam and I could depart, with the contingency that we'd make formal statements tomorrow. Renata's presence, however, was required at the station tonight. One look at Ethan assured me he wouldn't be leaving her side.

"Okay," Renata said, "but Terror stays with me. That's non-negotiable."

"I accept your terms," Clarke said. "Now, let's get you in front of a heater." She led Renata and Ethan toward the car.

Raul watched them go. Then he shook hands with Sam and locked eyes with me. "Callie, I don't know what to say. If you hadn't shown up, my sister might be…"

His voice turned gravelly, and I hugged him. "I'm just glad I got here when I did. She was smart to call me back and keep the line open. Must be genetic." He gave me a lopsided grin, then trotted off after Renata.

Sam and I walked down the street to my car and settled Woody and Carl into the back. I handed Sam my keys and fell into the passenger seat, exhausted and aching. He climbed behind the wheel and turned the key in the ignition, ratcheting up the heater. While the wipers flapped the accumulated snow off the windshield, he leaned over and kissed me. "We have to stop meeting like this."

I wrapped my arm around his neck. "Thank you for always coming when I need you. I don't deserve you, but I'm going to change that." I gave him a secretive grin. "I think you'll enjoy what I have planned for Friday."

He kissed me again. "I don't need a special plan, Callie. I only need you."

***

My phone buzzed nonstop as word of Theo's arrest traveled lightning fast across the town's communication channels. I called Mom and Dad first and told them we were on our way to their place and would fill them in when we arrived.

As Sam drove down Evergreen Way toward the lodge, I also returned a text from Tonya, assuring her everyone was all right and asking her to let Jessica and Summer know. I ended with, *Thanks for checking on me after all that's happened between us.*

She responded quickly. *I was actually checking on Renata.* Then she added a smiley face and heart emoji.

At that moment, I felt hopeful. Maybe our friendship could heal.

I glanced at Sam. His eyes squinted as he focused on the road. The crinkly lines around his mouth and eyes were deepening with the years—laugh lines, I knew. The signs of a well-lived life. But there were creases on his forehead, too, representing concerns and worries. Also necessary parts of a well-lived life.

He sensed my gaze and darted a look at me. "What?"

"Nothing," I said. "I'm just glad to have you by my side."

He reached over and squeezed the fingers that poked from my cast. "Nowhere I'd rather be."

39

The second we pulled into the parking lot of the lodge, Mom stepped through the lodge's glass doors. Sam got out and opened the back door, and the creatures scampered to her. We hurried across the parking lot after them.

"Mom, get inside," I said. "It's freezing, and you're not even wearing a coat."

She pulled me into her arms. "You had me so worried."

I hugged her back so hard my ribs protested. "I'm fine, Mom."

She lifted an eyebrow. "Yes, fine. Always fine. What age do you have to be before I stop fretting over your well-being?"

She gave Sam a warm smile as she led us into the lodge. "Thank you, dear, for being there for my daughter. For all of us."

He put an arm around Mom. "It's my pleasure, Maggie."

Inside, Jamal called out a greeting from behind the desk. I waved and scanned the lobby. Other than the few guests curled up on the couches near the fireplace, the place was quiet. "Where's Dad?"

"Upstairs making sandwiches," Mom said. "We figured you hadn't eaten yet."

My stomach rumbled in response. "You figured right. Speaking for myself, at least."

Sam rubbed his hands together. "I can always polish off a sandwich." Then I noticed him glance at Jamal. "Why don't you two head upstairs?" he said to me and Mom. "I'll be right along.

Maggie, please make sure Callie doesn't devour all the sandwiches before I get there."

I watched him as he set off toward the desk. "What's that about?" I asked Mom.

She made a "my-lips-are-sealed" gesture. "Not my place to share, darling."

I sighed, too exhausted to protest.

In the kitchen, my father was putting the finishing touches on a stack of sandwiches massive enough to feed the village. I selected a roast beef on rye and took a hearty bite, savoring the tender meat, Swiss cheese, and spicy mustard.

"Darling, do sit down at the table," my mother admonished. "Let's behave like civilized folks."

I wiped a dribble of mustard off my chin and picked up a plate, loading it with another half sandwich and a large scoop of potato salad. When I'd settled into a chair, Mom opened a cabinet and took out a glass. "Milk?" she asked.

"How about wine? It's been a long day."

"All right, but just one glass. Can't have you falling asleep at the table."

Sam came in then, fixed himself a plate, and sat beside me. Dad brought Sam a beer, and he and Mom settled into chairs across from us. Dad clasped his hands on the table like a school principal. "Okay, Sundance, tell us everything."

Between bites, I filled them in on the evening's events, from the moment I spotted Terror in the street to Renata swatting Theo's legs out from beneath him. "Her athletic instincts are amazing," I said. "It was the same move I've seen pro hockey players make—just before they end up in the penalty box."

"It's a wonder no one was seriously hurt," Mom said. "Or worse. Thank goodness."

From the kitchen, a cell phone rang, and my mother rose to answer it. Dad looked at me and shook his head. "You sure get yourself involved in some sticky situations."

I raised my palms. "None of this is my doing. This whole fiasco...I've been a victim of circumstances."

"I suppose you have a point. Still, I sometimes wonder what life would be like if you'd chosen a career as a librarian."

"Dad, I've known plenty of librarians, and I think your image of them may be misguided. One librarian I interviewed went on African safaris and slept in the jungle. Another…" I waved. "Stories for another time. But you get the idea."

Mom returned and set her cell phone on the table. "That was Mrs. Finney. She allowed me to provide the highlights of this evening's events, but Callie, she strongly suggests you appear at Rocky Mountain High tomorrow so she can hear the story from you." Mom grinned. "And I quote: 'The woman who ignores her duty to her elders is doomed to a life without coffee or pastries.'"

We all laughed, and I promised to present myself bright and early. After a brief pause, Dad gave me a searching look. "Tell me, Sundance—does Theo's arrest give you closure?"

I scrunched up my face. Leave it to Dad to sense my misgivings. Perhaps he, too, was experiencing some doubt. "Well, I suppose it makes sense," I began. "Theo's rage toward Jeffrey escalated over the years, to the point that it could have culminated in murder. There's just something…I don't know…*off* about the whole thing."

"Anything you can put your finger on?" Dad asked.

Three sets of eyes fixed on me, and I shrugged. "I can't explain it. It's just an instinct, I guess. Theo literally attempted to kill Renata. He admitted hating his brother and being glad he was dead, but then he so passionately—and persuasively—denied murdering him. It's hard to understand the logic."

My father considered. "Here's the thing, Sundance. Theo's actions toward Renata prove the man is capable of murder. And as you've said, he's a troubled soul. The sincerity might have been authentic—in his own mind." He leaned back in his chair. "I know of situations in which criminals beat lie detector tests because they convinced themselves they were telling the truth. Could be the case here."

My mind flashed to Theo standing on the bridge. "*It's all because of her,*" he'd said forcibly, pointing at Renata.

My brain felt overloaded, on the verge of shutting down. I yawned, even though I tried to avoid it. "You may be right," I said. "But I'm too worn out to think about it anymore."

"A full stomach and a clean conscience," Mom said. "You'll sleep well tonight."

***

Sam and I drove down Evergreen Way and parked in front of the studio. We left Woody and Carl snoozing in the back seat and went inside long enough for me to put a Closed for the Day sign in the window. I needed a day to regroup, and since Thursdays tended to be slow, the timing worked well.

We locked up and walked a half block down the deserted sidewalk to Snow Plow Chow so Sam could pick up ingredients to make breakfast for us tomorrow. While he bagged items, I tapped out a text to Braden and Banner. *Closing the studio for tomorrow. Have a fun afternoon.*

The response was immediate. *Heard about Theo. Sure you want to close? We can handle the gallery if you just need a day off.*

I texted back, *Thanks, but we could all use a break. The podcast airs tomorrow, so hope we'll be extra busy on Friday. Rest up.*

Arm-in-arm, Sam and I strolled back to the car. My pets barely roused when we got in. Sam turned on the heated seat, and I leaned against the headrest and let my eyelids drift shut as he drove down the empty streets. My mind floated over the day's events, settling on something I'd been meaning to ask him. "What were you talking to Jamal about earlier?"

"I wondered when you'd get around to that."

I rolled my head toward him and opened my eyes. "'Fess up."

"It's no big deal," he said. "I've decided to make some changes, that's all."

"What do you mean, changes?"

He shrugged. "I want to cut back on my workload, and Jamal and I have been discussing the possibility of him coming on board. I'm at Snow Plow Chow almost every day, from before sunrise to after sunset. It's taking a toll on me—and on my

214

relationships. I can't sustain the pace anymore."

I sat upright. "Sam, I hope you're not doing this because of me. The problems we've had—they're not because of your work."

He sighed. "I know that. Much as I care about you, Callie, I do make a few decisions just for me. Now that Elyse has decided to quit commuting and stay in Boulder, I want to be able to visit her whenever I feel like it. I'd like to travel to Florida to see my parents more often. And there are so many other places in the world I'd like to explore. Plus, working so much is making me short-tempered." He rolled his shoulders. "It's not like I'm selling the place. Just slowing down."

I nodded, thinking about the long hours Sam kept. Even with Rodger and Dan to shoulder some of the load, the schedule had to be grueling for him, especially since he'd been doing it for over a decade. "I think it's a great idea. You can sleep in once in a while. How did you decide to team up with Jamal, by the way? And more important, how do my parents feel about you snatching him away?"

He smiled. "They're fully on board. Jamal would have to leave Knotty Pine even if I wasn't involved. In order to graduate culinary school next fall, Jamal needs to complete an internship rotation as a chef in a full-fledged restaurant. It makes perfect sense for him to work at the Chow, and the timing couldn't be better. I'll turn the lion's share of the cooking over to Jamal and Rodger, while I focus on the business end of things. I can still experiment with recipes and prepare new dishes, but it'll be on a want-to basis, not have-to."

I laid my hand on his knee. "That sounds perfect."

"I think it will be. As you know, Jamal is talented, and his work ethic is superior. Maybe he'll even end up staying at the Chow for a while after graduation—until he's ready to move on, that is."

"If the stars align, you'll have Jamal, and I'll have Ethan," I said. "I could take a couple of those trips with you."

"Sounds good," he said. "How about if we start with Vegas? I hear there might be a wedding this fall worth attending."

"That'd be great, I said, but inwardly I winced. It was a good plan—assuming I was still invited to the wedding.

40

I was asleep as soon as my head hit the pillow, and after nine hours of dreamless slumber, I woke refreshed and hungry. While Sam cooked, I filled pet bowls—though the aroma of frying bacon meant Woody wasn't at all interested in kibble. He didn't venture far from Sam's side—and neither did I.

As Sam drizzled syrup over the blueberry-raspberry-pecan pancakes, the doorbell rang. I glanced down at my fuzzy slippers and flannel robe and ran my fingers through the pre-shower frizz in my hair.

"Want me to get it?" Sam asked, amused.

"That's okay. People who show up here before eight in the morning get what they get."

I opened the door, and a woman in a delivery uniform took one look at me and smiled apologetically. "Sorry to wake you. Rush order." She handed over a bouquet of white lilies and roses, dotted with blue forget-me-nots. I tucked it into the crook of my elbow above the cast and signed the form.

"One more item." She held out a box tied with a shiny blue ribbon. "You're on someone's good list."

My purse was on the table in the foyer, and I rummaged in it for a tip and thanked the woman. I carried the gifts to the kitchen and set the vase on the counter.

"Secret admirer?" Sam asked.

"I'm sure you're right." I plucked the card from the flowers and read it aloud. *"I knew I'd come to the right place for help. We can't thank you, Woody, and Carl enough. Love, Renata and Terror."*

I untied the ribbon and opened the box, unveiling an array of gourmet pet treats. I lobbed one to Woody, who caught it mid-air and swallowed it whole. Beside him, Carl looked interested, so I tossed a treat to him, too. He watched it fall to the floor and sniffed it before delicately nibbling at its edges.

Sam put our breakfast on the table then, and I wasn't nearly so delicate.

***

After we ate and made ourselves presentable, Sam and I headed to the police station to make our formal statements. Marilyn poured us each a cup of coffee and escorted us to the interview room. Sam opened the container of homemade lemon meringue scones he'd brought along and offered her one. When she took her first bite, she practically swooned. I thought she might ask him to marry her.

Raul and Detective Clarke entered the room then, and Marilyn placed a protective hand over her scone as she passed them, as if they might try to steal it. Raul looked at us quizzically. "I guess she likes the scones," I whispered, gesturing toward the box on the table.

"Help yourself," Sam said.

Raul responded with enthusiasm, but Detective Clarke outdid him. She scarfed one down without taking a breath and reached for another. "Sorry," she said, holding a hand in front of her mouth as crumbs fell from her lips. "I haven't eaten anything but a handful of peanuts since lunch yesterday."

I laughed. "I don't think either of us worries much about manners, Detective Clarke."

"Lynn," she said, still chewing. "It's time you started calling me Lynn."

Finally, I thought. "Lynn it is." I smiled at her, then turned to Raul. "Looks like you're allowed on the case now."

"I'm assisting the lead detective." He tilted his head toward

218

Lynn, and I could see the two of them had made their peace. Nothing like catching a killer to turn everyone into bosom buddies.

"Renata sent me a lovely gift this morning," I said. "I assume she's doing okay?"

"I'd say she was a little shook up," Raul said, "though she'd never admit it. Overall, though, she seems to be holding up well. We finished up with her interview about ten last night, and she said she planned to go to school today like normal. I'm not surprised. Ever since she was a little girl, she's had the fortitude of a gladiator."

"What about Ethan? Was he here the whole time?"

Raul smirked. "Couldn't pry them apart. I'm guessing he'll be joining our family dinners from here on out."

"Your family could do worse," I said.

"Sure could," he said wistfully. "Jeffrey Forte is evidence of that. Which brings us to the matter at hand."

He gestured to Lynn, yielding the interview to her. She opened her notebook and pressed a button on the recorder in the center of the table. After getting the basics on tape—my name, the date, the case number—she said, "In your own words, Ms. Cassidy, please take us through yesterday's events."

I told my story succinctly while making sure to cover all the details. This wasn't my first rodeo, after all. Then Sam took a few minutes to recap his own actions and observations.

Lynn jotted down the highlights, slapped her notebook shut, and turned off the recorder. "That should do it. We'll get this typed up and ready for your signatures by tomorrow."

I put up a hand. "Not so fast, please. Now it's my turn. I'd like to know what's going on with Theo."

Lynn glanced at Raul. "Okay by me," he said.

She folded her hands on the table. "Well, there's not a lot to tell yet. They examined Theo at the hospital and released him. He was transferred to the station, where he spent the night in a cell. We can't interview him, not until a public defender shows up to represent him. Should be soon. In the meantime, Theo continually—and loudly—denies killing his brother."

"So, no confession," I mused. "Makes for a pretty circumstantial case. No solid proof that he murdered Jeffrey."

Lynn nodded. "Not so far. But considering the kidnapping and the attempted murder of Renata, which are indisputable thanks to you and the other witnesses, we'll have no trouble getting a D.A. to file charges. And we're still digging for more evidence."

I twirled a strand of hair around my finger and considered the situation. After a few seconds, I noticed Raul staring at me. "What?" I asked. "Do I have something in my teeth?"

"No, you have something on your face. That look that says even though the crime has been solved, you're not satisfied."

I felt a pang, and it had nothing to do with the case. Raul knew me so well he could read my thoughts. And soon, he might leave for a new job in Boulder. I wanted to ask him where things stood on that, but now wasn't the time. Instead, I tried to make my face appear convinced. "Oh, I'm sure Theo did it. Nothing else makes sense. If two professional detectives believe it, why shouldn't I?"

Raul narrowed his eyes at me. "Uh huh."

***

Sam had left his car at the cafe overnight, so we drove into the upper village together. I dropped him off at the cafe and parked in my usual spot behind the gallery, ready for a walk down to Rocky Mountain High so I could fulfill my duty to Mrs. Finney.

As I stepped through the alcove and onto the sidewalk, the air began to sparkle. I squealed in delight when I realized the village was in the midst of a rare weather phenomenon, one I'd witnessed only twice before. Diamond dust. It occurred when tiny ice crystals fell from a clear, cloudless sky. The sun's rays reflected from the crystals as they floated in the air, appearing suspended there. I lifted my palms and did a slow spin. It was as if the gods were tossing glitter from the peaks of the mountains, and the event served as a reminder from Mother Nature that miracles existed all around me.

A few minutes later, I entered Rocky Mountain High, and the

scent of roasted coffee beans promised yet another miracle. The morning rush had dispersed, but a few patrons lingered over steaming mugs. I strolled past them to the counter, where Mrs. Finney awaited me.

"Good morning, Callahan," she said.

"A fine morning indeed," I replied. "Did you see the diamond dust?"

She gave a clap of appreciation. "A lovely sight. So very peaceful. Perfect for the day following a murderer's apprehension."

I held up a finger. "Alleged murderer, Mrs. Finney. Mustn't get ahead of ourselves."

She placed a steaming cup of coffee in front of me. After I refused the offer of a pastry, citing my huge breakfast, she leaned her elbows on the counter. "Sit down, dear. Tell me all about it."

For the third time in less than a day, I replayed the events of the night before, pausing only when customers approached the counter for refills. I ended my story with the visit to the police station this morning and the few details I'd extracted from Lynn and Raul.

"I'm relieved everyone made it through safely." Mrs. Finney stroked her chin and gazed into the distance. "My, my, it's all wrapped up in a neat little bow, isn't it?"

At her tone, the seeds of uncertainty I'd carried since yesterday sprouted a bit more. "Are you thinking it's not that simple?"

"I don't know, Callahan. The outcome seems obvious. Yet…something about the ordeal feels unfinished."

"That's what I said." I leaned forward and lowered my voice. "When Theo denied killing Jeffrey, he seemed so earnest. So fervent."

"Perhaps he's a skilled dissembler. Addicts often are."

"I suppose." I drummed my fingers on the counter. "But the logistics bother me, too. You've seen Theo. He's scrawny. His brother, on the other hand, apparently never missed a meal. When I try to picture Theo lifting Jeffrey over the guardrail…"

"Just playing devil's advocate, dear, but Theo subdued Renata, and she has the strength of a bull."

"True," I said. "Though strength doesn't matter so much when a gun is involved." A moment of silence stretched between us. "Ah, well," I said at last. "I'm sure the detectives have it right. I should just let it go."

"Yet one's instincts must not be ignored. They serve as our guideposts in the darkness of night." She pulled her notebook from beneath the counter. "Just let me jot that down."

Perhaps, I mused as she wrote. But I'd also seen instincts steer people down a decidedly misguided path.

The bell above the coffee shop door jingled, and Tonya breezed inside. Her open coat revealed a tailored burgundy pantsuit. She was a vision, as always, but my stomach clutched at the sight of her.

"Tonya, dear," Mrs. Finney cooed. "Look at you, lovely as a portrait."

My friend smiled and pulled off her gloves. "The same to you, Mrs. Finney. Your lavender pantsuit sets off your eyes. You must spend all day fighting off suitors."

Mrs. Finney blushed and tittered like a schoolgirl as she began preparing Tonya's usual: A foamy latte. When it was ready, she passed it across the counter with a flourish. "Can I interest you in a pastry?"

"Tempting as it is, I'll pass." Tonya patted her waist. "No wedding dress bulge blues, please."

The two of them chatted for a few minutes. I sat on a stool with a polite smile plastered on my face, but my nerves ran high. When Mrs. Finney trotted off to tend to a customer, Tonya dropped her eyes, then looked up at me through long, thick lashes. I realized we were both confronting a shyness we hadn't faced around each other since we'd met in middle school.

"Shall we find a table?" Tonya asked.

I followed her to a spot in the corner. We sat and took long sips of coffee. I knew it was up to me to break the silence. "Tonya, I'm so sorry. I feel terrible about the whole situation."

"David told me you apologized. That was gracious of you."

"I meant everything I said. Scrounging around in his past, keeping my actions secret from you, it was all so wrong. I have no excuse. I just hope you can forgive me."

Her red lips curved down. "Well, Callie, I don't know. I just don't know."

Tears welled in my eyes. I'd been so afraid of this.

She took another sip of coffee. When she looked at me again, I noticed the glint in her eye. "Perhaps if you sink to your knees and pledge eternal loyalty, all the while chanting, 'Tonya is a goddess, and I will obey her until my dying day.'"

I froze for a second, then burst out laughing. Tonya and I jumped up at the same time and wrapped our arms around each other, giggling and crying. I repeated her words, swearing to serve as her obedient minion.

When we returned to our seats, I placed my hand on hers. "There's still one more order of business we need to address."

She arched an eyebrow. "Goddess."

"Sorry. One more order of business, goddess."

"And what might that be?"

"My title. Am I to be Best Woman, or did you settle on Grande Dame?"

41

N ow that we'd made up, Tonya wanted to interview me for the story she was writing for *The Gazette* chronicling the events of the past few days. We agreed to meet at my house later that evening. She hurried off for a scheduled meeting with Lynn Clarke, and I headed back down the street. Though the diamond dust had dissipated, the village still seemed sparkly to me. Perhaps that's what joy looked like.

I entered the gallery and locked the door behind me, leaving the sign turned to Closed alongside the note I'd posted last night. I had no intention of opening for business. In fact, I'd only stopped by to make sure I had enough stock to satisfy the droves of customers Bradley and Tim predicted.

First, I took a count of the postcards and the smaller, matted photos we kept on a table near the door. Then I walked around the gallery. The twins had done a good job maintaining the canvases, with a healthy blend of landscapes, wildlife shots, and village photos. The freestanding partitions, which I used for themed arrangements, displayed winter sports shots—skiing, snowshoeing, skating, tobogganing. It all looked good.

Next stop was the storage room, where I flipped through the stock of canvases from our recent delivery. If we sold more than ten or twelve photos, I'd need additional stock. This was the toughest challenge for me as a gallery owner—determining how much to spend on back stock and how to navigate the ordering timeline. I decided I'd rather be overstocked than empty-handed. Heading to my office, I booted up the computer and scanned my most recent photo shoot, sending my printing company an order of a dozen additional canvases. A response from my sales consultant assured me they'd be delivered next Tuesday.

I sat back in my chair, contemplating whether there was anything else that needed my attention. My eyes drifted to the storage cabinet. I thought of my Nikon inside, the one I'd used at the rink on the day of Jeffrey's murder. And that thought led to the deleted photos and the retrieval software Preston had promised to send.

Ugh. Why couldn't I let it go? Why couldn't I spend my day off as carefree as Braden and Banner's friends, twirling their shirts over their heads and pressing their bellies against the window?

Well, perhaps that wasn't the best example…

But I supposed it was a bit like asking why Carl wasn't cuddlier. It just wasn't the nature of things. My innate curiosity, my hunger for justice, wouldn't allow me to spend much time immersed in oblivion. I'd never be one to ignore catwalks and crime scenes, killers and cover-ups.

Thoughts tumbled through my head again. Even if Theo hadn't murdered his brother—which he surely had—it wasn't as if I believed he was a good guy. He'd been prepared to kill Renata, and he'd even threatened her dog. And me. A man like that didn't deserve any extraordinary interventions on his behalf.

No, it was two other considerations that propelled my pursuit of the truth. First, if Theo hadn't murdered his brother, it meant someone else had. And if someone killed once and got away with it, what would keep them from doing it again if it proved expedient?

Second, and perhaps even more compelling: My need to know the truth. It was difficult for me to rest until a puzzle was properly and satisfyingly complete.

Even though Jeffrey's killer was supposedly in custody, I was determined to see whatever images I could recover from that memory card.

I skimmed through my recent emails and found nothing from Preston, so I picked up my phone and called his direct line. I'd expected to leave a message, as I usually had to, and it surprised me when he answered. "Hello, stranger," he said. "Heard you caught your killer. Didn't hear it from you, of course, which makes me—"

"Sorry for not calling you about the arrest," I interrupted. "I'll fill you in later, but right now, I have a quick question."

He chuckled. "What Callie wants, Callie gets. What do you need?"

"I never got that photo retrieval software from you."

"Well, that's not a question, but to answer you anyway, I sent it yesterday. Don't you check your email?"

"I'm scrolling through it now. There's nothing."

"Hmm." I listened to the sound of fingers tapping on his keyboard. "Here it is in my Sent file. Three in the afternoon, my time. Says the recipient hasn't opened the email. Have you looked in your Spam folder?"

I slapped my palm against my forehead. I rarely thought about checking Spam. Whenever I did, I found myself bombarded by surefire cures for male issues or letters from foreign princes requesting cash to help them unlock their shackled bank accounts.

Clicking on the folder, I scrolled through a pile of garbage until...voilà! An email from Preston titled RetrieveIt. Perhaps the title had thrown the bots into a censorship tizzy. I moved it from Spam to Inbox.

"Found it," I said. "Thank you so much, Preston. I'm going to hang up now and see if I can learn how to use it."

"Don't bother calling me if you can't. Technology is above my pay grade. But I can connect you with one of our photo editors if need be."

I snickered. As editor-in-chief, nothing was above Preston's pay grade. He simply hired people to do that kind of work for him. "I'm sure I'll be able to figure it out. I haven't been out of the game that long. I'll call you when I get results."

"Sure you will," he said. "I'll have to find out from Mrs. Finney."

***

I clicked on the attachment in Preston's email and downloaded the software. It was a large file, and it took several minutes. While I waited, I went to the storage cabinet and got the Nikon. Then I unzipped the pocket in my purse and took out the memory card I'd stashed there. That done, I tapped my fingers on the desk, cautioning myself to lower my expectations. Even if the software worked, I wasn't sure there was even an image there to retrieve. Maybe my memory was playing tricks on me, and I hadn't snapped the shutter before Jeffrey fell after all.

At last, the download completed. I opened the software and skimmed through the instructions. After a couple of minutes, I threw up my hands. It was like reading a foreign language. Either the people who wrote these instructional guides possessed a sadistic streak, or I'd been out of the game longer than I thought. I felt like an old fogey. "In my day, we didn't use retrieval software. If something got deleted, we shook our fist and moved on."

Thank goodness Ethan and the twins had taught me about the all-encompassing usefulness of YouTube. I searched for how-to videos on RetrieveIt and hit pay dirt. Three minutes of real world instruction, explained by someone who spoke in words I understood, and I was ready to try it.

I connected my Nikon to the computer and followed the steps I'd jotted down during the video. The software flashed a message warning me there were no guarantees.

The rainbow ball on the screen rotated, indicating deep thoughts in the computer's brain. I realized I was placing way too much importance on the images that might or might not be on this card. Everyone else seemed satisfied that Theo was guilty, other than Mrs. Finney and me. And possibly Dad. So why did my instincts keep trying to persuade me that the dead man's brother was telling the truth?

Finally, the rainbow ball stopped turning. Two seconds later, a message flashed in all caps: SUCCESS! Seven thumbnail photos appeared. I held down the shift button and clicked, enlarging them to full size.

First up were the hockey team photos—six shots of the Rock Creek Rockets, lined up and scowling. I clicked through them. Then my pulse quickened. Only one last photo remained.

When the picture filled my screen, I experienced a surge of disappointment. Though I had indeed snapped a shot just before Jeffrey fell, it revealed nothing except darkness and indeterminate blobs.

Zooming in, I scrolled across the image. Then I pulled up the editing palette, lightened the image, increased contrast, and attempted to sharpen the photo. The only thing those efforts accomplished was to convince me the closest blob was blue, likely Jeffrey in his fancy coat. When I squinted, I could sort of make out a black shape near the blue one, and perhaps a stroke of red. Might have been Theo wearing his leather coat...

I sighed. Nothing ventured, nothing gained, I supposed. The picture didn't answer my questions, didn't ease my doubts. But at least now I had a tangible reason to abandon the hunt.

And there was one more positive outcome, I realized—I could give Lars a copy of the team photo he'd wanted for the locker room wall. I chose the best of the images and did a quick crop and edit. After I printed it, I tucked it into a large manila envelope. I could drop it off at the rink on my way home.

42

I drove toward the rink feeling an unexpected lightness. Even though I hadn't uncovered a definitive answer as to Theo's guilt, I'd done everything in my power to obtain it. I accepted that the outcome did not rest in my hands. Now I could turn my attention back to running the gallery—and planning Sam's Valentine's present.

On weekdays during winter months, the rink closed after Early Skate and reopened in the evening after school let out, so it was no surprise to find the parking lot empty except for Lars' white pickup truck. I pulled in beside it and turned off the ignition, taking a moment to relish the beauty and peace of my surroundings. To my right, Mt. O'Connell rose into the sky. Skiers swooped down its slope, and I could almost feel the spray of snow pelting their cheeks. Turning my head, I watched the skaters on the lake across the street. Little ones stumbled around wearing their first pair of blades, and their grownups shuffled behind to scoop them up when they fell.

A casino would have ruined these picturesque tableaus. Though I wasn't happy Jeffrey was dead, I had to admit I felt a sense of relief that his plan had perished with him.

I glanced toward Pinkerton's Place and saw Pinky outside sweeping snow off his front stoop. Next door, a line of people waiting to rent equipment snaked into the door of The Ski Shop. Did local business owners even have a clue how close they'd come to a potential crisis?

Enough ruminating over what might have happened, I told myself. Time to take my friend Summer's meditation advice and live in the present moment. I got out of the car and tramped through the snow to drop off Lars's gift.

Inside the arena, dim lights glowed above the rink, giving it a ghostly appearance. For a moment, I heard no sound. I shivered, but it wasn't from the chilly air. A sense of disembodiment settled over me, as if I'd been dropped into a phantom world.

From above, I heard the clatter of metal on metal, followed by what had to be the sound of a drill. Lars was probably doing some work on the catwalk.

I put my foot on the first step, intending to climb up and present Lars with the photo, but I found myself hesitating. Jeffrey Forte had died up there. Did I want to stand in the spot where it had happened? Apprehension warred with curiosity. But for me, curiosity always won.

When I got to the top of the stairs, I saw Lars halfway down the catwalk. He was half turned away from me, crouched over a bundle of metal beams. Nearby, a toolbox and a coiled rope rested on the grating. My eyes traveled across the guardrails, which were higher now across a third of the walkway's length. Lars was adding a level of height to the railing. A good idea—though it came too late for Jeffrey.

I cleared my throat to keep from startling Lars. He looked up and caught sight of me. His expression seemed confused, then wary. He rested the drill on the floor and rose, brushing his hands across his jacket.

His black jacket. With red piping on the sleeves.

Immediately, the deleted photo I'd recovered popped into my mind. The black blob. The red streak. The answer hit me like one of those metal beams, and I reeled. In an instant, I saw the scene as it must have played out. Lars had gotten wind of Jeffrey's plan to build a casino and found out Jeffrey had his sights on this land. The arena Lars loved like a second home would be bulldozed and erased. His anger must have reached a boiling point.

Saturday morning, he'd seen Jeffrey climb the catwalk stairs, and he had snapped.

It was all speculative, but if I was right, it meant I was perched thirty feet above the ice with a killer striding toward me.

I backed toward the stairs, but Lars's long legs covered the distance between us fast. I'd never be able to outrun him, if it came to that. I plastered on a fake smile and tried to act oblivious. "Hi, Lars," I said cheerfully. "I was hoping to find you."

He eyed me, but after a moment, he smiled back. "Vat you doing up here, Callie?" Though he kept his tone light, the accent I'd found so charming now sounded malevolent in my ears.

"I brought you something." I saw him tense when I unzipped my bag, but he didn't stop me. As I reached inside, my fingers brushed against my phone. *Should I try to make a call? Text someone for help?* Lars's gaze never wavered, and I knew I couldn't risk it. Instead, I pulled out the manila envelope and held it out to him. "It's the team photo you asked for. You can hang it in the locker room, like you wanted."

He took it from me, looking puzzled. I cringed when I realized what I'd done.

He stared at me. "You said ze pictures vere erased."

"I…well, most of them were. There was just this one…"

We looked at each other, and both of us knew the gig was up. I made a move toward the stairs, and Lars snatched my arm. His grip was gentle but firm. It said he didn't want to hurt me, but I wasn't getting away.

Still holding my arm, he reached into my unzipped bag and plucked out my phone. Then he pulled me a few steps toward the middle of the catwalk and spun me around so that he was between me and the staircase. He released me and crossed his arms over his massive chest.

I was trapped.

He shook his head sadly. "Vy you come here, Callie? The police, they arrest Theo. Vy you cannot leave it alone?"

I stared at him, my mind scrambling. Neither of us moved for almost a minute.

231

I took a deep breath. "Lars, you're a good man who has done a bad thing. It must be tearing you apart inside. Tell me about it. It's the only way you'll relieve the guilt."

A series of emotions played across his face: Fear, pain, guilt. He dropped his hands to his sides. His eyes shimmered as he turned away, unable to meet my scrutiny.

Then he took a step toward the catwalk rail. For a brief, panicky moment, I thought he'd decided to throw himself over. Instead, he surveyed the rink below us. "I vill tell you, Callie. But first, I vant you to understand me."

He swept a hand around the arena. "Zis is ze only place I ever felt whole. Fitting in…it never come easy for me. Always ze giant troll, tromping around on clay feet. But on ze ice…I become ze ballerina."

He paused, and a tiny smile played on his lips. "Zat sounds stupid to you, but here, I am at home in my own skin. Ven zey put me in charge here…It vas like a gift from God."

He gazed into the distance. "Ze people in Rock Creek Village velcomed me. I vas home. How did I get so lucky?"

I risked a tentative smile. "We're lucky, too, Lars. Our village is a better place because you're in it."

He gave me a hockey player grin, one that revealed his teeth—and two empty spaces where teeth used to be. Then the grin disappeared, and his fist clenched around my phone so tightly I thought he might shatter it. "Everything vas perfect until zat Jeffrey Forte shows up. He comes by one day and tells me he is buying zis land. Vill tear down rink and put up casino. Not to vorry, he says, zere vill be job for me. Maybe vash dishes, bus tables."

"He was a jerk," I said, my voice tight. "He wanted to hurt Renata, and he didn't care about anyone or anything else. But we wouldn't have let him destroy our village. The townspeople would have banded together and stopped him."

"In my experience, greed alvays vins." Lars heaved a mournful breath. "Forte vould have gotten vat he vanted. And I vould have lost everything."

He drew a hand through his hair. "Vat to do? Should I try to fight his plans? Look for other job in village? Give up and move back to Sveden? Zen, Saturday, I see Forte come into ze arena and climb stairs to catwalk, as if he already owns ze place. My mind...I don't know how to describe. It vent blank. I vasn't thinking, just moving. My legs carry me to stairs. My eyes see hockey stick leaning against vall. My hand grabs it. I have no plan, you must believe me..."

I nodded. "I do, Lars."

"Ven I get to catwalk, Forte look at me. At first, he seems surprised, but zen he gets a stupid smirk on his face. My fingers tighten around ze stick. I think ze rage might burst through my skin. I manage to rein in my anger and try to talk to Forte man to man. If he sees me as a person, he might show compassion. I tell him how I love it here. Zat I've been saving every dime, hoping to buy ze arena myself. I beg him to find someplace else for ze casino."

I pictured the scene—Lars's desperation juxtaposed with Jeffrey's haughty arrogance. One selfish, hateful man could destroy so much. "What happened next?" I asked.

Lars scoffed. "Forte laugh at me. Calls me an idealistic dreamer, like everyone else in zis stupid village. He says ze whole town belong to him soon and I can accept zat or go back home." He lifted his chin. "But zis is my home. Not being born here doesn't make it less so."

His face reminded me of a wounded deer I'd once spotted near the side of the road. The animal's eyes carried a deep pain, but even more haunting was the plea for help I'd seen in them. Before I could decide what to do, the injured doe had risen and limped off into the forest. Realistically, I knew I couldn't have helped her anyway, but the memory of those eyes still tortured me on occasion.

Lars's eyes would haunt me, too. As with the doe, I sympathized with him and wished I could help him. But as I looked at the big man standing between me and the staircase, his hand gripping my cellphone, I knew my compassion would have to wait. Right now, my focus needed to be on my own safety.

"Finish the story, Lars," I said. "It's the only way you'll quiet your torment."

He shrugged. "You must know ze rest already. My arm rises, ze stick comes down on ze man's head. I feel surprised, like someone else is hitting him. Same arm swings again. Forte falls to his knees. Ze stick hits him von more time, and…" Lars clenched his jaw, his eyes focused on the memory. "By ze time I come back inside myself, he is already dead. I check for pulse, but nothing."

We were both silent for a moment, picturing the scene. Then I asked, "Why did you throw him onto the ice?"

He grimaced. "An impulse. At zat moment, I vant him far away from me. I don't zink about ze people down zere—you, ze children. For me, zat is worse than…" He took my hand, and a single tear spilled down his cheek. "Can you forgive me, Callie?"

I didn't even have to think about it. "Yes, Lars. I can forgive you. I already have."

He closed his eyes and breathed deeply, his relief evident. Then he asked one more question. "Vill you let me go?"

43

I couldn't easily answer Lars's last question. Could I turn the other way—pretend I didn't know the truth?

Part of me wanted to do just that. I believed Lars's story that he'd acted in a fit of passion. It wasn't as if society would be in imminent danger if this decent man went free.

I knew it wasn't that simple, though. Lars had murdered Jeffrey Forte, then remained mute as they questioned Renata, then as they arrested Theo for the crime. Would a truly decent man do that?

I bit my lip, staying silent as the tears pooled in my eyes and slid down my cheeks. Lars studied my face, then lifted his eyes to the ceiling. After a moment, he exhaled a long, decisive breath. "I vas afraid of zat."

When he pulled me toward him, my first thought was that he wanted to hug me, a goodbye of sorts. It was only when he twisted me around and pressed me against the catwalk railing that I realized my mistake.

Lars meant to kill me, too.

When I yelped, he looked surprised and loosened his grip—though not by much. "I vould not hurt you, Callie. Never. I vish you never figured zis out. I erased zat card to keep you from knowing. Later, I worried I hadn't done a good job, so I vent to your office to destroy ze card completely. If only I had located it, perhaps we would not be in zis position. Ven Theo is arrested, I zink, now ze problem vill go avay." He shook his head sadly. "But it vas not to be. Now, I must make my escape. I see American movies. Your prisons—I could not tolerate."

In two large strides, he reached the rope coiled beside his toolbox and was back almost before I could move. In the shuffle, my phone slipped from his hand and slid beneath the catwalk's bottom rail. We both watched as it cartwheeled through the air and smashed against the ice below. I swallowed hard.

"Please, Lars. I won't say anything. We'll go on like normal. You'll run the rink, and I'll shoot team portraits. It'll all be fine."

His body stilled, and I sensed he was considering it. Eventually, he shook his head. "You might mean it now," he said. "But people like you, ze morals run deep. You'd crack. Maybe not today, or next veek, but someday. Better zat I leave Rock Creek Village behind. I need only a…a head start. In a few hours, people vill come to ze rink for hockey practice. You vill call out to zem, and zey vill free you."

He drew my right hand behind me, but when he reached for my left arm, snug in its cast, he hesitated. I realized he was worried about hurting me.

This was my moment to act, the only moment I might have. I swung my arm back, striking Lars in the temple with my cast. The thud sent a bolt of agony through my broken bone. I gritted my teeth and pushed through it.

Lars grunted, and his grip on me slackened. Adrenaline surged through me, muting the pain. I twisted my right arm and spun around, thrusting my cast at him again, this time connecting with his face. A torn bit of the cast's fiberglass caught the tender skin above his eye, ripping open a gash. It was only a flesh wound, but blood trickled into his eye. He lifted his hand to wipe it away. I stepped around him and used the cast once more to whack him on the back of the head. That blow sent the big man to his knees.

Here was my chance. I took off toward the stairs, but Lars snapped out a hand in time to grab my ankle. I tumbled to the metal floor, and a spasm roared through my ribcage. My foot slid over the edge of the catwalk. For a sickening moment, I visualized my body careening toward the ice and landing shattered beside my phone.

I screamed. The gap between the catwalk floor and the bottom guardrail wasn't wide enough for Lars to slide through, or Jeffrey, but for me, it would be a close call. A fleeting thought rushed through my brain: If only I'd eaten a few more scones…

The fingers of my right hand scrambled on the floor, trying to latch onto something, anything, but my body continued its slow slide. My eyes darted around and fell on Lars, still on his hands and knees. "Help me," I pleaded.

He lifted his head, and I saw the indecision on his face. I rolled onto my side, hoping my forty-something hips were too wide to squeeze through the gap. It didn't work. As I reached up in a last-ditch effort to wrap my arm around the bottom rail, my momentum abruptly stopped. Strong hands seized my armpits. Lars pulled me back from the precipice and onto the catwalk floor.

He lifted me to my feet. My entire body began shaking, and Lars held me tight. I could feel him trembling, too. "You're okay, Callie. I von't let anyzing happen to you. I am not a bad man. I just—"

He choked on a sob, and I wrapped my arm around him. "I believe you. You'd never have let me fall."

Then came the sound of footsteps pounding up the stairs. This was the end for him. "Oh, Lars," I whispered.

His expression seemed resigned—almost content. "It is for ze best."

Seconds later, Lynn appeared on the catwalk and positioned herself in a classic cop stance, feet hip-width apart and weapon trained on Lars. "Hold it right there!"

I stepped in front of Lars and lifted my hands, gesturing for calm. "We're okay here, Detective Clarke. Lars just saved me from…" My voice caught in my throat as the full weight of what might have happened hit me.

Lynn looked from me to Lars, then to the rope on the floor. Her aim never faltered. "Callie, step away. That's an order."

"It's all right, Callie," Lars said. "It is over. I must pay for vat I have done."

He raised his hands in surrender and moved out from behind me. More footsteps thumped up the stairs, and Raul appeared. Within seconds, he'd assessed the situation and moved toward Lars, ordering him to put his hands behind his back. Lars complied, and Raul cuffed him. When she heard them clink, Lynn holstered her gun.

Lars lifted his chin. "Now I vill tell you—"

"Hold that thought," Lynn said. "First, let's get off this blasted catwalk. Then I'll read you your rights. If you still want to talk after that, we'll be happy to hear you out."

Raul guided Lars down the stairs. I followed, and Lynn brought up the rear. When we made it to ground level, she drew a plastic-coated card from her belt. As she read Lars his Miranda rights, Raul pulled me aside. "Again?" he asked simply.

"How did you know to come?"

He tilted his head toward Lynn. "She called me for backup."

Lynn finished reading from the card and turned to us, keeping a hand on Lars' arm. Her fingers didn't wrap even halfway around his bicep. "I was driving by on my way to the station and saw your red Honda in the lot," she said to me. "I just had a bad feeling."

"Intuition is one of Lynn's talents," Raul said. "And since one of yours, Callie, seems to be finding trouble…"

Lynn smirked. "Anyway, I figured I might as well check it out. I called Raul and told him where I was—"

"Because that's what people do when they might be treading into a perilous situation," Raul interrupted. "Not that you'd understand."

"Let me finish," Lynn said. "I came inside and was standing near the bleachers when a ruckus broke out above me. I looked up and saw legs dangling over the side of the catwalk."

Raul shuddered slightly and shoved his hands in his pockets, dropping the lecture. "This one was too close for comfort, Callie."

I looked at Lars, whose rounded shoulders gave him the appearance of a deflated balloon. "He saved me, though."

A scowl crossed Raul's face. "You seem to forget it's because of him you were at risk in the first place."

I sighed. He had a point, of course, but it didn't make me any less sad for Lars.

44

When five o'clock rolled around on Sunday, I turned the sign to Closed and locked the gallery door.

Braden, Banner, and Ethan stayed long enough to help me with the end-of-day chores, and then I shooed them home. These past few days had been a whirlwind, and I'd never been happier that Sundance Studio was closed on Mondays.

Bradley and Tim's podcast had created the desired effect—a rush of customers swarmed through the gallery from Friday morning through the weekend. Even Bradley and Tim had shown up—mostly to pester me about doing a podcast interview on Jeffrey Forte's murder and my catwalk encounter with his alleged killer. Still, they bought two canvases to go with the five they'd purchased last summer, and they posted rave reviews on social media, adding to the fuss. We sold fourteen high-end canvases in person and another ten online. I hadn't even begun to inventory the smaller items, but the bins and racks looked as picked over as a cornfield in September. It was exhilarating—and exhausting. I needed a day to reboot.

I put on my coat and gathered my things, planning how I'd spend my solo day off tomorrow. Jamal had begun his internship at Snow Plow Chow on Friday, and by this morning, Sam was already secure enough to put the cafe in the hands of his team while he made an overnight visit to Elyse in Boulder. He'd been reluctant to leave me, even for a single night, but I'd reassured him I was doing fine. I'd also hinted it would be nice to have a little time alone to plan his Valentine's Day surprise.

Before that, though, I'd sleep in—that was a no-brainer. Then perhaps Woody and I would take a trail hike. Afterwards, I'd marinate in the lodge's hot tub. I sighed in anticipation. The plan sounded ideal. And maybe focusing on my physical well-being would keep me from thinking about Lars. Or Theo. Or Jeffrey.

Of course, immersing myself in the hot tub meant I'd need to wrestle this blasted cast into a waterproof bag. But it could be worse, I supposed. Following the events on the catwalk, Mom had insisted I see Dr. Graves for a reassessment. He'd stayed after hours on Thursday evening to tend to me. Another round of X-rays had satisfied him that I hadn't further aggravated my prior injuries. All I needed was a minor repair to my damaged cast, and I was good to go. A few Tylenol did the trick for my aches and pains, and by Saturday morning, all traces of my most recent ordeal had vanished.

All physical traces, anyway. Emotionally, I was still shaky. I startled easily and sometimes found myself on the verge of tears for no apparent reason. The appointment I'd made with my counselor next week would surely soothe some of those rough edges. In the meantime, dinner at Mom and Dad's tonight would provide a therapeutic benefit of its own.

I was out the door and in the car before my body registered the frigid temperature. The sun had set about a half hour earlier, but there was still enough dusky light to see what a beautiful day I must have missed while cooped up indoors. I vowed to change that tomorrow.

A quick drive down Evergreen Way, and I was at the lodge. It was strange to walk through the doors and not see Jamal. My parents had hired someone new—Sid Farmington, a friendly retired history teacher Mom knew from her days at the high school—but it gave me a jolt to see a different face smiling at me from behind the desk.

I plodded up the stairs and was greeted at the door by an exuberant dog and a less enthusiastic cat. Mom came out of the kitchen, took one look at me, and sat me down at the dinner table with a glass of wine. "You look exhausted, Angelface," she said.

"I am. But it's a good tired. Productive. Even so, my bed is going to feel like heaven tonight."

"Well, dinner's ready. We can finish eating by six-thirty—six-fifteen, the way you devour a meal—and you can be home ten minutes later."

I grinned. "Bedtime by seven? Does that make me an old fogey?"

"Not at all, darling. It just means you've been through the wringer this week. And that reminds me: I've warned your father already, and now I'll caution you. I've declared a moratorium on any discussion of crime or arrests or related subjects. Not one word. Serious penalties await offenders."

I took a sip of wine. "I shall dutifully obey your pronouncement, Your Majesty."

Dad came out of the study then, carrying the scrapbook Mom had created for him. He seemed almost giddy. The gift had clearly been a booming success.

"You have to see this, Sundance," he said. "Your mother made it for me." He looked at her with such deep affection that I thought I could swim in it. Forty-five years of marriage, and they still felt that way about each other. I wanted that for myself someday.

Reverently, he placed the book on the table. "I've seen it, Dad, and it's amazing. But why did Mom give it to you so early? Valentine's Day isn't until Friday."

He put an arm around Mom. "When you have someone like this beside you, every day is the day of love."

She kissed his cheek. "Forty-eight Valentine's Days together, counting our dating years, and you still make my heart go pitter pat."

"You two are about to make me gag," I said with a grin.

The meal was delicious—pork chops, homemade macaroni and cheese, braised Brussels sprouts, and biscuits. As promised, we ate fast, with no talk of dark topics. Instead, we discussed Jamal's new internship.

"You mark my words," Mom said. "That young man will be running a Michelin-rated restaurant within five years. And in the meantime, he's agreed to spend his free time teaching Sid the ins and outs of successful hors d'oeuvre creation. Though Sid insists on referring to them as appetizers, much to Jamal's chagrin."

The evening was just what I'd needed. I felt relaxed and drowsy as I drove home, already decompressing from the wearisome week. Woody and Carl snuggled together in the back seat. I'd heard doggie and kitty snores before we even pulled out of the lodge's parking lot.

When I stopped for a light next to Pinkerton's Place, I glanced toward the store and saw Pinky carrying a load of flattened cardboard boxes, no doubt heading toward the recycling bin out back. On impulse, I pulled into the parking lot. Those boxes would be just what I needed to complete my Valentine's project.

I got out of the car and hurried toward him, waving my hand. "Hey, Pinky."

He turned to face me, and I pointed at the boxes. "If you're just throwing those out, I wonder if I could have a few?"

"You want my trash?" he asked.

"Well, yeah. As they say, one man's trash…" I said, smiling.

He frowned. "Don't know what you're talking about, but sure, take what you want."

I plucked several of the boxes from his stack. "Thank you," I said. "These'll work just fine."

I started back to my car, then shot a glance at the nearby arena and hesitated. "Are you doing all right, Pinky? Everything that's happened must have been tough on you. You and Lars seemed to be friends."

"Well, I don't know about friends," he said in a husky voice. "But we got along fine. He was a good neighbor. Woulda had no problems if not for that Forte character. A menace, that guy. We shoulda run him right outta town as soon as he got here."

I nodded. "I agree with you there."

He shifted the boxes in his arms. "Lars's lawyer told me he's pleading guilty. Gotta tell you, I'm glad to hear that. A man needs to accept the consequences of his actions."

I knew Pinky was right, but still, grief rippled through me. Lars had done a terrible thing, but I still cared about the man, and I couldn't help feeling sorry for him.

"His lawyer asked me to write a letter for his sentencing hearing," Pinky continued. "Character reference, she called it. Told her I gotta think about it. I can't excuse what he did. A man who commits murder deserves to be punished, no matter why he did it. But…" He paused. "Everything's just not as cut and dried as I used to think."

"I know exactly what you mean," I said. "It's like there's a spectrum between good and bad, and we all fall somewhere in between."

Pinky's face flushed. "Yeah, well. I gotta finish up. Store ain't gonna close itself."

"Sure, Pinky," I said. "Thank you for the boxes."

He trudged around the corner of his store as I shoved the boxes inside my car and drove the rest of the way home. Someday, I'd spend some time figuring out my views on justice and mercy. But not right now. Tonight I needed to tend to myself—and that meant pajamas and a good book. Chick lit, I decided. I didn't think I could handle a mystery.

As soon as I'd changed and settled onto the couch, a knock came at the door. I sighed. Why would anyone show up unannounced at this late hour? Then I glanced at the clock and saw it was just past seven.

After a peek through the side window, I opened the door for Raul. He glanced at my flannel robe and fuzzy slippers. "Kind of early, isn't it?"

"If you'd had the weekend I've had…"

"Who says I didn't?" He held up a box. "I don't do flowers like Renata, but I have this."

We walked into the kitchen, and he set the box on the counter. When he opened it, I gasped. "Is that…?"

"French silk pie," he confirmed. "Store bought—sorry—but it'll have to do."

"How'd you know that's my favorite?"

The corner of his mouth twitched. "I'm a detective, remember?"

I took two plates from the cabinet, and Raul cut each of us an enormous slice. We carried our pie to the living room and dug in.

"Anything new on the case?" I asked, licking whipped cream from my lips. "Other than what I read in Tonya's *Gazette* article, that is?"

"Haven't read her story, but I can tell you what I know."

He began ticking off the details of the case. Theo and Lars were now wards of the state, living in nine-by-nine cells at the Chilula County Prison. Charges against Theo included felony kidnapping and attempted murder. Prosecutors had also thrown in an animal endangerment citation, which pleased me. Terror deserved that bit of justice.

"Theo pleaded not guilty," Raul said, "but since he doesn't have the money to make bail, he'll spend the next few months before the trial locked up."

"I think that's for the best," I said. "Time behind bars might help him stay sober. I've done stories on convicts who came out of prison better people than when they'd gone in. I can't say I'm optimistic, but miracles happen."

We talked about Lars then and his guilty plea on voluntary manslaughter charges. "What do you think about that?" I asked. "Is the charge appropriate?"

"I'm good with it," he said. "I don't believe Lars premeditated Jeffrey's murder, but he killed a man. And that started a chain of events that put my sister in danger. And you. I

245

can't forgive that."

In my view, though, the chain of events had actually begun when Jeffrey came to Rock Creek Village to harass Renata. The victim in this case had provided the catalyst for everything that came after. That reminded me of another loose end. "Did you ever find out how Jeffrey got into Renata's apartment at the start of all this?"

"Lynn talked to the apartment building manager," Raul said. "Jeffrey told the guy he was her ex-husband and she'd asked him to check on the dog."

"So he just let Jeffrey in?"

"Loaned him a key, actually. But after Lynn got through with him, you can bet he won't make that mistake again."

I polished off my last bite of pie and set my plate on the coffee table, thinking about everything Raul had told me. I had one more unanswered question. "What's the news on Jeffrey's will?" I asked. "Is your sister a wealthy woman now?"

Raul snorted. "Nah, nothing on that front yet. Renata's lawyer seems pretty sure she'll get the money, but it'll take months to get the will through probate."

"How much?" It was none of my business, but since when had that ever stopped me?

"Seven-figure range, sounds like. Hard to believe." He stood up and carried our plates to the sink. "Now you know everything I do. I'm going to get out of here and let you get some sleep."

I followed him into the kitchen and crossed my arms. "Not yet," I said. "We have another matter to discuss. I can't keep *not* asking. What's up with the job in Boulder?"

Raul leaned against the counter. "As a matter of fact, the chief of police called me just this morning and offered me the job."

My stomach dropped. Though the news inwardly devastated me, I made myself put on a cheerful face. Raul deserved that. "Oh. That's…wonderful. They're lucky to get you, Raul. When…um, when do you start?"

His eyes twinkled. "I didn't say I took the job, Callie."

I frowned. "Are you telling me you turned it down? Deputy chief? That would be a step up the ladder career-wise. And a bump in pay, I imagine."

"Maybe," he said. "But the truth is, my family and friends are here. Rock Creek Village is home. You can't put a price on that." He grinned. "Besides, my sister is going to be rich. She can always take care of me, if need be."

I put a hand on my chest, unable to hide my relief and delight. "This makes me so happy, Raul. I couldn't imagine the village without you in it."

He shifted from one foot to another and said nothing. After a moment, he suddenly snapped his fingers.

"Oh, one more thing I forgot to tell you. I'm getting a partner."

I raised my eyebrows. "Oh?"

"It's not official yet, but Frank met with the Town Council on Friday. If they approve it, which I'm sure they will, he'll be hiring Lynn Clarke sometime next week."

"Wow. That's quite a bombshell. I didn't realize Frank was even looking for a new detective—or that Lynn would be interested. She's willing to move here from Pine Haven?"

"Yeah. She says she loves Rock Creek Village and wants to raise her daughters here. We're not too far from Pine Haven, so there won't be any problems with visitation."

"Visitation?"

"Her ex-husband has the girls every other weekend, but she says their relationship is amicable. He's on board with the move."

Hmm. So Raul's soon-to-be partner was divorced. Not that her marital status mattered in any way. Except maybe to Raul...

I put that thought straight out of my mind. Lynn would be a great fit here, I had to admit. In one short week, she'd proven herself skilled and loyal. We'd had a rocky start, maybe, but I liked her. She might even blend in well with our girlfriend group.

I walked Raul to the door, and we gave each other an awkward, one-armed hug. Once I'd bolted the door behind him, I climbed the stairs and got in bed with my book and my creatures. I had a hard time concentrating, though. The whole information dump from Raul had keyed me up, and I couldn't make myself relax.

The phone rang, and I saw the caller was Sam. "Hi, beautiful," he said when I answered.

And just like that, I felt calm. We talked about Elyse, the creatures, Jamal, my weekend sales—little things that wove together to create the tapestry of life. By the time we hung up a half hour later, I knew sleep would come easily. It had been an exhausting day, but a good one. In fact, things couldn't get much better.

Now, if I could just pull off Sam's Valentine's Day surprise.

45

Valentine's Day had finally arrived. I inspected the gallery one last time, satisfied with the presentation. The scene had come together just as I'd visualized. In fact, everything looked perfect. Sam was going to love it.

Still, my nerves fluttered. What if he didn't? This kind of grand gesture didn't come naturally to me, and I was feeling especially vulnerable at the moment. I remembered a strategy my therapist had given me once. She called it, "What's the worst?"

What's the worst thing that could happen? He won't like his surprise.

And if that happens? It'll hurt my feelings.

And if that happens? Well…I'll get over it.

I smiled to myself. Hurt feelings I could manage. Besides, I knew Sam. He'd never mock my efforts. He wasn't that kind of person.

I glanced in the mirror for the hundredth time. My dark hair hung loose around my shoulders, and I gave it a quick poof. I'd applied a bit of makeup to my eyes and lips, and I thought it looked pretty good. I wore a cranberry-colored tunic over a pair of dark jeans, the closest I could get to my high school wardrobe.

I felt Woody and Carl watching me, and I did a spin. "What do you think, guys?"

Woody wagged his whole body with enthusiasm. Carl wound around my ankles—a ringing endorsement from the reserved cat.

There was a tap at the door. When I opened it, Sam stood before me, looking so much like he did on our first date that it took my breath away. He wore jeans, too, and a blue plaid flannel shirt that set off his eyes. The breeze carried his scent into the room—the spicy, earthy smell that would always say "Sam" to me. It mingled with the fragrance of the bouquet he handed me—white roses, just like the ones he'd given me in high school.

I took the flowers and kissed him before ushering him inside. "What do you think?" I asked, gesturing toward the room.

His eyes roamed across the scene. A net of white lights hung across the ceiling, the best imitation of stars I could produce. Along the far wall, I'd set up a large white screen. On it, a projector shone a photo I'd lifted from our senior yearbook: The two of us gazing into each other's eyes as we danced at Homecoming.

Facing the screen was a brown leather loveseat my father had dropped off this afternoon. In front of it, I'd fashioned a fake dashboard and steering wheel. I'd painted Pinky's cardboard boxes and placed them on the sides as car doors.

For a moment, Sam stared, bewildered. I looped my cast through his arm and leaned into him. "Do you like it?"

At last, a smile wreathed across his face. "Our drive-in."

"Closest I could come."

He faced me and put his hands on my shoulders, his eyes bright. "You did all this for me. Because I said that drive-in was one of my favorite memories."

I nodded and touched his cheek. "Sam, I've loved you ever

since I can remember. When I came back to Rock Creek Village last year, when we found each other again, it almost seemed too good to be true. So I held a part of myself back from you, I think, in case it was. It's like…like I moved halfway toward you and then got stuck. Frozen in motion, like an action photo. But I don't feel stuck anymore. I'm ready to go all in. If you'll have me, I mean."

The kiss we shared gave me his answer. We held each other for a long time until Woody nudged himself between us. Laughing, Sam gestured to the screen. "So, is there a movie, or are we just going to make out in the front seat of the car?"

"I was thinking maybe both." I took his hand and led him to the loveseat, opening the fake passenger door for him. "I'll take the driver's side today," I said, lifting my cast.

"Works for me." He dropped onto the loveseat. I closed the cardboard and walked to the counter, returning with a picnic basket. As I placed it on the loveseat, Sam said, "You just crashed through the windshield."

"The inventor of the fantasy gets a little poetic license in its execution," I responded. Just the same, I opened the pretend driver's door and scooted through it.

When I handed him his turkey sandwich and a can of Coke, he looked at me, wide-eyed. "This is the same meal you brought that night."

I nodded. "When you're going for nostalgia, details matter."

As we ate, I picked up the remote and clicked play. When the opening scene of *Waterworld* appeared, Sam burst out laughing. "You're too much. I can't believe you did this. You hated this movie the first time."

I moved the picnic basket to the floor and nestled against him as the opening credits played. "But I love you. From now on, I'm going to spend way more time showing you how much."

He wrapped an arm around me and put his lips on mine. A knock at the door a few minutes later interrupted us.

"Who could that be?" I muttered, glancing at my watch.

"The studio has been closed for hours."

As I walked to the door, Sam picked up the remote and hit pause. "Whoever it is, they're about to experience my wrath," he said. "I hate it when people come late to the movies."

Peeking through the blinds, I saw Tonya and David standing on the stoop. I turned the bolt and opened the door. Tonya walked past me. David followed, pausing to kiss my cheek. "Ciao, *cara amica*," he said. "Apologies for the intrusion, but *mia bella signorina* insisted. There's no saying no when she sets her mind on something."

I nodded in sympathy. "Don't I know it."

"We were in the bookstore and heard the music," Tonya said. "Sounded like a movie."

"It is," I said. "Or was. Until we had to pause."

She looked around the gallery. "What's all this?"

Sam beamed. "Callie recreated one of our first dates. The drive-in."

Tonya gave me an appreciative smile. "Since when did Ms. Practicality turn into Ms. Romance?"

"I've always been a romantic," I said, to which Tonya and Sam laughed. "At heart, I mean."

"Well, we might as well join you," Tonya said.

David looked aghast. "No, *mi amore*, we mustn't interrupt this charming moment."

"Pish," Tonya said, waving him off. "They're drinking soda and watching *Waterworld*. Plus, when we were in high school, I intruded on any number of their romantic moments. I'm making the memory more realistic."

I glanced at Sam. He smiled. "She's right. Let's rustle up a back seat."

David helped him carry over two of the gallery's padded visitor chairs. When everyone had settled in, I pressed play.

Tonya leaned forward and tapped me on the shoulder. "By the way, David and I have some news."

"I hate when people talk during the movie," Sam said.

"As if you were even watching it before we came in."

"Well, we weren't talking," Sam said.

Suddenly, another knock echoed at the door. "What's going on here?" I said, annoyed.

This time, it was Jessica and Summer. "We were walking by from the yoga studio and saw the lights," Jessica said, brushing past me. "A movie party? Why weren't we invited?"

I sighed. "Sure, come on in."

"What are we watching?" Summer asked. They pulled chairs next to Tonya and David's.

Then a key turned in the front lock. Ethan and Renata entered, looking surprised to see us. Renata was holding Terror, who yapped at the sight of Woody. Carl hissed in response.

"I wasn't expecting to see you all here," Ethan said. "I left my iPad in the office, and we stopped by to pick it up." He narrowed his eyes. "So, Callie, this was the reason you closed an hour early. What's it supposed to be, a drive-in?"

"Oooh, I've heard of those," Renata said, bouncing on her feet. "They're so retro."

I glanced at Sam, and he smiled. "Care to join us?"

Renata put Terror on the floor, and the creatures darted off toward the office. Ethan followed them and came back with more chairs. I went to the kitchen and got more Cokes from the refrigerator.

I snuggled next to Sam again and restarted the movie. Everyone nibbled and slurped and watched—for about two minutes.

"Sorry to interrupt," Tonya said, earning a groan from Sam. "I'm not trying to cut in on this masterpiece of filmmaking, but David and I have an announcement. Who wants to know?"

Everyone raised a hand, including me. Sam hit pause again. Tonya stood and pulled David to his feet. She smiled coyly. I reached across the back of the loveseat and swatted her leg. "You're such a diva. Just tell us already."

She clasped her hands to her chest. "David and I are getting married."

"That's old news," Summer said.

"Well, we've picked a date and a location."

"For your destination wedding," I said. "Vegas?"

"Nope," she said. "Our destination is…" She paused, as if waiting for a drumroll, then spread her arms wide. "Here!"

I furrowed my brow. "In Sundance Studio?"

"No, silly. Here in Rock Creek Village." She looked up at David, who gazed at her with adoration. "We considered Las Vegas."

"And we looked into several beautiful, remote island paradises," David added.

"Italy, too," Tonya said. "But we decided we already had our own paradise, surrounded by friends in this enchanting mountain village. Why travel elsewhere when everything we want is right here?"

I leapt through the cardboard car door and hugged them both. "I think that's a fantastic idea."

The others joined in for a group hug. Then the bell above the door jingled, and I looked over to see Mom and Dad enter. Mom swept toward us, brandishing a large Tupperware container. "Darling, you forgot to pick up the brownies you had me make for your special date. I didn't realize it was a group date."

I sighed. "Neither did I. Thanks for bringing these." I opened the container and passed it around so everyone could grab a brownie. "Since you're here, Mom and Dad, let Tonya tell you the good news."

Renata held up her phone. "Hey, Callie, do you mind if I call Raul and tell him to drop by? He's just sitting home by himself on Valentine's Day."

I winced, then glanced at Sam. "Sure. Why not?"

Everyone began chattering. I took Sam's hand and drew him away from the commotion. "I'm sorry about all this," I said. "Our romantic evening took a detour."

"Nothing to be sorry for." He bit into his brownie and lifted his chin to our group of crazy, loving, devoted friends. "This'll do just fine. In fact, this is exactly what I want out of life."

Woody nuzzled against my thigh. Terror settled between his paws, and Carl purred at my feet. Heart full, I took in everyone and everything around the room. Friends and family I cared about, a business that brought me pride, furry creatures I loved, a boyfriend with whom I could hopefully build a future. I touched the smile lines around Sam's mouth, glad I'd contributed to their depth tonight.

A quote I'd once read floated into my thoughts. *Joy is the most magnetic force in the universe.* I was being sucked toward that joy right now, as it radiated from the people and animals in this room.

I looked up at Sam and smiled. "You couldn't be more right," I said. "This is just about perfect."

Coming Sept. 13, 2022:

Photo Finished
Callie Cassidy Mysteries Book 4

When a visit to a Colorado dude ranch turns deadly, it's up to photographer Callie Cassidy to corral the killer...

Callie believes she has planned the perfect bridal shower for her best friend Tonya: a week-long girls' trip to Moonglow Ranch, where they can bask in nature and enjoy each other's company. Then, a conniving local woman publicly threatens the ranch's owners, and Callie worries the trip may be destined for disaster. The next morning, she and her golden retriever Woody and tabby cat Carl discover the woman's body in the stable, trampled by a horse. Or did she die from a snakebite? Or—as Callie suspects—could something even more sinister be at play? Answers are as difficult to find as a needle in a haystack. And when the police chief accuses the ranch owners of murder, Callie realizes she'll need to lasso the real outlaw—*before the wrong people end up in the pokey.*

**Subscribe to the newsletter for updates:
www.lorirobertsherbst.com**

About the Author

Lori Roberts Herbst lives in Dallas, Texas, but spends a lot of time she should be writing staring out the window and wishing she owned a home in Colorado mountains, too. She is a wife, mother, grandmother (gasp!), cozy mystery author, and former journalism teacher. Lori serves as secretary of the Sisters in Crime North Dallas chapter and is a member of the SinC Guppies and Mystery Writers of America. You can (and should!) follow Lori on Facebook, Instagram, Goodreads, Amazon, and Bookbub. Subscribe to her newsletter at **www.lorirobertsherbst.com** for fun stuff (including FREE Callie Cassidy prequel stories).

Made in the USA
Columbia, SC
14 September 2022